Praise for Adriana Locke

"Adriana Locke creates magic with unforgettable romances and captivating characters. She's a go-to author if I want to escape into a great read."

—*New York Times* bestselling author S.L. Scott

"Adriana Locke writes the most delicious heroes and sassy heroines who bring them to their knees. Her books are funny, raw, and heartfelt. She also has a great smile, but that's beside the point."

—*USA Today* bestselling author L.J. Shen

"No one does blue collar, small town, "everyman" (and woman!) romance like Adriana Locke. She masterfully creates truly epic love stories for characters who could be your neighbor, your best friend— you! Each one is more addictive and heart-stoppingly romantic than the last."

—Bestselling author Kennedy Ryan

"Adriana's sharp prose, witty dialogue, and flawless blend of humor and steam meld together to create unputdownable, up-all-night reads!"

—*Wall Street Journal* bestselling author Winter Renshaw

Tumble

OTHER TITLES BY ADRIANA LOCKE

The Exception Series

The Exception
The Connection: An Exception Novella
The Perception
The Exception Series Box Set

Landry Family Series

Sway

Swing

Switch

Swear

Swink

Sweet

The Landry Family Series: Part One
The Landry Family Series: Part Two

The Gibson Boys Series

Crank

Craft

Cross (a novella)

Crave

Crazy

Dogwood Lane Series

Tumble

Stand-Alone Novels

Sacrifice
Wherever It Leads
Written in the Scars
Battle of the Sexes
Lucky Number Eleven

A DOGWOOD LANE NOVEL

ADRIANA LOCKE

Montlake
Romance

Published by Montlake Romance, Seattle

www.apub.com

Amazon, the Amazon logo, and Montlake Romance are trademarks of Amazon.com, Inc., or its affiliates.

ISBN-13: 9781503905146
ISBN-10: 1503905144

Cover design by Tammy Seidick

Cover photography by Wander Aguiar

Printed in the United States of America

To Saul.
We will always find one another.

CHAPTER ONE

NEELY

Y ou've got to be kidding me."
I hit the brakes, and my little rental car, not much bigger than a cracker box, rolls to a complete stop. The hound dog lying in the middle of the road, right where the yellow stripes would be if this were a town with more than a thousand people, lifts his head. I tap the horn. He lays his head back down and yawns.

"Hang on, Grace." I sigh, pulling the phone away from my ear. Wincing as the window slides down and the sun washes across my face, I wonder vaguely when I last saw a morning this bright. The sun doesn't do *this* in New York City.

My head pokes out the window. "Come on, Blue. Move it!"

He doesn't. He doesn't even bother to blink.

"Who's Blue?" Grace asks. "Like the color blue?"

"He's a dog."

"I thought you were in the car?"

"I am," I grumble. "Blue, come on, boy. Get out of the way. *Please?*"

"Why are you negotiating with a dog?"

Ignoring her, I watch Blue lazily yawn again and then close his eyes without a second thought to my request. His fur is sprinkled with gray, his eyes droopier than when we used to load him up in the back of a pickup truck and cruise town with him all weekend. It's kind of sad.

"Fine," I tell him, frowning. "Have it your way."

Piloting the car in a wide berth around his body, I forge ahead.

"I can't believe you just had a conversation with a dog," Grace says. "You've been in Tennessee for, what, twelve hours, and you're already losing your mind."

"How sweet of you to insinuate I still have a mind."

A long pause stretches between us as I heed a stop sign.

When Grace dropped me off at the airport last night to catch the red-eye back to Tennessee, I stained her new cream blazer with my mascara-laced tears. It was the first time she'd seen me cry in the handful of years we've been friends. Crying is not something I do well. Years of gymnastics competitions broke me of shedding tears easily.

"I know you still have a mind," Grace scoffs. "And I know you're okay, even if you don't, because you're one of the strongest women I know. But I will admit, your tears last night kind of screwed me up."

"Oh, sure. Make this totally about you." I shake my head, wishing we were having this discussion over coffee instead.

"I didn't mean it like that."

"Don't worry about it. It was more of an angry cry than anything." Flipping the visor down with a little more force than necessary, I accelerate through the intersection. "The tears are over."

"They don't have to be over, and you're allowed to be pissed. Just promise me you're okay."

I consider this. It would be so easy to not be okay right now. I'm unemployed. My New York City rent is awful, and I quit my job without thinking it through and don't even have a backup plan.

And I'm here. The one place I've avoided in every single way since the day I left.

As the pine trees roll by, there's no sourness in my stomach at being back in Dogwood Lane. There's no regret at buying the plane ticket last night and jumping on a plane to come home without telling my mother until I landed. I expected at least a little of each. It's confusing.

"I'm not okay by any means, but I'm better this morning." I shrug, trying to find a way to rationalize it. "You know what they say—sunshine brings opportunities."

"Um, no one says that."

"They should."

"If the southern sunshine cures problems that fast, I'm on my way."

I slow to make a turn. "My problems aren't cured, but there is something about the air down here. It just purifies the soul or something."

She laughs. "I'll take credit for your purification since you going home was my idea. That's me—the one with good ideas."

"Hardly. The last advice I took from you got me a warning from security at a very expensive hotel downtown."

"You should listen to me more. I guarantee you'd have more smiles, sunshine, and, quite possibly, a lot more sex. *Great* sex."

"God knows I need more of all three of those. But I didn't have time for that stuff before I decided to storm into my boss's office and quit like some silver-spoon princess who doesn't need money. I definitely don't have time for it now."

"You have time for what you make time for. We have to remember there are twenty-four hours in a day, and if we're going to be boss women in New York, we have to use all twenty-four."

Just hearing that feels like a weight squats on my shoulders. "I know. You're right. I should give up the four hours of sleep I get at night and get a social calendar instead." I fake cry at the idea. "I see now why some women are gold diggers. If I would've dated the stockbroker from the deli, I wouldn't have this worry."

"No. No stockbrokers." The line muffles. "Hang on for a sec, Neely."

Her voice mixes with another, getting louder and then softer before she returns. "Sorry. They're trying to not run my article on women's tennis, and I'm digging in my heels. It's the best thing I've ever written."

The line muffles again, and my mind wanders to the last piece I wrote for the sports magazine I work—*worked*—for. It followed a collegiate soccer player who came from nothing and won the starting goalie position at an elite school. A tale of hard work and overcoming obstacles, it was the type of story my soul craves.

It's the kind of article I became a sports journalist to write.

It would've been the perfect story to kick off the new division at the magazine.

Forcing a swallow in an attempt to quell the bitter taste in my mouth, I flip my attention back to my friend.

"You still here?" Grace asks.

"Yup."

"Okay. Had to do a little 'my balls are bigger than yours' show to the boys. You know how it goes." She sighs. "I love when they think they can make decisions and not include me. Imbeciles."

That hits home a little too hard. I force another swallow. "Totally."

Grace must hear the slight wobble in my voice, because her tone lowers. "You know what? I'm gonna steer this conversation in another direction."

"It's fine," I promise. "You're allowed to talk about your job."

She ignores me. "I'm stuck at work dreaming about a vacation and dealing with office politics. You, my friend, are free. You should totally live it up for a few days."

"Livin' it up in good ole Dogwood Lane," I say with a laugh. A little yellow-painted building with a patched roof passes on my right. "Maybe I'll pull into the Bait Shop over there and count the worms."

"Worms? Gross. But on the bright side, I bet there are cute country boys in there, probably even in flannel."

"Flannel?" I laugh. "That's random."

"Yes, flannel. Your job is to find a hot country boy in flannel and roll around in some hay. Drink some lemonade in mason jars. Ride around in old pickup trucks. Do whatever it is you do down there and forget life for a couple of days. I'll be working some angles around here."

My spirits slip, just like the sun slips behind the clouds. My life in New York City was anchored by my position at the magazine. My entire routine was centered around my job. The stories. The people.

The magnitude of the situation, of starting over from scratch, combats the feel-good energy from the pine-scented air. I cringe. "Remind me again I didn't just screw up my life."

"Stop that," Grace warns. "You didn't screw up anything, and this will all work out for the best. I know it."

"I hope so, but, man, now that the adrenaline has worn off . . ." I try to laugh, to play it off as a joke, but no sound comes out.

"Look, I have friends in high places. Getting you a job will be as hard as the musician I slept with last night. And trust me, that's a good thing for you."

"I gather he wasn't amazing since you're calling him by his job instead of by his name."

"He told me it was Gabriel. But since I told him mine was Lydia, who knows if that's true. But now you're distracting me." She shouts at someone before coming back to the phone. "I have a list of people I'm going to call this week to see if anyone is looking for a brilliant sports journalist."

My fingers grip the steering wheel. Grace is a bloodhound: once she sets her sights on something, there's no turning back. We met a few years ago at a conference and realized we lived the New York equivalent of "right around the corner" from one another. We bonded over cereal from the box, afternoon movies, and ballpark hot dogs. Grace decided we were friends, and that was that. I love her for it.

"I know you want to help," I tell her. "But I'll find something. I already sent my résumé out this morning to a couple of places. I got this."

"Okay, but I can't be blamed if something just falls in my lap while you're on vacation."

"I wouldn't call this a vacation," I note. "More like a chance to see my mama."

"Well, I still think you should make the best of it. Just don't fall back in love with your hometown too much, because you aren't leaving me."

I drive through the center of town and take in the quaint buildings and the kids riding bicycles on the sidewalks. There are no drive-through coffee shops, no chain restaurants. The closest dry cleaner is two towns over, and if you want more than the cheap toilet paper, you're out of luck. Nothing has changed in the decade I've been gone. Not physically, anyway. My stomach bottoms out as I think about the people and the things I've avoided all my adult life. My spirits sink as I consider the topics I've forbidden my mom from even mentioning over the years.

Shoving them out of my mind, I sigh. "Trust me. I won't fall in love with this place. I'll be home before you know it."

"Why? What's wrong with Dogwood Lane, Tennessee?" she asks in her best southern voice.

"Your New Yorker attempt at a southern drawl is pathetic."

"I'll work on it. Now, tell me what you see. Paint me a picture of whatever you're looking at. Bonus if it includes flannel."

I take in the first building on my right. "The post office was built a hundred years ago and has needed a new coat of paint for at least the last twenty years." I flip my turn signal on. "Across the street is a church with musket balls from the Civil War lodged in the steeple."

"You're joking."

"I'm afraid not," I tell her. "The whiskey barrels lining the main drag are filled with pansies because the first year they planted those, the high school football team made it to the state finals. That never made sense to me because they lost, but apparently that's close enough and no one wants to rock the boat. Superstitions and all."

Grace goes into a monologue just to hear her newfound accent while I watch Dogwood Lane roll by. Styrofoam cups spell out GOOD LUCK to the softball team in the chain-link fence surrounding the high school.

"Okay," I say. "I'm now stopping at the Dogwood Café, the only place in town where you can get a cup of coffee besides the gas station, because even I am not that desperate."

"Doesn't your mom have a Keurig?"

"My mom started drinking decaf." I pucker, flipping off the ignition. "It's like I don't even know her."

"Ew. Okay. Call me later."

"Bye, friend."

My blonde hair is piled on top of my head, my face free of makeup save for a dash of mascara, as I make my way toward the front door of the café. I step up on the patio and nearly get run into.

"Whoa," I say, scooting out of the way as a little girl finishes her gymnastics trick. "That's pretty good."

She turns to look at me, her strawberry-blonde hair and spattering of freckles across the bridge of her nose reminding me of a younger version of myself. A grin splits her cheeks.

"That's all I'm allowed to do out here," she says, straightening her lavender shirt with AERIAL's emblazoned across the front in gold lettering. "My nanny says I'll bust my head open and she'll have to take me for stitches. Have you ever had stitches?"

"No," I say, laughing at the way her little nose crinkles like a bunny's. "Have you?"

"Once. I fell off the trampoline and busted the side of my leg wide open. You could see my bones," she says, her voice growing conspiratorial. "It was *so* gross."

7

"That *is* gross."

She watches me, her bright-blue eyes sparkling. There's an ease about her that draws me in. It's a charm, a charismatic element I've felt in only a handful of people over my entire life. Most people don't have it, but she does in spades.

With a shrug, she flips a lock of hair off her shoulder. "Got lots of ice cream for dinner, though, so it wasn't totally a bad thing."

"Ice cream cures everything."

"Yup. My leg is stronger than ever. I'm almost ready to get my back tuck with no help."

Now she's speaking my language.

I grin. "That's awesome. I didn't get mine forever. I think I was almost twelve."

"Well, I'm almost ten. You weren't that far behind me. But I have been doing this since I was three."

Stifling a giggle, I nod. "Do you take classes at Aerial's?"

"Yup. The Summer Show is coming up. It's going to be amazing. Miss Aerial says it's the best one ever!"

The pride in her little singsong voice hits my heart. The Summer Show is the biggest thing this town has to offer. It started off when I was a little girl as a dance recital. It now encompasses an entire weekend with gymnastics displays, dance-offs, and a parade. People come from all over to support the children's charities Aerial's sponsors. It's the highlight of the entire town's year.

"You should come," she insists.

"I'll try."

The café door opens, and a woman with long black hair and glossy lips smiles and steps onto the patio. "You ready, rascal?" She turns and sees me standing next to the windows. "Oh, hello. I didn't see you there."

"No worries," I say. "Just coming by for coffee and got caught up in talks of the Summer Show with . . ."

"Mia," the little girl chirps.

"With Mia," I add. "Sounds like it's going to be great."

The woman nods, side-eyeing the child. "Is it wrong to say I'll be glad when it's over?"

"Yes," the little girl and I say in unison, making her laugh.

"Well, I'll keep that to myself then," she jokes. "You ready to get some work done?"

Mia nods.

"Have a good day," I tell them, reaching for the door.

"You too," the lady calls out over her shoulder.

"Bye!" The little girl tosses me a big wave as they step into the parking lot.

Scents of bacon and sweet-smelling syrup lie thick in the air as I pull on the door handle. Chatter from the remaining customers telling stories mixes with the clatter of silverware and dishes from the kitchen.

Stepping inside the cozy little café is like stepping back in time. The walls are the same white with a touch of yellow from the deep fryers in the back. There's a country-blue chair rail lining the four walls of the dining area. A bar separates the front from the kitchen area, and the vinyl barstools sport a brown faux leather that crackles when you sit on them. Or, at least, I suppose they still do.

The cash register pings as I force my feet forward toward the bar. I don't look at anyone. I just need coffee.

I take another step toward the counter and then jolt to a stop. My hip knocks a table, salt and pepper shakers rattling on the top.

Eyes the color of leaves at the beginning of spring snatch my gaze and pin me in place from a few feet away. They're a green so bright, so lively, *so familiar*.

Oh, crap.

CHAPTER TWO

Neely

My brain goes dead. All coherent thoughts and processes come to a screeching halt. A low-keyed hum whispers through my head as I watch Dane Madden's eyes sparkle. Flecks of golds and blues catch the light as the corners of his lips tug toward the ceiling.

No, no, no.

Self-preservation kicks in, and I take a step back. He takes one toward me.

"Hi, Neely." His voice is grittier than I remember it. Deeper. Gravelly, even. The timbre rushes across my skin without permission, slipping deep into my inner workings and flipping switches like it's second nature. I can feel the struggle between us as we wrestle silently for control.

I clear my throat. "Hi, Dane." My voice is even, *practiced,* and I send up a prayer of gratitude for the communication classes forced upon me in college.

His heavy brows, a shade darker than his sandy-colored hair, pull together. Back and forth goes his squared jawline as the hint of a smile disappears.

"Didn't expect to see you here," he says.

"That makes two of us."

My breath is hot as it passes my lips, like his gaze actually upped the thermostat in my body. Moisture accumulates on my palms, and I slide them down my shorts as the waitress pulls his attention away. I vaguely hear him order coffee.

A heather-gray T-shirt stretches across his broad chest, hanging loose enough to not be pretentious but tight enough to skim the tapering of his waist. There's a hole in one leg of his jeans a few inches below the pocket and a pair of dirty brown work boots on his feet.

He's as different from the stockbroker at the deli as I could get. *There's a reason for that,* I remind myself.

As my eyes travel up his abdomen and my brain attempts to use facts and logic to put out the fire starting to smolder in my core, Dane plucks my gaze out of the air with his own.

"What are you doing here?" he asks.

"Getting coffee."

"That's not what I meant," he says, his Adam's apple bobbing in his throat.

I struggle to take a lungful of air from beneath his gaze. "Am I not allowed here?"

"That's not what I meant either."

The lack of oxygen makes it difficult to come up with words. I just look at him like we should break into chatter about our lives, joke about things that used to make us laugh. Only we can't. There's a wall between us we can't skirt. It's built with just as many tears and just as much betrayal as it is any good times we shared.

I shift my weight, lift my chin, and feel my guard start to wane. My lips part to speak when I'm cut off by the sound of a high-pitched squeal.

"Neely! Is that you?"

I rip my eyes off Dane, and they settle on a set of bright-red curls. "Claire! Oh my gosh. How are you?" I pull her into a hug as she holds a cup out to each side.

"I'm so excited to see you, girl," she says. "I haven't seen you in, what? Ten years?"

"Close enough." I laugh. "How are you? What have you been up to? Still seeing Happy?" I ask, pointing to his name tattooed on her wrist.

"Oh, hell no. That was a drunken mistake years ago." She sighs, rolling her eyes. "I just tell people I got it for my cheerful demeanor."

"That's a crock of shit," Dane mutters. Claire bumps him with her hip, careful not to spill the coffee in her hands.

"I have to jet to the back and help pack up an order for the fire department." She hands Dane a cup. "This one's for you. And this one," she says, turning to me, "must be for you."

"I didn't order anything yet. I do want a cup of coffee, though. Black, please."

She bites her lip. "Coffee. Black." Nodding toward the cup, she extends her hand again. "Dane ordered it for you. Or I guess it was for you."

I glance at Dane. He nods, tossing me a little smile that throws me. My insides flop like a fish out of water, one direction one second, another the next. My attention flips to him in an unguarded moment.

He takes a sip of his drink—coffee with two sugars and one creamer, if he still takes it the same as before. To anyone watching, he'd seem cool and collected. I, however, see the fire hidden in his eyes. Feel the heat in his gaze. Hear the questions sitting on his tongue.

The last time we saw each other came with a finality that was as hard to accept as it was necessary. It came with more pain than anything I've ever endured on the gymnastics floor or in the business world. All the reasons why come flooding back as I feel him burn through my defenses.

Forcing a swallow, I make myself look at Claire. "How much is it?"

"Stick it on my tab," Dane says.

"No. I'll pay for it." I put my hand into my pocket.

"If you think I'm taking your money when he's standing there, you've forgotten where you are, Neely. I'm not getting on his bad side over a cup of coffee." She shrugs. "Now take this. I need to get to the kitchen."

She shoves the cup into my hand.

"Um, thanks," I say, still uncertain whether to accept it. "Let me at least give you a tip."

"I add ten percent on Dane's bill every month. No worries." She winks, moving to miss Dane's shoulder bump. "Will you be in town long? I want to catch up."

"Probably not. A couple of days at most."

"Well, I'll find you." She glances toward the kitchen. "I really do gotta go. Talk to you soon."

"Okay. Bye, Claire," I say, giving her a little wave.

With each step she takes away from us, the air grows thicker. I used to know without looking when Dane walked into biology class. I swore the air changed. Standing this close to him now, I believe my assessment back then was probably true. The space around him is charged with some invisible, magnetic energy I can't describe but that pricks at the very fiber of my being.

Jerk.

"Thank you for the coffee," I say, finding my voice. "I will say I'm kind of surprised you remembered how I like it."

"Not a big deal."

My stomach flutters like a teenage girl's, and I try to override the sensation and remind myself I'm a grown woman. A capable woman. A smart one—a smart enough one not to be dazzled by his smirk.

He's a couple of steps away, but it feels as if he's right up against me. My shirt clings to my chest, the air so warm my lungs almost refuse it.

He twists his Dodgers cap backward. As if I need more of a reason for my heartbeat to go wild, I get a better look at his face. His skin is tanned, a couple of days' worth of stubble scattered on his cheeks. Under his left eye is a purplish mar, and I can only begin to imagine where that came from.

"How have you been?" he asks, tapping his thumb against the side of his cup.

"Great."

"Where you living these days?"

"New York," I say, wishing I'd prepared more for this scenario. As I stand in front of him, I mentally smack myself for not thinking this through.

"New York? Nice."

"Yeah. I love it there. What about you? How have you been?"

"Doing good. Been working on a house up on Zion's Hill. Some lawyer from Nashville bought it and is completely redoing the whole place. About done with it, though."

"Carpentry?"

His lips purse and he nods.

"Took after your dad, after all."

We exchange a soft, genuine smile. The mention of his father settles over the ball of frayed nerves in my stomach, softening it a touch.

I always loved Nick Madden. He worked hard, was kind of a hard-ass, but was as sweet as pie when you got to know him. He loved me too. He taught me how to change the oil in my car and to throw a punch—just in case I ever needed to know.

"How is he?" I ask, knowing I shouldn't.

"Same. Busting my ass all the time."

"You probably need it." I grin, ignoring the ease of the words. "There are worse things than taking after him, you know."

"I kind of fell into it." Dane shrugs, bringing a hand to his cheek and sliding it over his chin. A yellow-and-green bracelet is wrapped around his wrist, the colors emulating the hues of his eyes. "Got laid off at the mill a few years back. Didn't really have a choice. But I kind of like it."

I bring my cup to my mouth. "Don't worry. I won't tell your dad you said that."

He laughs. "Please don't. I'd never hear the end of it."

My laugh melts together with his, and for this one split second, I breathe easy and enjoy a familiarity I haven't had with anyone in so long. "How's your brother?"

"Same. Total asshole. But Matt works for me now, so that gives me some leverage."

"I bet that's a fun day on the jobsite."

"It's a real treat." He regrips his cup, the veins in his forearm flexing. "We work together pretty well, actually. We have quite a little crew. Get a lot of work."

My eyes travel up his muscled bicep, over his wide shoulders, and up his thick neck. I gulp. "I bet you're good at it." I think back to the way he could strum a guitar or fix practically anything. "You always were good with your hands."

As soon as the words pass my lips, I realize what I've done. He fights a smirk. I want to die.

"Thanks," he quips, the smirk growing by the second.

Sticking the coffee between us, I shake my head. "I didn't mean it like that."

"I'm sure you didn't."

Pulling the cup to my lips to hide my errant blush, I override the part of my brain telling me to leave. A grin kisses his lips, and I hold my breath for whatever is to come.

"If anyone would know how good I am at anything, it would be you," he says.

It's true at face value, but the innuendo is right there for the taking. My thighs clench together as I consider what Dane could do to me now. With that body. With those lips. With that damn smirk.

The latter grows deeper. He thinks he has me. He might be right. But just as he might not completely be the bad boy next door anymore, I'm also not the naive teenager who wears her heart on her sleeve. And I'm definitely not a fool.

Tossing my shoulders back, I shrug. "It's hard to remember after all these years. You've kind of faded from my mind." *Lies, lies. All lies.*

We stand eye to eye, our chests rising and falling in time. I need to leave. I need fresh, un-Dane-scented air. But if I do, he may misinterpret it, and I refuse to let him have the upper hand.

"You married?" he asks nonchalantly, but there's a hint of deception in his eyes. He's bracing himself for my reaction, knowing, or at least suspecting, his tiptoe into these waters won't be met with grace.

He'd be right.

A bucket of cold water douses the warmth of the moment, and I shiver. My guard comes up and locks into place. "I think the real question is, are you?"

"Nope. Never been married."

My eyes grow wide before I can catch them. Why that answer surprises me I don't know, and before I can think about it too much, I change the topic.

"Nice shiner you got there," I note, nodding toward his eye.

"If I told you how I got this, you wouldn't believe me."

"That's a fact," I tell him. Biting my lip to suppress the tangent I'm about to go on, about how I wouldn't believe much at face value with him, I give up. It's time to go. "You know what? I gotta go. Thanks for the coffee."

"I know you think back then, before you left, that I . . . that things . . ." He removes his hat and roughs a hand through his hair. "You know what? It doesn't matter." He drops his hand, his jaw set.

"You're right," I say, my mouth hot as I gulp in a steadying breath of air. "It doesn't matter. Good to see you, Dane. Take care." I tip my coffee toward him.

He doesn't move as I step around him toward the door. He doesn't call out as my palm grips the handle and twists it. He doesn't follow me as I walk by the windows toward my car with a step quicker than can be explained as natural.

He also doesn't stop watching me, because his gaze burns a hole in my profile.

It's the second time he's burned me. It'll be the last.

CHAPTER THREE

DANE

Splat!

The sound of the hammer—swung with more force than was necessary, to boot—crushing my thumb ricochets across the front lawn. The tool falls from my hand, striking against the sawhorse, and flips into the soft grass with a gentle thud.

"Son of a . . . *Shit!*" My hand shakes, the top of my thumb threatening to explode. I tilt my head to the sky and try to find some peace in the clouds.

I come up empty.

"Matt!" I call to my younger brother. "I'm taking ten."

He nods from halfway up the ladder leaned against the side of the house.

Wrapping my good hand around my thumb, I head toward my truck. Sounds of construction ring out behind me. It's usually music to my ears, the lifeblood of the Madden name. But each cut of a sawblade, buzz of a power drill, and swing of a hammer feels like a distraction this morning. I have a throbbing thumb to show for it.

Beads of sweat cluster along my forehead. I remove my hat with my good hand and run the back of my forearm along my brow.

"Damn it." Everything feels sticky. Mildly irritating. And the progress on the project that usually energizes me has failed me epically this morning. I just don't want to be *here*. Not that I have a better place to be. Quite frankly, I have a lot of places I shouldn't be, and with Neely, or thinking about Neely, is one of them.

I would've recognized her anywhere. Same gray eyes that glimmer like she's about to tell you a secret. Full lips that spread into a smile so infectious you can't help but feel your own mouth following suit. The hint of floral perfume, the golden hair that may as well be silk, and the aura about her that's just as strong as the day she left Dogwood Lane and me—it's all the same. It's like time forgot to age her. She somehow has become more beautiful, sexier, stronger.

The world hates me. I've postulated this for a long time, but it's obvious today.

The tailgate of my truck lowers. I scoop a handful of ice from the cooler in the bed into a bandanna and wrap it around my injured digit. The relief lasts only a few moments.

"What are you doing down here?" Penn rests his forearms over the side of the truck, the tattoos carved in his skin like mini masterpieces on full display. He eyes my makeshift bandage. "What happened to you?"

"Hammer," I groan, adjusting the ice.

"That's interesting."

"How you figure?"

"Never knew you to hit yourself with a hammer before. I find that interesting."

"If that's interesting, you need a hobby. Or you could work like I'm paying you to do . . ."

"I have a hobby, thank you, and you should've seen her last night," he says, smacking his lips together. "Lord Almighty, she's a—"

"Penn."

"Yeah?"

The tip of my finger sticks out of the bandanna. It's bright red and hot to the touch despite the ice packed around it. "All your escapades really sound the same at this point."

"Is that jealousy I hear?" He cups his hand around his ear. "I thought so. Not my fault you're in a dry spell."

Leaning against the truck, I look at him. "Jealousy isn't how I'd describe it. But if that makes ya feel good, go for it."

"My *hobby* makes me feel good." He moves his lips around, like he's fighting the next words trying to pop out. He does this when he knows he shouldn't say something but can't quite convince himself not to. "From the looks of you, I'd say you're more than jealous. I'd say you're . . . *tempted*."

My tongue presses on the roof of my mouth. "Tempted to what?"

He leans against the truck, too, the gold St. Christopher's medal he's worn since elementary school clamoring against the side. The corners of his lips nearly touch the corners of his eyes. *He knows.*

"Word travels fast, huh?" I say, prodding around to see if my guess is right.

He slow blinks. Twice.

"What?" I ask.

"That's all you have to say about Neely being back in town? 'Word travels fast.' For fuck's sake, Dane. What's wrong with you?"

We don't have time for that conversation.

I sigh. "What do you want me to say?"

"I'd love to have been a fly on the wall for that little run-in." Penn snickers. "Did you stutter around like I imagine? Or did you not manage to say an entire sentence?"

Working my jaw back and forth, I point a finger his way. "You better stop while you're ahead."

He reads me correctly, and his animation drops a notch. "You just stuttered?"

"You're such an asshole."

"You say that like it's new info," he says, continuing his amusement at my expense. "Really, though. How'd it go? But before you answer that, let me toss out there that I heard sparks were flying all over the diner so hot Claire had to call the fire department."

I shake my head. "Shut up."

"Just telling you what I heard."

"The firemen were there to order food, you idiot."

He thinks he's onto something. There's a glee in his face that means only one thing: it's going to be a long day around here.

"So, what happened?" he asks, resting his arms over the truck bed.

"You know, sometimes I think you should've been a girl with all the gossiping you do."

"This isn't gossip," he contends. "This is Neely-freaking-Kimber, man. Every memory I have of my entire adolescence has her in it. She bailed me out of jail when I was too scared to call my dad and you and Matt were passed out on moonshine. Remember that?"

My chuckle is so hard, it causes my thumb to throb. "I forgot about that. She was pissed."

"I didn't prostitute myself. The cop was just pissed off. He wanted to nail . . . What was her name? Claire's cousin? Anyway, doesn't matter. He wanted her and I got her first." He shakes his head. "Neely came through, though. God, I miss her."

Those last words echo through my mind.

I have shoved her out of my head for the last few years. Took over Dad's business, took care of my business. Trudged forward without her because that was the only choice I had. I hardly even think about her anymore unless someone brings her up in conversation.

So why do I itch to crawl into the truck and hunt her down?

Because I'm a fucking idiot.

My hand squeezes my finger harder.

"I gotta get back to work," I tell Penn, shoving away from the truck. "So do you."

"Wait. You haven't even told me anything yet."

"What do you want to know?" I ask. "I went into the café for a cup of coffee. She came in. We said hello. She left."

He looks nonplussed. "And?"

"And what? There's no more to say."

"You know how you know when there's more to say? When someone says, 'There's no more to say.'"

Fiddling with the bandanna, I consider that.

Of course there's more to say. But if I tell him I bought her coffee or noticed the new freckles across the bridge of her nose or thought about her so much in the last hour I wrecked my finger, he'll never let it go.

He needs to let it go.

I need to let it go.

I wipe my brow again. "She's visiting for a couple of days. Living in New York. Seems happy."

"That's your answer?" Penn deadpans.

"Yeah. That's my answer."

He scratches the top of his head. "Really, Dane? It's like you withhold the good stuff just to be a dick."

"What good stuff?" I laugh. "You want to know if she's hot? Hell yes, she's hot. No," I backtrack, realizing that's not quite right. "She's not hot. She's fucking beautiful."

My brain starts to send words to my mouth at a speed my lips can't quite keep up with. I start and stop four sentences before giving up with a shrug.

"Yeah, you're fucked." Penn smiles, but this time, it's a tiny bit less asshole-ish.

"What are you talking about?" Twisting my hat around backward, I let the sun hit my face. It'll be a decent excuse for the heat in my cheeks if Penn calls me out on it. "She's just a girl from my past. I ran into her. People run into their exes all the time."

"Just a girl from your past, huh? So if I tell you Brandon Atwood has a date with her tonight, you're cool with that?"

"He fucking what?" I bark, not giving a damn that my cheeks are blazing. "How do you know that?"

"I don't. It was a litmus test."

Shoulders slumping, a breath rushing from my lungs, I glare at him and try not to laugh. "You're a cocksucker."

"And you're a liar. What's worse?"

"Does the cocksucker charge for sucking cock?" Matt slides up to the truck and looks at each of us. "If so, that's worse. If not, I'll go with the liar." When we fail to respond, he grins. "This is going to be good, isn't it?"

"What?" I ask.

"Whatever the two of you are arguing about."

"We aren't arguing," Penn tells him. "I was making a point he didn't want me to make."

Matt pulls his brows together. "You made a point? Okay. This I gotta hear."

"I don't even have to make it," Penn says. "Let Dane tell you, and then you'll see my point. That's the magic of all this."

"Will you shut the hell up?" I ask. "Why do you have to make such a big deal about everything?"

"Uh, because this *is* a big deal."

Matt's head goes back and forth like he's watching a volleyball match. "Is someone gonna tell me or what?"

"Fine." I look at my brother, ignoring the shit-eating grin on Penn's face. "Neely is home."

His eyes grow wide. "No kidding?"

"No kidding."

"When did this happen?"

"I don't know. Saw her this morning at the café." My voice is calm as her face streams through my mind. "Yes, she was hot, if that's the first thing you wanted to know like dumbass over here."

"You said *beautiful*." Penn holds his hands to his sides. "What? You said it. I didn't."

"She was always beautiful," Matt admits. "That's nothing new."

"Yeah, but you should see her now. Fucking hell, Matt."

Their raised brows let me know they're curious where I'm going with this.

Answer: *nowhere.*

I open the cab of the truck and pretend to search for something just to stop the banter. Just to get a second to myself.

The vein in my temple begins to pulse along with the heartbeat in my thumb. My skin itches as if it can't keep all my emotions contained. I can't focus on one thing, one part of *this thing*, long enough to make sense of it without jumping to the next. I shouldn't give a shit. She's here for a few days. She said so herself. Even if she were here indefinitely, it doesn't mean she would give me the time of day or that I should even want her to. Or that I could actually do it.

I broke her heart. I broke her heart in the worst way I could, and the fact she didn't tell me to fuck right off is more than I really deserve. It's more than I would've given me.

A box of screws falls from the passenger's seat onto the floorboard. Penn's voice calls from the other side of the truck, giving me shit about my state of mind. I flip him the bird before going back to rustling through the middle console.

I can't make things not have happened. I can't undo actions taken years ago.

My hand stills over a packet of spearmint gum. Eyes resting on the little tree-shaped air freshener, I sigh.

I wouldn't undo them. Even if I could. Even if it would have saved her the heartbreak.

My shoulders slump as I back out of the cab.

"All that for some gum?" Penn asks, looking at the packet in my hand.

I deliberately open a stick and shove it in my mouth. "Want one?"

"Just in case you poisoned it, I'm good." He stretches his arms overhead. "So can we call off today and go see Neely?"

"No. Both of you go back to work." The gum crackles as I put way too much effort into chewing. "Now."

"You wanting to go alone?" Matt cracks.

"Why do I like either one of you again?" I look from one to the other.

"Because I'm your brother and saved you from drowning when you were ten. And we keep Penn around . . ." Matt looks at our best friend and shrugs. "Why do we keep you around?"

"I'm assuming so you can get pussy. So many come at me I can't possibly handle them all."

"How does that shit taste comin' outta your mouth?" Matt asks.

I watch the two of them spar back and forth. Despite the near-constant jabbing between each other, Penn's refusal to ever show up on time, and Matt's perpetual state of looking for something he's lost, they're the two I can count on.

As I realize they have stopped bantering and are both looking at me, I frown. I can't do this all day. "I'm going for lumber," I tell them.

"Is that what we're calling her now?" Penn tries to bite back a laugh and fails. Matt joins in, and their entertainment at my expense grates my nerves.

"If you need anything," I say, ignoring them, "you have about two minutes to tell me."

"I need about a dozen two-by-fours," Matt says, trying to wave Penn off. "And a couple boxes of nails."

"I figured we were going to come up short."

Penn digs a water bottle from the cooler in the back of my truck. "That's what you get for letting Matt do the calculations."

They chat about something quietly as I busy myself with picking up the screws on the floorboard of my truck. It would be a completely normal day if I didn't have a knot winding in the pit of my stomach so tight I can feel it radiating through my core.

By the time I get the screws back in the box and the passenger's door shut, there's a peace in the air. The bantering has stopped, and a stillness settles across the lawn.

Matt wipes his mouth with the back of his hand as he gazes over the forest below. "Can you imagine walking out your door in the morning to take a piss and then seeing this?"

"I don't normally piss out my front door, but I see your point," I say, admiring the acres of forest surrounding the building site.

"Well, I do and I get it." Penn takes a few steps in front of us. "Nice chunk of land."

"Nah, it's more than that," I say. I can imagine the yard full of toys, the house smelling like roast beef. "It's the perfect spot for a home."

Matt takes a deep breath and works his neck back and forth. "You know, I've been thinkin' . . ."

Penn groans. "Thanks for the warning."

"I'm being serious," Matt protests. "Hear me out, will ya?"

"We're listening," I tell him, preparing myself. Absolutely anything in the world could topple out of his mouth. Nothing would surprise me. A few things would irritate me, and I have a feeling he's headed that direction.

Matt pauses, possibly to get his courage up, and takes another drink. His lips pull together as he screws the top back on. "We're getting old, guys. Maybe it wouldn't be bad, having a house like this with a woman and—"

"Did you just suggest monogamy to me?" Penn gasps. "Do you know me at all?"

I give them both a look. "This day gets stranger by the minute."

"Fuck you, guys." Matt chuckles, shaking his head. "I'm just saying maybe there's something to be said for predictable pussy."

Shoving away from the truck, I laugh. "That's an oxymoron. Pussy is never predictable."

Matt nods. "Yeah. You're right. Bad choice of words. What about consistent pussy?"

I was right. I know where he's going with this, and I'm not about to let him get there without a few attempts at redirection.

"Consistent pussy means a consistent headache," I say.

Penn shrugs. "I don't know what either of you are talking about. If there's one thing in my life that's consistent, it's women."

Matt's head swings side to side. "You know what I'm getting at."

"Do we?" I raise a brow. It's more of a warning than a question.

"I do, and I think Matt better tread lightly." Penn points a finger his way. "If he kills you, I'm helping bury your body."

Matt and I have a standoff—him trying to make a point and me trying to deflect it. I have no clue why he thinks today of all days is the day to go *there*, but I refuse. He doesn't agree.

"Seriously. Do you ever wonder what might've been?" Matt asks, ignoring my glare.

I twist so we're face-to-face. I don't want anything getting lost in translation. "No," I state. "I don't. If you have to wonder why I don't, you better walk your ass away before I knock you upside the head."

Matt slumps as my point sinks in.

"What might have been wasn't for a damn good reason. It wasn't and it won't. How pretty she is or how long we dated or how many fucking sparks flew this morning doesn't make any difference." I look at my brother and then at my friend. "Get it?"

"Yeah. I'm sorry," Matt says, his eyes falling to his boots.

"I figured you might be." Glancing up the path, I succumb to the realization that if I stay here with these two, all we're going to do is rehash the past. I can't do that until I sort it out in my head. I need to go now. "I'm going to town. I'll be back."

"Got ya." Penn tosses his empty bottle in the back of my truck. "Sorry we're assholes."

"I know." Making my way to the driver's side, I pop open the door. "I'll go by Mucker's and bring us back some lunch."

"Excellent peace offering," Matt says. "I'll make sure I get the front done today just to be nice."

"Whatever." I climb inside the cab as they back away from the bed.

I sit, engine off, watching my friends make their way back to the jobsite, and I kind of regret biting their heads off. It was them just being them. They're always jackasses, but at the end of the day, I can't blame them.

Everyone was devastated when things between Neely and me ended. We were as much a part of Dogwood Lane as the train tracks through the middle of town. Baseball captain and elite gymnast. The all-American couple who would have a slew of babies if anything were right and fair in the world. Turns out, there's nothing right or fair about the world at all.

For reasons both good and bad, Neely changed who I am in every capacity. I don't think about her every day anymore. But when I see a ditch full of tiger lilies on a country road in the summer or find myself arguing to some unknowing soul that cheerleading is a sport, I think of her. Then let it go. It's all I can do. I had to let her go for her own good. I had to let her memory go for mine.

I start the engine, and as the makeshift ice packet falls to the floor, I slam my truck in reverse and back out of the driveway.

CHAPTER FOUR

NEELY

"S he goes into this half-hour-long dissertation about how adorable her granddaughter looks in her flamingo outfit," Mom says, relaying a part of her day. "I don't understand why people do that. It's not like I'm going to agree her family is the prettiest bunch of girls on the planet when I happened to birth the actual one myself." She looks over her shoulder and smiles. "Maybe next time I'll whip out pictures of you."

"Um, I'm not in a onesie anymore." I laugh. "I don't think it's a direct comparison."

"I bet I have some of those around here somewhere . . ."

"Oh, I bet you do. About fifty million."

She chuckles, going back to the chicken pasta dish she's stirring on the stove. The kitchen is flooded with the warmth of a home-cooked meal. My mouth waters, ready to eat more than my share to cap off a long-but-not-altogether-unbearable day. I might go as far as to say today was halfway enjoyable.

After the Dogwood Café incident with Dane, I slid into the bank to see Mom and ended up spending an hour chatting with her and her coworkers. They reminded me how I used to call Mom at work at three thirty when I got home from school and proceeded to keep calling to ask a million questions every few minutes until she got off an hour later. Apparently, I was quite the handful as a child. The term they used was "distracting." They don't know what distracting is.

Distracting is the way a certain pair of green eyes refuse to leave your brain even after the air clears of his cologne.

"Neely."

"What?" I ask, jumping at the intrusion.

"What?" Mom's brow furrows.

"What what?"

"Your entire demeanor just changed."

I hop off the counter and sigh. It's so much easier keeping things from her when she's in Tennessee and I'm in New York. "Just thinking. That's all."

She places the spatula on the spoon rest we picked up in Philadelphia last year on a quick mother-daughter getaway. Mini vacations are how we see each other unless she comes to see me in New York. I tell myself she needs to get away from here, that it does her good.

Facing me, the confused look melts into one of concern. "Do you want to talk about it yet?"

"Talk about what?"

"Why you're here. I don't want to pressure you, honey, but I would like to be there for you because I know good and well something spurred this."

Grabbing my glass, I head to the refrigerator and add some water. "I can't just miss my mom?"

"I hope you do," she says. "But you haven't just hopped on a plane and come home. Ever."

I lug in a deep breath. "Maybe I was wrong for not coming home before now. I just . . ."

"I know it's hard to face things here. We all have things we don't talk about in life. It took years before I even wanted to hear your father's name."

"I still don't want to hear that."

"Me either."

I take in my mother in her kitchen, wearing her apron with a relaxed air about her I never see in New York or while on vacation in a random city. A person looks like that only in their home. As I watch her move easily around the room, I realize I'm more relaxed here than I recall being in a long time.

"If it helps," I say, "I did miss home. Even if don't say it a lot."

"It does help to hear that. I'm thrilled to have you in my kitchen and eating my food, even if I don't know what's on your mind."

"Yeah . . ." I blow out a breath. Leaning against the counter, I watch her as I sip the drink.

Once I open up to my mom, it's all over. I keep everything in a neat little box mentally when talking to Grace. I'm "New York" Neely with her—composed, professional, aggressive. But with Mom, I'm basically a fourteen-year-old girl standing in front of the woman who can read me like an open book. My stomach twists into a tight knot as I prepare to recount everything that happened.

"It's not fair for me to come back here and not even tell you why." I place my cup on the counter. "Thanks for giving me a little while to deal with it on my own."

"This house is your home whether you actually live here or not. You don't need a reason to be here, and you don't owe me an explanation. I just want you to know that whatever it is, I'm on your side."

"I know. I appreciate that."

She bites her lip as if to keep herself from saying more.

My heart thumps wildly in my chest. Her support was never a question. She'd stand up for me even if I were wrong. What I don't want to happen is for her to worry I'm going to starve to death or cast me a look of pity because of the decision I made.

I throw my shoulders back. "I quit my job."

"Oh, Neely." Mom's eyes grow wide. "Are you okay?"

My sigh betrays the confidence I usually go out of my way to depict. The sound is filled with the pressure and stress I've been carrying around for a few days, and my mother picks up on it right away.

"Want some tea?" she asks.

"Tea isn't going to fix this. Turn off your burner, though. The pan is starting to smoke."

"Darn it." She flips off the switch and gives the pan a final stir before scooting it to an unlit burner. It's a few moments before she's sitting at the table with two mugs of hot tea.

I don't know if it's the weight of the moment that sinks me into the chair across from her or the exhaustion I'm just starting to acknowledge deep in my bones. Regardless, there's a mug in my hands before I know it.

"So . . ." Blowing out a breath, I watch the steam billow from the tea. "Remember a few months ago, I called and told you I thought I'd convinced my boss to start a new magazine focused solely on females in sports?"

"Yes," she says. With a nod, she smiles brightly. "I believe you said you were 'knocking down walls,' or something similar. You were really excited."

My heart burns in the center of my chest. I close my eyes briefly, swallowing the taste of betrayal. The bitterness makes my face sour.

"Neely?"

"So Mark, my boss, called me a couple of weeks ago," I say past the lump in my throat. "We had lunch. He took my idea, the entire proposal he had me create from my vision of what this new monthly could be, and delivered it to his boss, Frank. It was really fantastic." My hands fold in front of me. "I worked with one of Grace's friends who does layout, and we created a visual of the website that would cater to mostly young girls and then one of the actual print version that would be for adults. I didn't sleep for two weeks, Mom. Just busted my butt to get this together to really sell it, you know?"

"And when you get that fire in your eyes, the one you have right now, you get what you want. I've seen you do it too many times."

Sitting back in my chair, I feel my spirits fade. "Mark said it was a go. Frank loved the idea. Said the market was wide open for something like this. Heck, Frank even sent me an email and told me he saw great things stemming from my proposal."

"So why are you telling me with no enthusiasm?"

A half laugh, half snort gets her attention. Wisely, she refrains from saying anything more, and instead gives me a few moments to remember I'm in front of my mother and not Grace. Word selection is important.

"I needed to apply for a position there," I tell her. "Put together a formal résumé as well as a sample six-month schedule of ideas."

"Even though the entire thing was your idea?"

"Protocol." I shrug, the anger I've been able to keep mostly buried shifting just below the surface. "I was talking to Lynne, another editor at the magazine—"

"We had lunch with her, didn't we?" Mom leans forward, resting her elbows on the table. Her gray eyes, like mine, are clear as she absorbs my story. "Isn't she the one who met us for paninis last year when I visited?"

"Yup."

"Why do I get the feeling I won't be having any more paninis with Lynne?"

"Because if justice is served, she'll choke on the next one," I say, shoving away from the table. Standing behind my chair, fingers wrapped around the top rung, I look at my mother. "She told me she wasn't interested in the position and to use her as a sounding board. Then she took my ideas and submitted her own application."

The words slip through my gritted teeth, coming out twisted and sharp. I bite down hard to avoid adding that I'm 99 percent sure she accessed my computer and found my mock-ups. Her layouts, her design ideas—things I didn't show her—were too similar to be happenstance.

My blood pressure soars so high my head almost explodes. But at the same time, my heart sinks. This wasn't just a coworker betrayal. That I could've handled. This was a betrayal of the worst kind—from a so-called friend.

Lynne was my friend. If she'd said she wanted the position, I would've cheered her on. I might've even ensured we went after different jobs. But to backstab me like she did? Over something she knew was so important to me? I can't.

"Oh, Neely, honey. I'm so sorry." Mom gets to her feet but doesn't come toward me.

"I had to quit," I tell her. "It felt like such a betrayal to have put so much work into this and then be overlooked. It was my idea. My brainchild. I just refuse to work there out of principle." I turn away so she doesn't see the wetness washing over my eyes. "I'll be fine. I promise."

"You can stay here as long as you want. Forever, if you feel like it."

Laughing, I sniffle and turn back to her. "I just need a couple of days to breathe. But thanks for the offer."

She comes around the table, and I almost fall into her arms. She holds me close, her hands around the small of my back as she sways gently back and forth.

"I'm so proud of you. You know that, right?" she asks, planting a kiss on my cheek as she lets me go. "I've done a lot of things wrong in my life, but every time I look at you, I know I got one right."

"Stop it," I tell her. "Don't make me cry. If I cry, I'm going to be mad."

"Well, it's true," she says, dabbing at her eyes with a napkin. "You've always been my little crusader. Remember when you sold lemonade that one summer because you saw the animal shelter didn't have enough funds for food?"

"I raised three hundred dollars," I remind her.

"You did." She laughs. "I think I spent a hundred on supplies."

"I'm sure the animals appreciated it." I lean against the counter again, my load a little lighter. After a quick sweep of my mother's face, I shake my head. "I'm going to be fine. I promise."

"I know, sweetheart," she says, lifting her tea. Her tone is soft. It's the one she always used when she'd come into my bedroom late at night right after my father left us and whisper to me that everything would be all right. "I worry. You know that."

"I'm not going to be homeless. There are people looking over my résumé as we speak. Besides, like Grace says, when is the last time I took a few days off? Maybe this is a good thing."

"I'll never argue with getting to spend more time with you."

"Right." Despite the resoluteness in my voice, my spirit feels less convinced. My pride stings. "I put my life into that company," I say before I can think twice. "I did everything right. I worked my butt off. I went out of my way to find gems of stories, the ones that resonate with readers. I had little girls sending me letters. Those things are . . ."

I don't know how to summarize what those things are to me. Looking at my mom, I shrug.

"Those things are what make your world go 'round," Mom whispers.

"It's why I wanted to do this in the first place," I say, my shoulders dropping. "That was my dream. *Is* my dream. To make a difference. To matter. To feel like I have a role in the world, and now . . ."

Mom sets her mug down, dabbing at her eyes with her fingertips. "This door closed, but another will open. It's how life works. As much as you loved it there, it's not where you are meant to be."

With a half laugh, I pick up a napkin off the table and touch it to my cheeks. "I could just take a job today at some random magazine, but I don't want just another job. I want to be needed. I want what I thought I had. The opportunity of a lifetime."

"Give it time," she says. "And who knows? Maybe a door will open here in Tennessee."

I laugh. "I love your optimism, Mom, but I think that's a stretch."

"Never know."

My growling stomach calls notice to the unattended pasta on the stove. Talk of work behind me for the time being, I want to move on. To anything. "I'm hungry. Let's eat."

She looks at the stovetop, then back at me. She takes in my cues, and a slow smile stretches across her pink-lined lips. "Let's go for margaritas."

"Really?" I laugh. "What's happened to you? I come home, and you're drinking decaf and tequila."

"Oh, the tequila isn't for me, sweetheart." She leads me into the dining room, where our purses sit on a little table my grandfather made when Mom was a child.

"Who's it for, then?" I ask, grabbing my purse.

"You." She looks at me and grins. "I feel like it'll help you tell me about seeing Dane at the café today."

"Dane," I whisper.

His name tastes like strawberry wine and balmy summer nights. As weird as it sounds coming out of my mouth, there's something so familiar. His name just rolls off my tongue like I've practiced it a million times. Probably because I have. And my tongue probably wonders why this time isn't followed by a curse word.

"I saw him in the bank last week. He's so handsome, Neely."

Rolling my eyes at the dreamy way she says it, like it's the epitome of her life's ambition to see the two of us together, I sigh dramatically.

"Well, I'm sure there's some kind of scandal brewing under all that handsome," I mutter, kind of hoping it's true. I don't want him to be nice. Or kind. Or anything reasonable that will make me not dislike him.

"I believe he lives a very boring life," Mom says. "You know, he spends all of his time—"

"No." I cut her off unapologetically. "I don't want to know how he spends his time or what he looked like in the bank or what he's doing with his life . . ."

I don't want to know anything about him. Not because I'm not curious, because I am. I've wondered about his life a thousand times since I saw him today. It's because I'm happier living with the little story I've created for him in my head than with any sort of reality that might be better.

"Let's go for margaritas, but there will be no talk of Dane Madden," I say firmly. "Deal?"

She laughs and almost dances toward the door. "Deal."

"Since when did you become a decaf-loving socialite liar?"

She just laughs some more.

CHAPTER FIVE

NEELY

There are no organic strawberries.

A little petulant, I eye the produce in front of me. Graber's is this town's only grocery store, and their fresh produce section is lacking. I'm not entirely sure Graber's even meets the definition of a true grocery store, but it's all I have to work with. After two giant peach margaritas last night, I have no desire to drive to the next town over for anything.

"This will have to do," I mutter, picking up a flat of blueberries.

"I thought you were allergic to blueberries." The man's tone behind me has a huskiness to it, like he hasn't been awake long. I jump, not because I don't recognize it but because I do.

My heart twists right along with my torso as I see Dane standing behind me. He's fresh from a morning shower. A blue-and-black flannel, top button undone, sleeves rolled to his elbows, should not look this good.

He shouldn't smell this good either. *Dear Lord Almighty.*

I must look like an idiot with my mouth agape because he takes a step back. Sticking his hands in his pockets, he rocks back on his heels like he might turn and go. The thought forces words from my mouth too quickly.

"What are you doing here?" I ask, shoving the cart between us like some kind of shield.

"Um, getting groceries."

"Yeah. Of course." *Stupid, stupid, stupid.*

I don't know what else to say or if I should say anything at all. We just look at each other like two people who once knew each other so intimately and are now as much strangers as people can get. Two people who know the depths of love and pain too great to ignore.

He holds a hand to his chest in a move I'm not sure he realizes he makes. My heart tugs as I look at the spot where my head used to lie while we snuggled on the couch and watched movies.

Stop. It. Neely.

"So, blueberries?" He nods toward my cart.

"Not my favorite, but there aren't any strawberries that look edible."

"But I thought you were allergic?" He nods to the container again. "Don't you blow up like that little girl on *Willy Wonka* when you eat those things?"

Laughing despite my insides collapsing that he remembered, I shrug. "How did you remember that?"

"Matt teased you about it for years." He chuckles. "How could I not?"

"Well, Matt will be happy to know I outgrew that allergy and no longer plump up like a, well, a berry when I eat them."

My laughter fades, but the smile remains. It doesn't vanish even when my brain tells it to. Before I know it, his smile pulls mine right along with it.

"I didn't know you could outgrow a fruit allergy," he says.

"Guess you can. Or maybe it wasn't the blueberries after all. I don't know."

"Did you wake up one day and decide to risk it? Seems pretty ballsy, if you ask me."

"Actually," I tell him, "I ordered a muffin at this little shop in New York that I love. I didn't know it had blueberries in it until after I ate the whole thing, and I didn't get sick."

"But you still could've," he counters. "Maybe that one muffin was an anomaly."

"Maybe. But I've had blueberries about a million times since then, and . . . nothing."

"You always were a gambler." He winks.

"*Were* a gambler. Were. Past tense. Trust me," I say. "Gambling is for the young and dumb, and I am not either anymore."

He tosses me a soft, genuine smile that makes my insides melt. "I never would've called you dumb."

I put the berries in my cart and consider how dumb I am right now to be talking to him like this. As I turn the corner, my phone buzzes in my bag. I don't have to look to know it's seven thirty and the call is from Grace. She's walking to work, probably venting about the sidewalks being closed and how slow people are walking. Instead of being in the office, laughing at her antics, I'm . . . *here*.

I look at Dane. *Dumb, dumb, dumb.*

Passing a swallow down my throat, I sigh. "I'm certainly not young anymore."

"You're not even thirty, Neely."

"True. But when you're close enough to thirty to say you're 'not even thirty,' that means you're basically thirty."

"It's just an age."

"True, I guess," I say. "But I'm old enough to need to be a little more sure-footed in things. I don't have my twenties in front of me to take risks and recoup quickly." I take in his somber expression and hear the buzz of my voice mail chirp in my purse. "I have to stop putting all my hopes on the line without some safety net. It's too big of a gamble. I've fallen too hard, too many times."

His chin drops and he looks away. My insides squeeze as if they're chastising me for causing this reaction. Ignoring the tightening in my gut, I eke out a breath.

"You probably think I meant that about you—" I rush, but he cuts me off.

"Yeah, and you're right. If you don't pay attention, life gets all messed up. I'm not fucked up about it."

The air is heavier than it was a few seconds ago, riding on our shoulders as we crawl past salad dressings. The force presses my sandals into the cheap linoleum floor, and I have to make an effort to pick them up and move them forward.

He chews on his bottom lip. "But you know, sometimes when things fall apart, you can learn something to help you the next time. Makes it less like gambling. You can still win."

"Good to hear."

"It's life, Neely," he says. "Live and learn."

"I guess when some of us fall, and we were all in, it must hurt a little more. You probably don't understand that," I fire back.

Our gazes snap together. He bites his lip harder—to keep from saying something? I'm not sure.

"Fair enough," he mutters.

The back of my neck tightens as his tone washes over me. I bite my lip, too, in the hope that it keeps me from saying anything else, but I succumb to guilt.

Despite whether that was deserved, why waste our time on it?

"I'm sorry. That wasn't fair," I say.

"Nah, it was."

"It *was*," I emphasize. "But I shouldn't have said it like that. It makes me seem classless."

"*Oh,*" he says, his grin returning. "You're sorry so you don't feel like an ass. Not because it might've hurt my feelings?"

"Exactly."

"So classy of you, Neely."

"The last time I talked to you, I was pretty convinced you didn't have feelings." I laugh. "So, pardon me."

He considers this as he plops a box of fruity cereal into his cart. "Okay. I can see where you're coming from there, and I can't argue it."

"Really?"

"I'm not saying you're right. Don't get excited."

"I was *so close*," I say, feigning defeat.

"Let's not get crazy, babe."

His term of endearment has me stutter-stepping around the end-cap. My shoulder hits a tower of potato chips, and the plastic rustles together, knocking one bag to the floor. I peek at him from the corner of my eye. He's looking at me with a dose of caution.

"Sorry." He winces. "It just slipped out."

"Apology accepted."

Our gazes refuse to break, although he's trying as hard as I am to look away. He finally bends to get the dropped chips as I fan my face to quell the blush in my cheeks.

"I don't think it's crushed too bad," he says, situating the bag on the rack.

"Just give it to me." I take it off the rack again and toss it in my cart. "I'll have a guilty conscience otherwise."

He laughs freely but doesn't comment. Instead, we continue down the aisle, going so slowly I could probably read every label as we pass. He points to little cakes shaped like stars with lime-green icing. Memories of those sitting in the passenger's seat of his car when he picked me up for school make my chest ache so hard it steals my breath.

"I haven't had one of those in forever," I say.

"I get them sometimes." He shrugs, the ridge of his shoulders flexing against the fabric of his shirt. "They're smaller than I remembered, though. They're half the size of my hand." He holds his hand out to demonstrate.

"What did you do to your thumb?" The nail is a gnarly shade of purple, and the end is almost double the size of his other fingers.

"Hammer." He makes a motion like he's swinging a tool toward his thumb and makes a popping noise.

"Guess you didn't take after your father after all," I goad.

"That's not nice."

"That's true. How many times has he hit his finger? Never. Because he's the best."

"You wound me." He tries to pout but ends up laughing. "He'd like to see you, you know."

My eyes dart to the floor. Leaving and never checking in with Nick was unfair. He was so good to me, loved me, even, and I just left. It was easy to rationalize then. He had Dane and his decisions to deal with, and I told myself having anything to do with either of them would only complicate things. That the responsible thing to do was just stay away.

That got harder as the years went on. I'd remember his birthday and want to send a card or see his favorite saltwater taffy and want to ship some his way.

I should see him. I want to, even. But the idea of being hit in the face with a family that isn't mine sends the lump in my throat rising.

"Yeah, well," I begin, clearing my throat. "I'm not sure I'll have time."

He nods, his face falling. "I get it. How long did you say you'll be around?"

"A few days, most likely," I say off the cuff. "Hopefully not longer than that."

I make a turn down the bread aisle, and he follows suit. I wonder how long he's going to follow me. I also wonder how much I'm going to buy before I have the balls to walk away.

"Why? You have something against this place?" he asks, his cart rolling to a stop. "Pretty sure Dogwood Lane is fond of you."

A swallow passes down his throat. I wait for his lopsided smile, but it doesn't come. Instead, a guarded hesitation is written across his face like he's afraid *he's* the something.

"I do have something against this place," I say, the lump in my throat evident. *You.* "My heart is in New York."

His brows pull together, and I have to look away.

Lurching my cart forward, the wheels spinning as fast as my heart, I push to the dairy case. I don't look over my shoulder to see if he's following because I don't have to. His energy wallops me from behind.

As I make the longest decision between almond and coconut milk in the history of dairy decisions, he stands behind me and waits.

"If you aren't going to be around long, Matt and Penn would love to see you," he offers finally, breaking the silence. "And Dad. A lot of people, Neely."

The disappointment in his tone, the slight accusatory nature, like I don't care for anyone anymore, pricks at my heart. "I've missed them, you know."

"They'd appreciate knowing that." He starts to laugh. "Just word it carefully around Penn . . ."

A giggle escapes my lips. "Is he still so ornery?"

"Time hasn't done Penn any favors in the growing-up department. Or Matt either, for that matter."

"Really? Neither have settled down? I figured Matt would have a wife and Penn . . . Well, I figured Penn would have ten kids."

"By ten women?" Dane chuckles.

"I didn't say that. But yeah," I add, laughing.

"Matt was almost married a few years ago to this chick he met at a bar in Nashville, but surprise, surprise. It didn't work out. And Penn . . ."

"Same Penn?"

"Same Penn," he admits. "Sleeping with anything that will move."

"That's so gross."

He holds his hands out like he's told him the same thing. "They'll be at Mucker's tomorrow night. I'm seeing them this morning if you want me to pass anything along."

I don't know what to pass along because I don't know them anymore. A "hello" seems pointless and a "call me sometime" ridiculous, and I just wish this weren't so weird.

Imagining their faces—Matt's huge smile and Penn's wisecracking grin—makes me want to tell Dane I'll swing by and see them. But as soon as the words are on my tongue, I consider how awkward it might be, and I chicken out.

My cart becomes super interesting as I flip my gaze to the random contents. The air between us moves as if on the precipice of something. Like it's waiting for us to switch into the next phase of this conversation, one I can't identify.

"Let them know I asked about them," I say finally.

Dane seems disappointed. "Will do."

I realize how much time I've spent walking the aisles for no reason, and if it were any other man standing with me, I'd pray to God he'd ask for my number. He is insanely attractive and remembers details about me and smells so good I want to attach myself to his chest and just breathe him in.

But it's not. It's Dane. And with all the comfortableness that comes with being around him, so do hope and worries and assumptions, and I find myself hating I ever turned around to see him today. Even more, I hate that I came home at all, because now I can't just hate him. Now things are messy.

A part of me will never forgive him for what he did. I may have found the pieces of my broken heart, but they'll never fit together the way they did before that Saturday morning when he destroyed it.

We can't be friends. I can't be a part of his life. I can't have that time of my life thrown in my face every time I see him or think about him.

The longer I stay here and chitchat with him, however harmless it may seem, the harder it's going to make forgetting him again. Because that's how our story ends. With goodbye.

I feel his gaze on my cheek, and when I look up, he's trying to see right through me. The greens swim with the yellows in his irises, and I could lose myself there so easily. So I look away.

"Neely . . ."

"I need to go," I say, giving him the best smile I can. "Good to see you again."

His exhale is hasty. He reaches for my cart but stops himself short.

My hand trembles against the red plastic cart handle, my palm sliding off and dropping to my side. I hate how his eyes make me want to reach out to him. I loathe that I will now remember this feeling tonight as I'm lying in bed and attempting to sleep. Wishing things could be different. Regretting that they can't, that I wasn't quite enough, and that he didn't even want to fight for me. For us.

He didn't even try.

"Want to meet up for drinks or something?" he asks, playing with a slice along the thigh of his jeans. "Just to catch up."

I pause, ignoring the burning sensation over the bridge of my nose and gathering myself before answering. "What do we have to talk about, Dane?"

He searches my face before speaking again.

"We don't have anything to talk about," he admits. "It's just been a hell of a long time since I've seen you, and I'd like to know how you are. *Who* you are."

It would be so easy to succumb to this. A bigger part of me than I want to admit wants to. His arms are the only ones I've ever felt safe in. His stories the only ones I've ever wanted to hear over and over. His scent is the one I think I smell on random streets in the city and find myself stopping, even now, to see where it's coming from.

But as I feel myself break, I remind myself I'm not eighteen anymore, and he doesn't deserve to know me. And I don't want to know him and all that his life entails.

"I'm just somebody you used to know that's home visiting her mom."

He scowls, unamused by my response. "It's that simple, huh?"

No. "Yeah. It's that simple." My heart drops to my sneakers, panic filling the void. I need air. I need space. I need a lobotomy for even talking to him. "It was good to see you. Take care, all right?"

We exchange a tentative smile, one that neither of us truly believes.

With a nod his direction, I flip my cart in a one-eighty and finally head to the cashier. He doesn't follow.

By the time I pull the oddball items I don't need from my cart and place them on the conveyor, the knot in my stomach has grown. I can't even remember why I came to the grocery store to start with.

My subconscious seems to be scanning the area on high alert for Dane's presence. I chastise myself again as I swipe my credit card.

It's that simple.

Yeah, right.

It's never that simple.

CHAPTER SIX

NEELY

There you are!"
Aerial's dark ponytail swishes as she propels herself across the gym. If the bright overhead halogens weren't enough to light up the room, her smile would do it.

Banners from competitions hang on the opposite wall, stretching the expanse of the room. They're visual proof of the excellent teaching staff. The other walls display motivational quotes, pictures of students in their glory, and a rack of trophies in all shapes and sizes. Couple all that with the faint smell of sweat and bleach, and it's like coming home.

"Get over here and give me a hug," Aerial insists, coming at me with arms wide open.

"How are you?" I ask as she pulls me in.

"I was at Mucker's last night and heard you were in town." She releases me but holds my hands in between us as she steps back. "I was going to swing by your mama's tonight and rail at you for not coming to see me."

"I've just needed a couple of days to myself," I say, curling my nose. It's a simple gesture, an automatic one, but it gives enough away for Aerial to pick up on it.

"Things not so hot in New York?" When I don't reply, just slump my shoulders for her benefit, she drops my hands. "Does this mean you're home for good?"

She starts along the edge of the mats toward her office, motioning me to follow. A few younger girls are stretching on the far side of the gym and wave in my direction. I lift my hand and move it back and forth, earning a giggle from the group.

There's a lightness in my steps as I follow Aerial. I've padded across these mats more times than I've ever walked anything in my life. They've caught my tears, heard my cheers, listened to my frustrations, and absorbed my perspiration. No matter what was happening in my life, what I was worried about or scared of, the gym was my sanctuary.

Aerial's office is a small, purple space that fits her to a T. She sits at her desk, and I slide into a chair across from her.

"Want to talk about it?" she asks.

"What? New York or the show?" I tilt my head toward a folder with SUMMER SHOW stamped across the front. "I heard you're in the throes of the best one ever."

"It's going to be great," she says, eyes twinkling. "The backdrops are overboard and totally too much in the best way. We somehow roped a band from Nashville to play after the final performance on Saturday, and someone from the mayor's office—Trudy, you won't remember her, she got here after you left—helped with the carnival. It's going to be incredible."

"I can't wait."

"So . . ." She sits back in her chair. "Any chance my star student could hang around and help out with it this year?"

My laugh dances through the room. "I don't think I'll be around for the actual show, but I'd love to help out until I leave."

"The girls would love that. You're kind of a legend around here."

"They're going to be so disappointed."

"Hardly," she says. "I bust out your Finals tape every year as motivation."

Memories from that epic night flicker through my mind, raising goose bumps across my arms. The roar of the crowd, the electricity floating through the air, the excitement rolling off my teammates as I stood in the center of the mat and waited for the music to start.

"I haven't thought about that in a long time," I admit.

"If I pulled out a perfect routine on national television, I'd think about it every day."

"I've had a lot of other things to think about, you know. Like rent."

She laughs with me.

"Trials of adulthood," she says.

"I'm really not enjoying adulthood as much as I once thought I might. It's freaking hard, Aerial."

She smiles softly. "It doesn't get any easier. But at least you're home for a bit. How does it feel to be back in God's country?"

It's not a loaded question, but it certainly feels like one. By the contented smile on her face, I know she expects an answer full of sunshine and roses. That coming back seems like a perfect fit and akin to a warm robe on a cool evening. Truth is, it's not. Not completely.

I struggle with how to explain that my adult memories take place on the streets of the city. How I love a good play in an antiquated theater and street food that may or may not make me sick. The museums brimming with history, the way you can sit in Central Park and lose yourself in the throngs of strangers, are my new normal. I miss them. I love them. I love them as much as I used to love the quiet streets of Dogwood Lane, especially when the streets here are filled with people who have lives and experiences I know nothing about anymore.

"It's strange," I say, tossing out the closest word I can find that gets near how I feel.

"Strange?"

"Yeah," I admit, shrugging. "I'm a fish out of water. I drive through town or wake up in my old bedroom, and for a split second, it feels like that's exactly where I'm supposed to be. But then I talk to people, even my own mother, and things aren't like I remembered them. How could they be? I mean, I'm not the same person I was when I left, so why would they be? Does that make any sense?"

"Absolutely. But I bet you won't feel so 'fish out of water' here long. You'll find your stride."

"I don't know." I cringe. "I'm used to being able to get a latte on every corner and Chinese at three in the morning. It's like I've gone back in time."

"No one needs Chinese at three in the morning."

"When you're putting together a piece that's due at six a.m., you need Chinese at three," I insist. "Trust me."

She leans back and assesses me. Arms over her chest, eyes narrowed, she sweeps her gaze over my face in a way that makes me squirm. "So, Neely, why are you really home?"

"What do you mean?"

"Why are you here? And don't give me the crap answer you're giving everyone."

Fidgeting in my seat, I shrug. "I'm visiting Mom."

"Remember when you used to fall off the balance beam," she says, "and I'd ask you girls why and you'd say you slipped. And I'd ask you why you slipped—what were you thinking?"

"Yes."

"What were you thinking that made you want to come back after all this time?"

"I quit my job," I say, shifting my weight.

"Maybe, but that's not why you're here." She stands and leans against her desk. "Shouldn't you be there job hunting?"

Scrubbing my hands down my face, I feel the weariness settle in my muscles. I should be there doing just that, but the thought of fighting that battle today is overwhelming. Being here, in the gym, at Mom's, seems weirdly more palatable.

"Have you ever become so tired you felt like you were running on autopilot? Like you go through every day in survival mode and you hope tomorrow is better?" I ask.

"I'm a mom. So yes."

I grin weakly. "I'm tired, Aerial. And not just from this whole job-loss, job-hunt thing—although I'm not enjoying that. But I'm just exhausted from life."

The words aren't a revelation, but saying them out loud seems to ring a lot truer than I even realized. I feel so much more run-down than I did when I ran in here, like verbalizing it to Aerial somehow gave me permission to feel it. As I wrap my brain around that, I imagine starting all over again—working my way up the ladder at a brand-new company—and I want to cry.

"Exhausted from life? How so?"

I suck in a deep breath and feel it fill my lungs. My chest is tight, too tight, almost, to fit all the oxygen I try to take in.

Standing, I pace a small circle around the office. "Do you ever feel like there's more for you out there? Like you love what you do and you find satisfaction in it, but like there's something else you could be doing that's important and you just can't quite get there?"

"Go on . . ."

"I thought the promotion I didn't get was that, and now I feel like I have no freaking clue what I'm supposed to really be doing."

She watches but doesn't respond.

"I love what I do," I insist. "I've done it for years, and the longer I do it, the months just add up and I expect to feel more validation, maybe, from it and it's just not coming. Not like I thought."

"You don't feel fulfilled. That's what you're saying."

"Maybe I don't. I don't know how to describe it." I shrug. "But when things went to hell, for the first time, I didn't overthink it. I came home."

She walks around the desk and places a hand on my shoulder. "And we're glad you did. But can I give you some advice?"

"Please?"

"There are some things in life you can't find outside yourself. What you're looking for is one of them." She drops her hand. "My mother-in-law taught me that after I had my second child. I kept thinking this perfect little baby was supposed to complete me, you know? That's what movies and books tell you. I had the house, the husband, the two cutest little girls, and yet I wanted something else. What I wanted, I found out, was to find me in the midst of all the things that make up me."

I nod, mulling that over.

"I am my family. My house. This gym," she says. "But I'm more than that, and it's easy to forget who you are and what you want and need and love when you're driven like we are. We want accolades. Trophies. Championships. Proof in tangible ways. That means we're worthy. But it's important, Neely, to reevaluate sometimes and be okay with wanting things you don't get a trophy for."

"I do need that," I admit. "I don't know why. There's probably a lot of therapy sitting right there."

She smiles. "Some people need parental approval. There are people who need a certain number in their bank accounts. Some get the same thing out of shoes. You and I do it with trophies."

I mull this over but am pulled back to the present by her gaze. "What?"

"I just want to add that sometimes what we want in life changes, Neely. And that's okay too."

"Oh, I still want what I want. That hasn't changed. I just want more, I guess. I just don't know how to define that."

Voices trickle through the open door as the evening round of classes begins to arrive. I glance over my shoulder to see a group of little girls huddled in a semicircle.

"You know some of their parents," Aerial tells me. "Competed with and against a lot of them. There's some talent out there."

Twisting around in my seat, I take in Aerial's narrowed eyes. "Why are you looking at me like that?"

"I have a favor to ask."

"Sure. Shoot."

"Is there any way you can come by tomorrow afternoon and help out? Jessica has a family obligation I just remembered, and I'm going to be shorthanded."

"Sure," I say, my brain still reconciling her speech. "It's not like I have anything else to do."

She stands as a voice calls her name from the gym floor.

"I can help out tonight too," I offer, getting to my feet.

"Not what I heard," she teases.

"What are you talking about? I don't have plans. And Mom splurged on margaritas last night, so she won't drink again for a year."

"I went into Dogwood Café this morning for an English muffin, and Claire told me you were going out with her tonight."

My eyes almost fall out of my head. "I have no idea what you're talking about."

"I think it might be a good idea." Aerial's arms cross over her chest, and she flips me a look only a well-seasoned coach can deliver. "When was the last time you did something really memorable? Just for you?"

I give her the look of a defiant student. "Three months ago. Rob Thomas, live. It was amazing."

Her arms fall to her sides. "If you're counting fun in months, you have a bigger problem than I realized."

"I may or may not have problems, but fun isn't one of them." When she tilts her head my way, I roll my eyes. "I have plenty of fun. Look at me, coming home on a whim. *I'm spontaneous.*"

"You might've forgotten, but you have people here who love you, Neely. People who would love to see you. Claire is only the tip of the iceberg."

"That's not true. They don't even know who I am anymore. It would be rehashing memories that don't matter."

Her head cocks to the side, and she considers my words. She draws in a long breath before speaking again. "Have you seen anyone but Claire?"

My throat squeezes. "Yeah."

"Who?"

"Dane," I admit, toeing the floor with my shoe.

The longer she goes without a reply, the faster my heart beats. The deeper the silence gets, the clearer the picture of him becomes in my mind and the harder the knot that I'm beginning to hate twists in my stomach.

Finally, I look up at her.

"How'd that go?" Her words are pronounced carefully, each syllable nice and even like I'm some kind of caged tiger that might pounce if mishandled.

"It went fine."

"Fine, huh?"

"Yup. Fine."

"All right. If that's all you want to say, then so be it."

I blow out a breath. "That's all I want to say. He's really just a guy I happen to have a history with whom I ran into recently. It's fine. It was just some stupid juvenile obsession, and that's over."

"You sure about that?"

No. "Absolutely."

"Miss Aerial!" Our attention turns toward the gym as the little girl from the café waves. "Is that Neely? From the videos?"

I give her a little wave, trying not to laugh as the troop of little faces look like a celebrity just walked in.

"Hi, girls," I say.

They give me a mix of waves, laughter, and a couple of shrieks that leaves me feeling like a million bucks.

"I thought you looked like Neely from the videos," Mia gushes. "But I didn't think it was really you."

"It's really me."

"Miss Neely is going to help us around here. Would you like that?" Aerial asks them, to which they wholeheartedly agree. "Good. Now, Mia, show me what you've been working on."

Mia turns toward the opposite end of the room, her chest rising and falling a couple of times before she sprints down the mats and tosses her small frame into a roundoff back handspring.

Her friends clap as she jogs toward us, a smile splitting her cheeks.

"Great job, Mia," Aerial exclaims.

"Very good," I tell her when she reaches us. "I didn't think you had that yet."

Aerial gives me a weird look. "How do you know her?"

"We met at the café," Mia tells her. "I told her about the show."

"Oh," Aerial draws out. "I see."

"Are you coming?" Mia asks me.

"I'm going to try. Okay?"

Aerial cuts in, giving Mia a pointer about her back handspring. I'm too distracted by my phone to pay much attention. It's a number local to Tennessee, but I don't know it.

"Hello?" I ask, turning away from Aerial.

"Neely? It's Claire."

"Oh, hey." I laugh. "How'd you get my number?"

"Your mom."

"Naturally," I say, shaking my head. "What's up?"

"Mucker's tonight. Nine o'clock. Be there. This is not a request."

"I don't know . . ."

"I do. Be there or I'm coming after you," she insists. "I've told everyone you'll be there, and I don't go back on my word. So, come. Okay?"

Glancing over my shoulder, I see Aerial smiling at me. I consider telling her no and spending the night brainstorming ways to get my life back together. But something about the way Aerial looks at me, and the way Claire seems so determined, makes me reconsider. Maybe I need a night away from the pressures of New York after all. If it's weird at Mucker's, I can always leave, and if nothing else, it will give me good stories to entertain Grace with.

"Okay," I relent. "I'll be there."

"Yay! Let me know if you need a ride."

"I'll be fine."

Except for the ache in my cheeks from smiling so hard.

CHAPTER SEVEN

NEELY

And then that movie star walked in. What's his name?" Grace asks. The phone muffles as she bobbles it on her end. "You know who I mean. He's in that movie I love."

"Oh, him," I reply, rolling my eyes. "I know exactly who you mean."

"Damn it. Now it's going to drive me nuts." She takes a breath before carrying on about her story from dinner. As she delves into the whos and whats of her evening, I tune out and focus on mine.

Mucker's sits before me like an old friend. The one-room sandwich shop, with its basket of fake ferns hanging by the front door, may as well be holding its arms wide open. It's been a staple of the community for fifty years. Focusing mostly on pizza and burgers with a decent selection of beer, it's the place to go in Dogwood Lane once the sun goes down. It's the only place, too, but that's beside the point.

There's a door inside that opens into a lot that was once a dilapidated basketball court. The owners bought it years ago and put a brick wall waist high around the perimeter. With some added shrubs and black iron fencing, it's a cozy little patio that gets more use than the seven or eight tables inside the actual pub.

As Grace chatters on, I do my best to figure out who's here. The shrubs are so big, and the only light comes from an outdoor lantern hanging above the door and haphazardly hung string lights around the fencing. It's difficult to make out anything, or anyone, for sure.

It's the "anyone" part that has my palms sweaty.

"And we were supposed to listen to a comedian uptown, but screw that." Grace sighs. "I've had enough action for one night."

"Sounds like it."

She snorts. "Whatever. You weren't even listening."

"I was too!" Moving up in the driver's seat, I shake the fog from my head. A warm breeze billows through the open car window. "You told me all about . . . dinner . . ." I scramble to come up with something else she talked about but fall short. "And your outfit?"

"It's a good thing I love you." She laughs. "What are you doing tonight?"

"Not what I should be doing." My index finger touches my lips, and despite all the germs I know are on my fingernail, I bite it anyway. "I'm so stupid, Grace."

"You better not tell me you're at home throwing a pity party. I swear to all that's holy I'll be on the next flight to Tennessee."

Someone stands on the other side of the fence. A blue cap rises just to the top of the shrub, and I can barely make out a Dodgers logo.

"Shit . . ." I whisper, but not soft enough to slip by Grace.

"Okay. What are you doing?"

A burst of laughter comes from the other side of the shrubbery. Several voices ring through the mix and swirl around me. My chest rises and falls in deep, steady succession, but it takes a lot of effort to keep it that way.

"I took your advice." I gulp. "Again."

"Does it involve hay and flannel? Because if it does, I'm jealous."

"No." I laugh. "I'm sitting in front of Mucker's."

"Which is?"

"A little pub sort of thing. I ran into an old friend, and she invited me out tonight."

"That's great. Exactly what you need. Go have fun and let your hair down."

My laughter fills the car. "That's a random saying for you to spout."

"I was with this banker last night, and he said it." She groans. "He had an accent that he said was British, but it kind of wore off in the middle of sex. I'm not sure about all that, but his skills in the sheets were sublime. I had no idea an investment banker would be that *thorough*."

Settling back into the leather seat, my eyes still glued to the patio, I blow out a breath. "Maybe that's the answer to my problems."

"Not following you."

"I need to find a thorough investment banker who takes care of everything, if you know what I mean. Then I could just sit at home and run my own magazine. It would be perfect."

"So you want a sugar daddy. That's what you're saying."

"No." I giggle. "There's nothing sexy about a grown man being called daddy—sugar or not."

"So true. Do you remember the—"

"Lion tamer," we say in unison before bursting into laughter.

"He couldn't have tamed a first grader. Where do you find these guys?" I laugh, wiping at my eyes. "His ponytail was epic, though. I—*ah!*"

When I jump at the sound of a knock to my left, my elbow hits the middle console. My phone goes flying across the car and lands in the passenger's seat with a thud. I barely register the glow leaned against the seat before I take in the white of a smile on the other side of my door.

My heart blips like it's been tased.

Dane grips the top of the car, the sleeves of a white T-shirt slipped back on his arms and exposing his solid biceps. The haze of the lights from the patio creates a spectacular shadow across his face that steals my breath.

"Neely!" Grace's voice shouts from the other seat. "What the heck just happened?"

"Hey," Dane says, ignoring the commotion next to me. His cologne, spicy and warm, percolates through the night air.

"Hey," I reply.

His mouth forms an easy curve. "You gonna get out?"

"Yeah, I . . ." Glancing down in response to the shouted demand from my phone, I sigh. Dealing with Grace, who is going to want answers, doesn't sound appealing. Neither does trying to tiptoe around the minefield that is Dane Madden. As Grace shouts again, my decision is made. "I need to get that."

"Sounds like it."

Bending over the console, I snatch the device. "I'm here. Sorry."

"What happened? And whose voice did I hear?"

"I dropped the phone." I look straight ahead, trying to keep my voice void of any emotion whatsoever. "Can I call you tomorrow?"

"No, you can't call me tomorrow. I mean, you can, but that voice—I need answers. It had that twang that makes me want to . . . This could get awkward."

"You think?" I choke back a laugh. "Let me call you tomorrow."

"Call me tonight. Unless you're taking more of my advice, and in that case, a call after breakfast would be sufficient, you little minx."

My eyes flip to Dane's. His arms are now flexed. The lines in his forearms are etched deeply, thicker than I remembered, and I wonder vaguely if they don't look bigger because of the delicate green and yellow strings around his wrist.

"Neely," Grace grumbles. "Don't ignore me."

"I'm sorry." Shaking my head, I pull my purse onto my lap. "I'll call you tomorrow."

"That's a good sign!"

"That's not what I meant."

"It could be," she chirps.

"Goodbye, Grace."

"Go get 'em, tiger."

Laughing at the purr she adds to the end of her goodbye, I end the call. That's all it takes to shift everything inside both me and the car.

Dane's presence is everywhere—outside my door, in the air, and rolling through my blood.

As I look up at his crooked smile brought on by Grace's antics, which I'm sure he overheard, another zap of energy catapults through my chest. "She's a bit of a handful," I say.

"I'd venture to say I'd like her. She sounds fun."

"She's fun all right."

With a chuckle that trickles across my skin, he opens my door. "Unless you drove all the way here just to spy on everyone from the parking lot, let's go."

"I'm not spying on anyone." Even as I say the words, I skim my eyes down his wide neck, the way his shirt drags over the length of his shoulders, and at the narrowing of his sides into the waistband of his jeans.

"Whatever you say." He steps back, giving me room to exit the car.

My sneakers hit the asphalt. I stand, my legs akin to Jell-O that's almost perfectly set. They're just a touch jiggly from the energy careening through me.

You're a big girl. You can handle this.

The door latches shut.

"I know you aren't here to see me," he says. "But I'm glad you're here anyway."

"Thanks." My lips twist, afraid to smile. I look up as a roar of laughter comes from inside the patio area, and the warmth in my chest spreads my lips into the biggest grin. "I'm glad I'm here too. I think."

"They'll be happy to see you." He tucks his chin to his chest and heads the opposite way of the front door.

"Where are you going?" I ask. Pointing the other way, I make a face. "The door's over there."

He stops and sighs. "Yeah, and if you go in that way, everyone will stop you, and it'll be closing time before you get outside. Follow me." He waits to ensure I do as instructed before turning around and making his way to the corner of the property.

As I walk along the row of hedges, picking out voices I remember, feeling my heart fill with memories, I watch him move. Confidence oozes from every step he takes. Curiosity takes root.

"Dane?"

"Yeah?" He stops at the corner. I can see a little opening where the two fences, each forming a separate wall of the patio, meet. His Adam's apple bobs, his hands going into the pockets of his jeans as he awaits my question.

I await it too. It was on the tip of my tongue, an inquiry as to what he's been up to. Not building houses or fishing with Matt or playing poker with Penn, but all the other things—the little things—that make up who a person is. The hours from one a.m. to four. The way you fill an early Saturday morning or a late Friday night. What you do on a rainy Wednesday evening.

I consider his responses and pair them to what I know about him to be true, and how some of those answers will be impossible to shake. I realize I don't want to know.

"You go first," I say, nodding to the opening in the fence.

He pulls his brows together. He starts to speak but stops himself short. A realization settles over his eyes, muddling the green that was cloudless only a few moments ago.

With a shrug, he brushes the shrubs out of the way and disappears on the other side.

The little pendant hanging around my neck, a heart my grandmother gave me, vibrates with each breath I take. My shirt clings to my skin. My shorts are suddenly too tight. As I hear a chorus of laughter float through the greenery, I almost wish I hadn't come.

Taking a deep breath, I grip the metal fencing. "Why are you so nervous?" I whisper to myself. "You're going to say hi. Trade some stories. And you'll be on a plane back to the city in a couple of days. Nothing to be nervous about."

The metal is warm to the touch as I slide between the poles. The brick paver patio is strewn with pieces of leaves and an occasional beer tab as I step through. Instantly, my nostrils are filled with scents of spilled beer and garlic from Mucker's famous pizza. Adjusting my shirt, getting my bearings, I watch as Dane slips into a seat beside Claire at the long table in the middle of the area.

Standing on the pavers, looking at a table of faces I love so much, all I can do is smile.

"Look who it is." Matt's voice rings out above the music playing in the little overhead speakers. His face splits with a wide, handsome grin. "It's a good thing you showed up."

"Or what?" I tease. "What were you going to do about it?"

He scoots his chair back and heads my way. Claire, Penn, Dane, and a couple of our other friends are watching us from the table.

"I was giving you until tomorrow, and then I was coming to find you." Matt's arms spread and I fall into them with no hesitation. "How are ya, Nee?"

"Good," I say. My entire body relaxes against him. "How are you?"

"As handsome as ever." He winks as he pulls back.

"That's the truth. I've been all over this country and have failed to find a guy as handsome as you," I joke.

"That's about right." His chest rumbles as he chuckles. "Damn, it's good to see you."

He takes his thumb and rubs it on my forehead, right between my eyes. It's something he started in fifth grade when Penn hit me in the face with a spitball. As I screamed on the playground and threatened Penn within an inch of his life, Matt came to my rescue. Or so

I thought. He wiped the area with his thumb to quiet me down, and then, as I stopped yelling and almost felt better, he whispered in my ear he was really rubbing it in.

I kicked him in the shin.

I also opened the door that afternoon to find Matt and his older brother, Dane, on my doorstep so he could apologize. Matt muttered through his apology while I wondered why my stomach felt like it was full of butterflies as I stared at the taller, slightly lighter version of the boy who tormented me. I may have forgotten about the spitball and what Matt's "sorry speech" entailed, but I never lost the butterflies.

"Okay, okay," Penn says, gripping my shoulder. "My turn." He spins me to face him, and then, before I know it, I'm lifted off the ground.

"Penn!" I laugh as he turns a circle with me in his arms. "You're a brat. Put me down."

"I'm a brat? What's that make you? The girl who jets off to the big city and forgets all about us." He sets me back on my feet. "I'll be a little pissed at you about that for the rest of my life. Just so we're clear."

"Forget about you?" I tilt my head and bat my lashes. "How could I forget about *the* Penn Etling?"

The corner of his lip lifts, a dimple settling deep in his cheek. "Well, that's what I was thinking. Forget these other fuckers, fine. But me? Kinda hard to believe."

Matt shoves his shoulder, knocking Penn off-balance. They both laugh, their carefree lilts caressing me and warming me in a way that starts on the inside—somewhere deep in my chest. The spot amps up a few degrees when I catch Dane's gaze. Before either of us can absorb it, our attention is drawn to the commotion beside me.

"Damn you!" Matt groans as Penn grabs him around the head. They start a friendly skirmish, bumping a table as they wrestle for control.

"Those two never grew up," Claire says, coming up beside me.

"What would be the fun in that? Ow!" Matt grimaces, his face turning red. Penn's hefty forearm is clenched just below Matt's chin. "Stop. It. You. Ow!"

Penn lets go. Matt staggers a few steps, his hands on his knees and his face beet red. Penn brushes his hands off.

"Made quick work of that." He laughs. "Now I need a beer."

"You're buying me one now," Matt tells him. He and Penn head to the table, waving for me to follow. Claire and I watch them go.

"I didn't think you'd come," she admits once the boys are out of earshot.

"I almost didn't."

"Why?"

"Well . . ." Quickly scanning the area, I shoot my gaze right over Dane. My heart strums in my chest. Standing near him is like a shot of adrenaline right to my veins. "A lot of reasons, I guess."

"Although I can't fathom what better things you had to do on a Friday night besides coming to Mucker's and hanging out with us, I'm glad you made the right choice."

The patio floods with our friends' laughter, and I can't help my grin. "Me too. What can it hurt, right?"

"Nothing, as long as you can manage not to combust. The way Dane is looking at you . . ." A sculpted brow shoots to the sky. "I'm just saying." She holds her hands between us in defense before giggling and turning toward the table.

"Don't make me regret this, Claire!"

My request is met with a full-bellied laugh.

CHAPTER EIGHT

NEELY

S it by me." Penn pulls out a chair. There are three open seats at the table, but this one just happens to be across from Dane. "I insist."

I lower myself into the blue plastic seat. Across the table, between Dane and Claire, is Brittney Blevins. She was a year older than Matt, Penn, and me in school and is stunning. Time has been kind to her. Her long blonde hair shines in the hazy light. Seeing her beside Dane loops a knot in the back of my neck.

"Hi, Brittney," I say as I get comfortable.

"How are you, Neely?"

"Good. Thanks. You?"

She brushes a lock of hair off her shoulder. "I'd be better if Patrick actually showed up tonight."

"You need to forget him," Claire tells her. "I know you like him, but he's no good."

"You can say that again," Matt grumbles.

Brittney sighs. "I like him, all right? I know he's unpredictable and won't commit and gets jealous, but I do like him. I can't help it."

I hold up a hand. "Wait. Who is Patrick? Why doesn't that ring a bell?"

"He's that fool who ran his truck off the bluff and into Dogwood Lake," Matt says, flipping a beer tab toward Dane.

"Oh." I look at Matt. "Didn't someone die in that accident?"

"That's what they say," he tells me.

Brittney rolls her eyes. "No one died. That was a stupid rumor."

Dane leans forward, flicking the beer tab back toward Matt. The bracelet around his wrist looks bright against his tanned skin. "It wasn't a stupid rumor. Bobby Jones went missing right around that time, and the last person who saw him was said to be Patrick."

"That's not what he says," Brittney retorts.

"Of course he doesn't," Penn chimes in. "That's gonna make him look even more suspicious."

I drag my gaze away from Penn to the other side of the table. Claire is taking a sip of her drink, hiding a smile as she watches me. I don't have to look at Dane to know he's watching me too. The feel of his gaze has me shifting in my seat.

Clearing my throat, I sit back in my chair. "You know how it goes. Small towns are always full of silly stories and conspiracy theories. You can't believe everything you hear."

"I agree with that," Penn says. "When Claire told me you and Dane were practically screwing in the middle of Dogwood Café—"

"Penn, I'm warning ya," Dane says through clenched teeth.

My cheeks heat as Matt and Brittney laugh, and I punch Penn on the shoulder.

"What?" Penn asks. He stretches an arm over the back of my chair in a clear joust aimed at Dane. "Don't lie to me, bud. I saw you right after that."

"Stop it," I tell him. "You're such a pesterer."

"That's a nice way of saying it." Dane's words are crisp. "He has nothing better to do with his time than needle me."

"Yes, I do. You just tell me my stories all sound the same." He leans closer to me, the smirk on his face clearly for Dane's benefit. "Maybe I'll work on a new story for ya, Dane."

"Penn, you're pushing it." I laugh, shoving him away.

The waitress stops by the table and drops off a few fresh beers for the crew. Claire orders the Rocket Razzle, a new Mucker's invention, for me and a plate of fried pickles for the table.

As the group chatters back and forth, Dane and I exchange a soft smile.

"Are you dating anyone?" Brittney asks, pulling my attention away from Dane.

"Who? Me?" I ask.

She grins. "Yes, you. I actually . . . This is a little embarrassing, but I follow your articles."

"Really?"

"Yeah," she says, looking briefly at the table. "I think it's totally awesome you got out of here and did something big with your life. Every time I see your name on the website or in print, it just makes me really proud of you in a weird way."

My cheeks ache at the compliment. "I don't know what to say. That's a really nice thing to tell me, Brittney."

"Yeah, well . . ." Her voice trails off into a laugh. "Anyway, I figured you had some big-shot boyfriend in the city. That's how you roll in my head."

Dane's movement beside her catches my attention, but I don't look at him. I force my eyes to stay trained on Brittney. I happily accept a large frosted cup with a mixture of bright-yellow and red liquids from the waitress. "I don't have a lot of time for a private life, actually. No big-shot boyfriend for me."

"That's good news," Penn says.

"Why?" I turn to him, my drink in hand, and take a long sip. The spiciness of the rum mixed with the sweetness of the pineapple and the sugar-rimmed glass lets me take in a little more than I intend on the first gulp.

"I don't know." He grins. "I don't have a lot to do tonight. What do you have going on?"

"I am not sleeping with you, Penn," I say, shaking my head before taking another drink.

His gaze skims over the top of my head, his face lit up like a Christmas tree. "Got something you wanna say, Dane?"

"Oh, I got a lot of things I'd like to say, but I'm not about to give you the satisfaction of saying them."

I glance over my shoulder. Dane is leaning back in his chair, one arm draped over the armrest. He appears completely cool. Relaxed, even, but the vein in his temple gives away his irritation.

Turning back to Penn, I shrug. "Sounds like he has your number."

Matt groans. "Everyone has his number."

"Back to the topic at hand," Brittney says. "I need you to have a super romantic life, Neely. Do it for me. Let me live vicariously through you."

"I just don't have time," I reiterate. "I work ten-hour days. Try to get my money out of my gym membership. Travel for work once a month or so and spend time with my friend Grace. Where do I fit in a private life?"

Mentally patting myself on the back at how believable that sounds, I take another drink. It's all true, anyway. I don't really have time for a boyfriend. Even if I found one, where would I fit him in, in the midst of my responsibilities?

My bed.

"You have to make time for a private life," Claire chimes in, ripping me away from my vision of a male form with a green-and-yellow bracelet tangled up in my sheets. "I learned that the hard way."

"How do you mean?" I avert my gaze from Dane's and hold up my glass to see it's empty.

"I work at the café to help pay my tuition at school. I'm going to be a dental hygienist," she tells me. She presses the slice of lime through the neck of her beer bottle. "I had a great boyfriend and thought life was good. Apparently, he didn't. I was too focused, according to him." She rolls her eyes. "So now I make sure I take time for myself."

Penn leans my way again. "She really just means she fucks me at least twice a week."

Claire throws a napkin at Penn, making him chuckle.

The waitress interrupts us, clearing off empty bottles and replacing them with fresh ones. As my friends give Penn hell, she comes back with another colorful Razzle for me. I waste no time diving in. The rum warms my blood and knocks off the edge of my anxiety. I can feel it rushing through my body and delivering a much-needed dose of comfort.

"Who did you get to replace me in New York?" Penn asks.

"Excuse me?" I laugh.

"Who is the devilishly handsome stud whom you secretly want?"

My snort is unavoidable. "I didn't realize that's what you are to me, but good to know."

"And?" he prods. "He's a musician, isn't he? I always felt I could've been a drummer."

Claire throws her head back and mutters something to the sky. All I can do is laugh.

"Well," I say, "you'll be happy to know you were irreplaceable. I spend all of my free time with my friend Grace."

"Is she hot?" Penn asks.

I turn to look at him. "She'd eat you alive, bud."

Why I'm surprised at the sparkle in his eye is beyond me, but it's there. Coupled with his little grin, the one that would tempt Grace in two seconds flat if she were here, I can only imagine the two of them together.

"When can I meet her?" he asks.

"So no boyfriend at all?" Dane asks, bringing my attention back to him. The sound of his voice sends a ripple of energy across my skin, and I glance up to see him looking at me.

"He really just means he wants to—" Penn starts, but is cut off by everyone's laughter.

"Stop," I say. Pointing my finger at him, I shoot him my best glare. It's not a great one with the rum in play. "Don't."

"I'm just trying to help things along. Help the inevitable."

"What's inevitable is that I'm gonna kick your ass if you don't shut up," Dane warns.

Penn extends his arm and shifts in his seat so he's sitting even closer to me. It's comical, watching his antics stir up a storm behind Dane's eyes. It's also gratifying.

"Can I get you all anything else?" The waitress places an oversize plate of fried pickles in the middle of the table.

"Ranch," Dane and I say at the same time.

"And I'm full of shit?" Penn laughs. "Please."

"It's salad dressing," I point out. "Everyone likes it. Claire likes ranch. Don't you?" Silently pleading with her, I watch the amusement roll across her features.

"Not with fried pickles," she says. "Just with salad."

"It's good on a baked potato too," Matt adds. "But these two," he says, motioning toward Dane and me, "are the only ones I know who eat it on everything."

Peering around Penn, I look at Matt. "It's Dane's fault. I was normal before he had me dipping chicken nuggets in it."

"That's gross." Brittney wrinkles her nose.

"It's really not." I bite my lip and pull my gaze to Dane. "Do you remember when we tried it on smoked sausage?"

"And macaroni and cheese," he adds. "I still do that, actually."

I cringe. "Me too."

We laugh as our friends call us disgusting and Matt orders another round of beers.

Despite the table full of people and the headlights shining through the shrubbery as people come and go, as Dane looks at me, it really feels like it's only him and me.

My heartbeat ricochets in my chest, my blood as hot as the late summer air. I take another sip of my drink and hope it cools me off. That, somehow, it negates the air simmering between Dane and me.

I'm struck by how handsome he is. How the lines around his eyes and the sharpness of his chin create a look of masculinity and experience. Yet when I allow myself to look deep enough, I see *him*. The little boy who lost his mother when he was ten. The teenager who had a hard time understanding his father's hard-nosed love. The young man who worried he'd never amount to anything. It's this Dane who has always pulled at me.

"I think you're being paged, Dane," Matt says, popping a fried pickle in his mouth.

Dane pulls his gaze away from mine, but mine follows. The woman from Dogwood Café is standing inside Mucker's and is waving at Dane. His face breaks into a wide smile.

I can feel my friends' eyes on me as I watch him react to the pretty brunette. His hand comes up as he signals to her.

"I'll be right back," he says.

He glances at me before putting his cap back on the right way. Shoving away from the table, he heads to the building. I watch him join her inside, next to a table. Her hands go flying through the air in animation. He shakes his head, his face splitting in an ear-to-ear smile.

Jealousy. I haven't felt it for years, at least not over a man. The occasional guys I've dated since Dane haven't been serious enough to really get torn up over. Yet here I am, watching him interact with that woman, and my stomach is smooshing together in the undeniable pit of envy.

Of course he has someone. Why wouldn't he? Hell, I'd want him, too, if things were different or if I lived here . . . *No.*

The expansive patio is suddenly too small. My shoes tap against the brick pavers, ready to flee as soon as my brain gives the go-ahead. Instead, I lift the glass to my lips and drag in a mouthful of Rocket Razzle. And then another. And then a third until there's nothing left but sugar granules along the brim and my head is covered with a thick fog that numbs me.

Everyone at the table is watching for my reaction. I could probably play it off—and I should play it off because what does Dane talking to some gorgeous woman matter to me?—but I can't.

I need air.

"Is there a bathroom out here?" I ask, looking at Claire.

She motions behind her, her eyes wary. "It's back there. Go around the tiki-bar thing, and you'll see the door. Want me to go with you?"

"I'm fine." I push away from the table. The alcohol hits my head in a hurry, and the shrubs along the far wall tilt to the right. Penn grabs my arm and steadies me.

"Easy there," Penn says softly.

"I'm fine."

"Didn't say you weren't." He watches me with a curious bend in his brow. "You want an escort?" He looks up with a wide grin. "I'll have everyone know that's the first time I've said that and didn't mean anything dirty."

My laugh sounds wobbly. "Thanks, but I'm fine. Honest."

"Okay. But if you fall and need CPR, I won't hold it against you."

I keep my hand on the back of his chair, and then Matt's, as I round the corner of the table. My instincts tell me to look toward the building and see if I see Dane, but I override them.

The inside of my skull screams with contradictory responses to this situation. One side of my brain tells me to waltz in there and stake a claim. The other side, the one that's logical and not completely buzzed, reminds me I have no claim to stake.

My heart lobbies for another drink.

CHAPTER NINE

Neely

The door is right where Claire said it would be. Before I tug it open, Penn rounds the corner.

"You found it?" he asks.

"It was pretty easy." I focus on his features, not sure if I missed something. "This is the right door, right?"

He nods. "I was just, uh, coming back here to see if they stuck the chalk in the tiki bar. They hide it from me."

I bite my lip, seeing right through his bullshit but appreciating it all the same. "You're all right, you know that?"

"Don't tell anyone and ruin my rep." He makes a face as he reaches over me and pulls open the bathroom door.

"Thanks, Penn."

"I'm holding a door," he deadpans.

"You're not just holding a door." I pat his shoulder as I walk by. "I appreciate you holding the door and checking on me. Don't worry," I say, laughing as he balks. "I'll never mention you being nice in public again."

"Good. We don't want to stir up the natives."

The door closes, capturing me and my giggle inside the little bathroom. I find the light switch. There's a little sink and a hand blower. The room bends into an L shape where I assume the toilet is located.

Fiddling with the lock, I try to latch it. It's old and a screw is missing, so it hangs haphazardly. The alcohol does me no favors either. After a few seconds of sliding it around, I get it. I think.

My back hits the wall, and I look at myself in the mirror above the sink. My cheeks are rosy, my eyes a wide, steely gray. The concrete block wall behind me is nothing like what I normally see in a bathroom mirror when I'm out and about. There are no chandeliers. No white cloth towels for drying your hands. No line of women with expensive clothes and perfect makeup waiting to use the facilities.

Just me.

A hollowness descends over me. I push off the wall, slipping my phone out of my pocket. Pulling up my emails, I sort through the names and subject lines. There's nothing there that I hope to see—no responses from companies looking for sports writers. Just a bunch of romance writers' newsletters and offers for dollar flip-flops and discounted shirts.

My shoes shuffle against the concrete floor as I turn the corner and spy the toilet. Just as I'm unbuttoning my pants, I hear the door squeak open and realize the lock must not have fastened after all. My heart flies to my throat, and the alcohol sloshes around like an angry volcano.

My breath stills in my lungs as I look into the dim light. Dane is standing at the sink. One hand is planted on each side, his head bowed.

I blow out a breath. "It's just you."

His head whips to mine as he staggers to his feet. "How'd you get in here?" He shakes his head, running a hand over his chin. "Dumb question and not what I meant." He sighs. "I didn't know you were in here."

"I know you didn't. You were inside with the girl from the café." The words come out before I have time to think about them. If I'd thought them through, I would've picked a better tone as well, because the accusatory way I said the words doesn't help much. There's nothing I can do, so I shrug.

"You mean Haley." He shifts his weight, his brows tugging together. His lips begin to tug toward the ceiling.

"I don't know what her name is."

"You got a problem with her?" He grins.

"I don't know her." The light appears to move above the sink, but I'm present enough to know it's really not. I lean against the wall and take a slow, deep breath. "She seems lovely."

"She is lovely," he says. "You'd like her."

"I'm sure we'd be besties."

He turns his back to me, but the way his shoulders vibrate tells me he's laughing.

I wonder who Haley is and who she is to him. Does he screw with her on the side, or does he know her little girl too? It's the last thought tonight, the one of Dane with a family, that draws my ire.

I do what comes natural: I throw my shoulders back, lift my chin, and pretend I have all the confidence in the world. It's an old gymnastics trick that works on the mat. It's not as effective against men. At least not this one.

Dane faces me, taking me in. "You know, if I didn't know any better, I'd think you were jealous."

"Of what?" I curl the corner of my lip like it's an absurd thought. "What would I have to be jealous of?"

"Haley."

A sound that isn't ladylike or explainable hiccups out of my mouth. I don't worry about it, though. I roll my eyes. The motion makes me a little sick, but it's worth it to make a point. "You obviously don't know me. I don't get jealous of pretty women, Dane."

"I didn't say you were jealous about *that*." He half laughs. "I mean, come on, Nee. You're the prettiest woman in any given room. Of course you aren't jealous about *that*."

My knees go limp, and I tell myself it's the rum. I also tell myself I misheard him, but when I look into his eyes, I know that's not true.

He takes a step toward me. And then another. With each step, my chest constricts harder. By the time he's standing in front of me, I can barely breathe.

"I hate it you're here," he says. His voice is almost a whisper, yet somehow, despite the softness, it doesn't lose a bit of grit. The words and texture are at odds, roughing over my ears and heart, and all I can do is take a step back against the wall. "I had just about forgotten you."

"I had forgotten you." I tuck a strand of hair behind my ear, my hand shaking against my neck.

The wall is cool against my back, the unfinished concrete rough. I fidget, and the edges of the material bite against the fabric of my shirt.

Dane closes the distance between us. We're so close that our chests are nearly touching. He towers over me with an intensity in his eyes that almost sets me aflame. Letting my jaw fall open in an attempt to breathe easier, I hear the vibration in my inhale. He hears it too. A smirk settles over his kissable lips.

"You hadn't forgotten about me," he says. "If you had, you wouldn't be reacting like this."

"Like what?"

"Like you know just how good it is between us."

"It *was* good between us," I admit. "'Was' being the key term."

"I have a feeling it would be even better these days."

I might gasp. I might whimper. I might confess that I was thinking the same thing, but my stomach is clenching so hard I'm not sure, and I can't hear anything over the echo of his words shooting through my mind.

Squeezing my eyes shut, I will my body to behave and my brain to take over and get me the heck out of here.

He reaches out and brushes another strand of hair out of my eyes. The back of his hand tickles against my cheek. A storm of goose bumps races across my skin, silently begging for more.

My stomach curls and I drop my hand to it to try to quell the ache. Before it makes it to my midsection, it bumps Dane's.

"I didn't mean to do that," I tell him.

"I'm not complaining."

He holds my gaze, a tempest brewing inside his green orbs. I peer into the swirls and feel his curiosity, hear the plethora of questions that mirror my own. Looking into his eyes doesn't put me on edge or feel like I'm invading someone's privacy like it does when you meet a stranger or go on a first date. It's the opposite. That's the problem.

The knot in my gut begins to unravel. My heartbeat slows. I start to lose myself in the pools of jade but am jolted back to reality by a drip of water falling into the sink from the faucet.

"I need to go," I say, shoving a swallow down my throat.

He shifts backward. "Need a ride home?"

"I drove here," I say, not moving a muscle.

"But you've been drinking and you're a lightweight."

Damn it. "I'll get Claire to drive me. Or Penn."

Tucking his hands in his pockets, he rocks back on his heels. "You afraid of me?"

"Hardly."

"Then let me drive you home. What could it hurt?"

Four simple words is all it takes to knock me sideways. I've replayed that exact line—*What could it hurt?*—over and over in my mind. Hearing it from his lips again is enough to nearly paralyze me.

He doesn't seem to remember. There's no light coming on over his head, no realization sweeping his features like I'm positive is happening on mine. He reacts to my reaction with narrowed eyes and a curious tip of his head, and somehow the fact he doesn't remember causes a pain to swell in my chest.

The force of emotion strikes a panic that radiates from deep inside my soul. I haven't allowed myself to delve too deeply into this situation for a long time. It's pointless. It will change nothing. But as my jaw hangs open and I try to bring precious oxygen into my lungs, I fight the urge to bound forward and smack him across the face—for what? For not remembering? For causing my chest to ache so painfully? For proving that everyone is a liar when they spout off you can have everything you want out of life?

Because I can't. I can't have him. And he doesn't even remember.

"Funny you should use that language," I say, clearing my throat.

"Why?" His face scrunches in puzzled confusion.

"It's like when you say, 'What could possibly go wrong?' and then everything actually goes wrong. When you say, 'What could it hurt?' I seem to remember it hurting so terribly I didn't think I'd survive." My voice breaks on the last word. Standing taller, desperate for him to get nothing from me but anger, I lift my chin. "Remember that, Dane?"

His gaze falls to the floor. His bottom lip sucks between his teeth as he toes his shoe against the concrete. "I don't remember that line specifically, but I get what you're getting at."

He looks up at me, the lines on his face etching into his skin. The water continues to drip in the sink behind him. Each ping of a droplet like a tick of a clock. Each second of our standoff like a fuse being burned.

The air crackles around us, wrought with an awkwardness neither of us can navigate. When I envision this late at night sometimes, I have a lot to say. Now, words seem impossible to articulate.

"You know," he says, bringing his eyes to mine, "I never got to tell you I'm sorry."

"I bet you are."

My response has his hands coming out of his pockets. He looks at me with an arched brow. "You know I didn't mean to hurt you."

The fuse has burned through.

"And that makes it all right, doesn't it? You didn't mean to hurt me. Gee, thanks, Dane." With a heated glare, I cross my arms over my chest. "I bet you were thinking that while you screwed Katie. I bet you were thinking, 'Boy, I hope this doesn't hurt Neely.'"

"It wasn't like that." He growls. "And you know it."

"I do? How would I know it?" I shake my head, fury singeing my veins. "Because all I remember is how bad it hurt to know you were—"

"We were broken up!"

"Because you broke up with me!" I shout back. Words pour out of my mouth, each syllable coated with so much pent-up emotion it surprises even me. "I thought we'd get back together. I knew it. I . . . loved you."

Blinking back tears, I step away.

"I loved you," he says softly. "I . . . You know, I didn't . . ." His Adam's apple bobs in his throat. "I didn't expect for what happened to happen."

My fists squeeze at my sides as my heart cracks. "You didn't mean to have a baby with my best friend while we were on a break."

The words sound wrapped in cotton, but they hit him squarely. His arm flexes like he's going to reach for me. He doesn't.

I squeeze my eyes shut to block out the picture of him standing in front of me. All I see is a nineteen-year-old version telling me that my best friend is having his baby followed by visions that have haunted me for so long of him holding a baby that's not mine. That should've been mine. He was mine.

When I open my eyes, he's in the same spot. Yet somehow, it feels like we've been shoved together. The drip of the water echoes through the stillness.

"Neely—"

I hold up a hand. "Like you said the other day, it doesn't matter."

"I know," he says. "It doesn't. Not really. But I would like to talk it out. Don't we owe it to ourselves?"

"I owe it to myself to not feel this way anymore." Running a hand through my hair, I notice the edges are damp from perspiration. "In a couple of days, I'll be back in New York doing whatever it is I do. You'll be here playing house or whatever it is you do with Katie and your kid. I mean, if you and she are still talking." Dropping my hand, I laugh angrily. "Probably not. You probably ruined our relationship for a one-night stand, didn't you? Good work."

"You have no idea what you're talking about." He cuts the distance between us in half.

"I know enough to know there's no reason to let you take me home. You made your choices and I made mine. Now we have to live with them, and I'm just fine with that."

He works his bottom lip between his teeth, absorbing my words. One of his hands claps against the back of his neck as he tries to release some of the stress in his shoulders. Finally, he shrugs. "You know what? You're right. Everything happens for a reason, Neely."

It takes everything I have not to fire back at him that I had to sacrifice my happily-ever-after because he decided to give some other woman a piece of him that was supposed to be mine. My tongue is heavy with questions. I want to demand he explain what reason is good enough to account for my suffering. But I don't. That will only give him more power. And *it doesn't matter*.

"Everything happens for a reason, huh?" I ask. "I don't know what caused you to sleep with Katie, but that's your problem. I won in the end."

His eyes darken. "Careful."

"Careful?" I laugh. "I'm not the one with a reckless history, bud. You got a kid by a woman you barely even knew, really. I got my dream job in the city. I'd say the end result was favorable to me."

He opens his mouth when someone pounds on the door.

"Hey, Dane. You in there?" Matt asks.

Dane doesn't look away from me. "What do you want?"

"Haley needs you."

"Guess it's a good thing I don't need a ride home, huh?" I shake my head, knowing he's going to go with her.

He does. He heads to the door but stops short of opening it. Looking at me over his shoulder, he flips me a look of pity. "Glad you got everything you wanted out of life, Neely."

The door squeals open, and I take a step toward him. "Dane . . ."

But he's gone.

CHAPTER TEN

NEELY

The sound of air whirling above my head lures me awake. My eyes open and expect to see the bulletin board across my childhood room that holds some of my gymnastics medals. Instead, there's a yellow-and-white-striped chair and a window overlooking a tobacco field.

My head pounding, I pop up on my elbows and try to remember where I am. Memories from last night filter through my mind. Matt and Penn singing karaoke. Mr. Mucker telling us it was time to go. Claire helping me to her car.

Dane's face in the bathroom.

I wince.

A soft knock raps on the white painted door, and it opens with a gentle push. Claire's head pokes around the corner. "Good morning," she says. She steps into the room. She's dressed for the day, her hair and makeup done.

"What time is it?" I ask, stretching my arms overhead.

"Noon. You're more than welcome to stay here, but I need to head to the café in about twenty."

"No," I say, coughing as the words get tangled in my throat. "I'm supposed to go to Aerial's today, and I don't want to be a pain in the butt." I throw the blankets off me and notice I'm in the same clothes as last night. "Do you mind if I ask how I got here? And maybe what happened last night? Because I don't think I've ever woken up in someone else's bed before. Except this one night in Boston, but that's a long story."

She laughs and sits on the edge of the bed. "We had fun at Mucker's. You sang some karaoke with Matt."

"I did?" I groan. "I apologize."

"You were terrible," she agrees. "But it was fun."

"What else?"

"Just normal Friday-night stuff. Penn found some sidewalk chalk and decorated the patio. Mr. Mucker isn't going to be thrilled when he sees that this morning."

"I bet not." I laugh.

"We ordered pizza and told stories and Patrick ended up coming by to see Brittney, and Matt . . ." She blows out a breath. "Let's just say Patrick will be avoiding Matt for a while."

I sit up. The pounding in my temples eases a bit as I prop myself up on some pillows. "What happened?"

"Nothing *happened*. It was what Matt threatened to make happen if Patrick didn't back off Britt. He's such an ass—Patrick, not Matt." She pats my leg. "Bet you missed the drama of Dogwood Lane, huh?"

"Right." I slide my legs off the bed and stretch my arms over my head. My joints crack as I work some life into them. "You should see the drama in the city. There are wars over parking spots and sidewalk space."

"For real?"

I nod.

"I couldn't live like that. No offense." She gets to her feet. "I'll be out of here, but if you want to stay, there's a key under the aloe vera plant on the porch."

I stand and my phone clatters from my pocket onto the floor. I retrieve it, no worse for the wear. "That's the most obvious place in the world to hide a key, you know," I say, giving my phone a final inspection.

She shrugs. "At least if they want to break in, they won't bust my windows or something."

"That's such a terrible way to look at it."

"It's a warped outlook, I know. I blame it on my mother." She heads to the doorway. "I'll let you know before I leave."

"I'll be ready in a second. Just need to wake up and find . . . Where's my car?"

"Mucker's," she tells me. "I can drop you off if you want."

"Please?"

"No problem. Be ready in ten."

Once she's gone, I sit back on the bed. The mattress bends under my weight, and I would have absolutely no issues with lying back and going to sleep. That is, until the room is quiet long enough for me to feel the niggle in my chest. It's a trigger that sends me right back to Dane.

Guilt sinks me deeper into the mattress. I shouldn't have been so hateful last night, even if I did want to hurt his feelings. Retaliating isn't my style, and the more I think about it, the worse I feel. I can't hold on to this and keep fanning flames that should've died out years ago. It is pointless and makes me feel nasty.

"Ugh," I groan, picking up my phone. Not in the mood for happy social media posts, I click the icon for email. Nestled in the middle of a shoe-sale notification and an alert for a new blog post on a sports website is an email from James Snow.

Dear Ms. Kimber,

Thank you for your application to Archon Sports. We were impressed with your résumé and body of work and would like to invite you to interview via telephone.

Please let me know a couple of dates and times that work for you, and I will send a confirmation email and instructions.

Looking forward to meeting you,
James Snow

Managing Editor, Archon Sports

Springing to my feet, I do a little dance in the middle of Claire's guest room.

"Did I miss something?" Claire asks, coming into the room.

"I just got an interview."

"Must be pretty special to elicit a dance this soon after waking up."

"It's okay," I say, picking up my shoes. "I actually just left my job, so I'm happy to get anything while I figure out where I really want to land."

Claire sits with me on the bed. She watches as I slip on my sneakers.

"Sometimes we all need a change of scenery," she says. "Did you work there long?"

"A few years. They screwed me over on a promotion, and I decided to go elsewhere." I bite my lip as I stand. "It wasn't the smartest thing I've ever done—just up and quitting my job. But I write stories telling little girls and grown women alike they can achieve anything they want. Not to let anyone knock them down. That they don't have a 'place' in society. Staying at my job would've felt really hypocritical, you know?"

"Sounds like you made the right choice." She gives me a quick hug. "Now I gotta get to the café, or I will be job hunting too."

"Let's go," I say, following her out the door.

"Great job, Mia!"

She shrieks and jumps up and down, the bun on top of her head wobbling with each leap. "I did it!" she says, grinning from ear to ear. "Keyarah! Did you see?"

"Do it again," her friend insists. "Hurry. When I did my back tuck the first time, I waited too long to do it again. Go."

"It'll be better this time," Madison says from the side of the mat by Keyarah. "You know you can do it now."

The three little girls banter back and forth while Mia gets settled at the corner of the mat. She looks at me with a hint of trepidation in her bright-green eyes. Her hands clench beside her.

"Hey," I say. "Breathe. You got this, girl. Remember to push off your toes."

"Okay." She nods and takes a long, deep breath.

Motioning for the girls to quiet down, I take a step off the mat. Remaining as still as I can, I meet her eyes.

My heart sprints with her as she barrels across the floor. I hold my breath as she turns her roundoff, and my torso pulls up as Mia leaps backward and rotates.

"Come on," I beg as she unwraps her body and sticks the landing. "Nailed it!"

Her friends cheer as I clap, watching Mia jet across the room toward me. Before I can congratulate her, she propels herself into me. "Thank you," she says, her arms wrapped around my waist.

"You did it. Not me." I laugh. "Aerial said you almost had it last week."

"Yeah, but having you tell me I could do it was different." Her eyes shine with gratitude, as if she really believes that.

My heart nearly bursts. "That had nothing to do with me. It was all you, kiddo."

"She's been working on that forever," Madison says as she and Keyarah come up to us. "Since we got out of school. That was the first day you tried it, wasn't it?"

Mia lets me go. "Yeah. The last day of school I tried it for the first time. I freaked out, and every time I tried it again, I remembered falling so hard. I didn't think I could do it."

"Let me tell you something," I say. "You're gonna fall a lot. Sometimes it'll hurt and sometimes it won't hurt as much as it will bruise you, and you'll have that scar for a really long time. But you can't let it stop you."

"Sounds like you're talking about life." Aerial walks by, flipping me a wink. "Nice job, Mia."

"Thanks!"

"Did you fall a lot?" Keyarah asks me.

"All the time," I tell them. "The worst one was in Iowa. I'll never forget it."

"What happened?" Madison asks.

"Well, I got on the mat. I had hit this routine all year, and if I hit it, I would win." I skip past the part about Dane and how my mind couldn't shake him and his baby drama that day. "It shouldn't have been hard at all. My foot slipped and I fell, whacking my head on the beam on my way down. It knocked me out cold."

The girls gasp.

"My left side was purple for a long time," I admit. "I had to miss a week of practices. But the worst part wasn't any of that." I look them each in the eye one at a time. "The worst part was the fear."

"I'd be scared," Keyarah says.

"But you're scared of the dark too," Madison tells her.

"Fear is healthy. It's normal." I shrug. "It's your body's way of saying, 'Hey, something scary is happening.' But anything you do that you haven't done before seems scary, right?"

They nod.

"Fear is also a way of saying, 'We don't really know how this is going to end, so you might want to double-check everything.' And that's a good thing. The key is to look at fear like your friend and not your enemy. And," I say, leaning forward like I'm telling them a secret, "that little burst of adrenaline never hurts."

"I could feel it." Mia giggles. "Right before I took off, I felt really excited."

"That's it. Just don't like it too much." I laugh.

"Why not?" Madison asks.

"That'll get you in trouble later. Adrenaline junkies have lots of bruises as they grow up."

"I'm not growing up," Mia informs us. "When you grow up you have to get a job and a house and bills."

"And laundry," Madison adds. "I hate putting up laundry, and I don't even have to wash it yet."

"Don't grow up. That's smart," I tell Mia as I glance at my watch. "I think it's quitting time, girls."

"Will you be here next time?" Keyarah asks.

"Yeah. Will you?" Mia looks up at me. "You're the best coach ever."

"I should be. I'll be here for a little while longer."

They celebrate, making me laugh. Their reactions cause a swell in my chest, a sense of satisfaction that's hard to achieve. Watching their purity for friendship, for cheering each other on, for a desire to achieve something new, spurs something inside me to want to do this again. I make a mental note to find a gym in New York where I can volunteer sometimes.

Aerial announces classes are over. The other two groups head into the locker-room area. Before my three girls can take off, I turn to them.

"One more time," I tell Mia.

She trots to the corner of the mat and takes a steadying breath.

"You can do it!" Madison tells her.

"Use the adrenaline," Keyarah yells.

Mia laughs, lifting her shoulders, and then sprints across the room and delivers.

"Yay!" I say, clapping. "Good one."

"Thank you," she says, bouncing on the balls of her feet. "I can't wait to show my—Dad!" Her face lights up, and she scurries across the mat, tripping off the edge.

"Don't hurt yourself now," I call out, laughing at her decent rebound. As I turn to see her leaping into a set of strong, tanned arms, my breath catches in my throat. Looking at me over the top of her head is a pair of green eyes that can belong to only one person.

Dane.

Oh my gosh.

My heel catches the edge of the mat, and I wobble backward, completely caught off guard.

"Careful, Miss Neely," Keyarah tells me as she and Madison head to the locker room. I barely hear her over the white noise flooding my ears.

He holds her tight, his hand flat against her back as she hugs him hard. It's an image I'll never unsee or forget.

Dane as a father.

Dane as Mia's father.

The things I said last night rattle through my brain. I cringe, wishing the mat beneath my feet would turn into a hole and swallow me. Guilt swallows me instead.

My chest refuses to expand. As every moment I've regretted him sleeping with Katie, as every terrible feeling I've had toward her and their child takes this opportunity to come barreling back, I think I might vomit.

Setting Mia back on her feet, he rips his eyes from mine and turns his attention back to his daughter.

His daughter.

Bile bubbles at the base of my throat.

"I did my back tuck, Dad." Mia's voice cuts through the chaos. "Miss Neely gives the best pep talks."

Dane lifts his gaze. There's no warmth there. It's filled with an indifference that may as well cut me in half.

"Good job, rascal," Dane says to Mia. His features change as he gives her a high five. "That calls for some ice cream, don't you think?"

"Two scoops, okay? Because the back tuck is a big deal."

He sighs, rolling his eyes. "Fine. Two scoops, but they have to be matching scoops. Two vanilla or two bubble gum, because the last time you got two weird flavors . . ."

She rubs her stomach. "Deal."

They share a laugh that tugs at my heartstrings. I want to interject, to tell him how great she did today, to apologize for last night, but it feels like there is a wall between them and me. A wall built from shame.

She heads into the locker room, leaving Dane and me alone. He jabs a hand in his pocket and starts to turn away.

"Dane—" I call but am interrupted by Keyarah.

"Madison and I are staying all night with you soon," Keyarah calls from the doorway of the locker room. "And we're kicking your butt in rummy."

"You two cheat," he tells her, making her laugh as he heads toward the door.

"And we're ordering pizza because you burn it."

"Once. I burned it *once*. You have no forgiveness."

"Nope." She laughs, skipping back into the locker room.

Mia emerges and hands her bag to her father. She looks at him adoringly before turning to me. "Bye, Miss Neely."

"Bye, Mia." I give her my best smile before looking at Dane. I open my mouth to say goodbye, to smile, to do something, but am stopped by the apathetic look he gives me in return.

The door opens, a stream of sunlight coming inside that does nothing to warm my chilled heart.

CHAPTER ELEVEN

DANE

Two plates. Two forks. Two glasses. One frying pan and a cereal bowl from breakfast are freshly washed and drying on a towel beside the sink. Scent from the lavender dish soap that Mia picked out because she liked the color wafts through the kitchen.

The pipes in the ceiling squeal, and the distant sound of the music Mia plays while she showers goes quiet. Her footsteps patter overhead, and it's just a few moments before I hear her run down the hallway and the door to her room slam shut.

I shake my head. She's been scared of that hallway her entire life. Only in the last six months or so has she managed to get out of the shower and get to her room without yelling at me to come upstairs. Why I always listen in hopes she'll call for me is anyone's guess.

Drying my hands and throwing the towel on the counter, I make my way through the kitchen and living room. I stop and pick up Mia's gym bag and hang it on the hook I put up for her near the door.

Flipping off the television and turning on a lamp by the sofa, I pause.

Artwork courtesy of my daughter hangs off an old board I fashioned with a few metal clips over the sofa. Pictures of her with her friends from Aerial's, and a few with me, are framed along the fireplace in the corner. She picked out the blue rug in front of the television—insisting it was perfect for relaxing and that she now needed only a puppy—and the various throw pillows that I'd never choose. But they make her happy. That's all that matters.

"Dad! Come tuck me in!"

"Coming," I call back. Taking the steps two at a time, I hit the landing. Passing the bathroom and the spare room across from it, I get to the door with the purple star cutout hung a little crooked. It opens with a gentle push.

She's curled on her side, her wet hair all over her polka-dot sheets. "Took you long enough," she teases.

"Some of us have to do the dishes and pick up gym bags." I give her a look as I sit on the edge of her bed. "Any reason why it missed the hook?"

"I'm lazy?" she offers.

"I think so." I laugh before kissing her on the forehead. "Sounds like you had a good practice tonight."

She rattles on about her back tuck, and I do my best to feign interest. As she goes into the mechanics of the trick, my mind wanders. But instead of going through a mental list of lumber needed in the morning or wondering if Penn put the saws up before he left today, my thoughts go straight to Neely.

The look on her face tonight is seared in my brain. But then again, so are the words she spat at me last night.

"I really like her, Dad."

Coming out of my reverie, I peer down at my girl. "Who?"

"Miss Neely. I really like her." She snuggles into her bedding. "She makes things seem so easy."

You're telling me.

"She was always really smart," I offer, figuring that's fair enough.

"You know her?" She pulls the blankets from her face. "You know Miss Neely?"

"Yeah, I know Miss Neely. We grew up together. She was in Uncle Matt's class." Rubbing the back of my neck, I laugh. "Why are you looking at me like I said I knew a rock star?"

"Did you know she was a college champion?"

"Yes. And she had many state titles before that. She also won the Spell Bowl in eighth grade and was on the Academic Bowl team in high school. Two or three years, I think."

She gasps. "How did I not know you knew her?"

"I know a lot of people you don't know I know." I wait for a response but am met with only a slack jaw. "What? Am I supposed to give you a list of all the people I've ever known?"

Mia tosses the blankets back and sits up. "Yes, if they're important."

"Lie back down," I tell her. Chuckling, I help her get situated again. Once she's under the covers, she waits patiently. I try to outwait her, but I know she'll win. With a sigh, I shake my head. "Fine. I knew Neely really well. At one point in my life, I thought I'd marry her."

The words slip easily by my lips. They sound right and that annoys me.

"Why didn't you? She's really pretty, Dad. And smart, like you said. And she's so nice."

"She's all those things, rascal."

My gaze settles on a picture of Mia and Katie, the only one we have. Mia is all bundled up in pink blankets the day we brought her home. It sits on top of her dresser in a little black frame. I never catch her looking at it, and she never moves it but insists it stays.

My heart cracks because that love, a mother's love, is one I don't think Mia will ever know. I'm not sure Katie has it in her to give that kind of affection. We never shared it in the ten months we were together, roughly speaking. And she didn't show it to our daughter in the month she stuck around after she gave birth.

My only solace in it all is that Katie knew enough to just leave. She packed her car, told me we were better off without her, that she had no inclination to be a mother, and left. My mother couldn't do that; she drank herself to death right in front of us.

"So . . ." Mia nudges my arm. "Why didn't you marry her?"

Because I broke up with her so she'd go to college. Got drunk. Got Katie pregnant. And never spoke to Neely again after telling her the news.

"There's more to getting married than finding a pretty, smart, nice person," I say. Standing up, I tuck the sheets in around her.

"I bet she would've married you."

I act like I'm shocked. "Are you saying I'm awesome?"

"No." She giggles. "I'm saying when you walked into the gym today, she made that face at you that Penn makes at Haley."

"Mia, Penn makes that face at everyone." I flip on her nightlight. "And if Penn ever does anything, you should do the opposite. Big lesson right there. Did I land it?"

"As good as I landed my tuck."

"Great." I kneel at the edge of her bed. She closes her eyes and folds her hands together in front of her face. "Dear God, thank you for all the blessings you've given us. Please protect us while we sleep. Amen."

"Amen." Her lashes flutter open as she yawns. "I love you, Dad."

"Love you, rascal." After a kiss to her forehead, I flip off the lamp and head to the door. "Don't even think about using the flashlight under your pillow to read after I leave."

"*Dad,*" she groans. "How'd you know?"

"Because I know everything," I whisper. "And if I pick up your bag off the floor again, you're taking out the trash. Understood?"

"Yes," she grumbles. "Good night."

"'Night, baby girl."

I make my way back into the kitchen. Fishing around in the refrigerator, I find a beer, and then I slip out the back door.

The sky is dark, the moon bright overhead and illuminating the good-size backyard. I plop on the swing and take a sip of the beer that's probably expired.

My heart is heavy as I push back and forth in the warm night air. From the corner of my eye, I see a flashlight on in Mia's room and laugh. She never listens. Dad says she gets it from me. I say she gets it from Matt.

She used to come up with new quirks—a way of saying a certain word or a new part in her hair—and tell me she got it from her mother. Then when Sara, a woman I really liked and saw a potential future with, moved in after our dating for a year, Mia latched on to her like a leech. And when six months went by and she left us, too, saying she wasn't prepared to raise someone else's child, Mia was broken.

I won't let that happen again. I won't fail her a third time.

I take another sip of the beer and free my mind to roam. It does the typical inventory list for work and runs through anything I might need to leave for Haley in the morning. And then it goes somewhere I usually don't let it: to Neely.

Resting back in the swing, a baby doll lying beside me, I imagine what life might've been like with her. Everything I said about her tonight is true. I'm not surprised Mia thinks the world of her. What I am surprised about is, despite her hateful words to me at Mucker's, I still think the world of her. How could I not? I'm the one to blame for things not working out between us.

Right or wrong, I broke up with her.

I gave her hope we'd work some kind of long-distance thing out.

I slept with Katie.

I had a kid.

Glancing up as the flashlight beam bounces off the window above me again, my heart fills with a love I've never felt for anyone else.

I wouldn't change it for the world.

CHAPTER TWELVE

NEELY

F ocus," I demand. Flexing my fingers, I start again.

Dear Mr. Snow,

Thank you very much for the invitation to interview.

My fingers stop working.

I throw my head back and sigh.

It's taken me twenty minutes to type twelve words I don't hate, and all I'm doing is thanking a man for an opportunity to interview. It's a basic email. I should've been done with this nineteen minutes ago.

Alas, I take a deep breath and start where I left off.

I can be available for an interview at several times next week.

I groan. "All week because I have no life." I start again but stop when a knock sounds on my bedroom door. "Come in."

"Hey," Mom says, poking her head around the corner. "I'm heading to the grocery for tea. You want anything?"

"I can't think of anything." Scooting my computer off my lap, I narrow my eyes. "You look different. What's going on?"

"Nothing." She says it too quickly. "Just running out for some tea."

"Eyeliner. You're wearing eyeliner."

"So?" Her cheeks turn a shade of blush that isn't natural. "Can't a woman my age wear eyeliner?"

Grinning, I swing my legs off the side of the bed. "Yup. Especially if you want to look hot. Who you looking all spiffy for, Mama?"

The blush deepens. "Will you stop it?"

"Not until you answer me." I walk across the room and pull the door open. "And you're wearing a skirt."

"A maxi skirt. For goodness' sake, Neely. It goes to my ankles."

"So you're going for a classy look. A 'you have to work for the goods with me' type of thing." I raise a brow. "I like it."

Her hands fly through the air in exasperation. "When do you go back to New York?"

"Needing this as a love pad?" I tease. "I can stay with Claire, you know."

"No, you may not. You're staying here." As she smooths down her skirt, the pink in her cheeks pales. "Mr. Rambis needed a few things, so we're going together."

"Mr. Rambis from across the street? The guy that taught algebra for a hundred years?"

"It wasn't a hundred years, but yes. That's him."

I consider this. "Not bad. He's cute. Could lose the mustache, though. But his lawn is impeccable. You might want to consider that."

"And why should I consider his lawn when I'm just getting some groceries with the man?"

"Because," I say, sitting back on the bed, "it starts with groceries. Then you start baking for him. Then he's staying late into the night, and the next thing you know, he's in your bed."

"Neely!"

"It's true. I've read articles on things like this because God knows I don't have any experience. And they say if a man's lawn is too tidy, that means he doesn't spend enough time inside." I waggle my brows. It brings the blush back to her face. "If you get what I'm saying."

"You've lost your mind."

With a roll of my eyes, I lean against the headboard and bring my laptop back to my lap. "It's been said."

The banner on the screen is for a cosmetics line, and the logo is a bright green. That's all it takes to send my spirits in a downward spiral.

I bite my thumbnail and try to shake the vision of Dane and Mia together from my brain. Looking up, I see my mother still standing in the doorway.

"What's the matter, Neely?"

"Nothing."

"Come on," she prods. "You owe me after that Mr. Rambis crap."

Guilt gnaws at my insides. I'd hoped it would be gone by now. I'd prayed that I would put some distance between us, get a shower, eat half a cheesecake, and fall into a carb-loaded bliss and not feel so bad about the things I said. Or implied. Or insinuated.

Didn't happen.

Instead, there might be a hole in the wall of my stomach from this evening alone. It grows a little deeper every minute.

"Have you ever had a Rocket Razzle?" I ask.

Her eyebrows shoot to the ceiling. "Yes. Why?"

"Well, it turns out those turn off a filter in me, and I say things I'm not proud of."

Mom sits on the end of my bed. "What did you say? And to whom?"

I can't look at her, so I look out the window at the dark night sky. "I said some questionable things to Dane."

"Questionable, huh?"

"Fine. Maybe nasty."

"Oh, Neely," she mutters. "You're better than that."

"I know."

She lays her hand on my foot and gives it a gentle squeeze. "Do I want details?"

"No." I look at her again. "I don't owe him an apology for anything. He hurt me. But I feel so freaking bad, Mom."

"Honey," she says, getting to her feet. "He might've hurt you, but hurting him back isn't going to sort anything. Because you're the one feeling bad right now, and if I were to guess, you hurt a lot worse than him."

"This is so not fair. Why do I have to be a good person?" I pout.

Mom laughs. "Because I raised you to be one. Now, I'm not going to tell you what to do because you're a grown woman and you know what you said and didn't say. But I'm going to give you some advice."

"Please do."

She faces me. "The last time you left here in a fight with Dane, it wore on you for years. I could hear it in your voice. I saw it in your pictures. Your gymnastics even lacked a certain *umph* you had before."

"Gee, thanks," I say, feeling worse.

"You're going to leave here in a few days. That's what you say, anyway."

I shift in the bed, unable to sit still. "What's your point?"

"Don't leave like that again. If you have to suck it up and apologize, do that. Be the bigger person. Then you can leave and go back to your life without any extra weight." She gives me a small smile, then disappears into the hallway. "That half a cheesecake missing from the fridge isn't going to help either!"

"Hush," I yell back at her. My laughter softens just as the snap of the door closing floats down the hall. I settle back against the pillows, mulling over her words.

I can certainly survive in New York without apologizing to him. Saying I was wrong after everything that's happened between us doesn't sound appetizing.

Glancing down at the unfinished email on my computer, I realize she's right. If this interview goes well, I could be gone by next weekend. It would be really nice to start fresh with a new job and a new hobby, if I can get back into teaching gymnastics, and without any old burdens I don't need to carry.

I hit "Save" on the draft, close my computer, and find my shoes.

I watch the house from the safety of my car like some kind of weirdo. There's a single light on in the front. Through the shadows of the curtains, I'm guessing it's a lamp.

Surely he's not in bed already.

Shivering despite the balmy outside temperature and lack of air conditioner inside the car, I kill the ignition. A dog barks somewhere in the distance. It just ups the awkwardness as I climb out of the car, as if I'm being filmed for some made-for-TV movie.

"I'll knock," I tell myself. "I won't ring the bell in case they're asleep. If they don't hear the knock, then I can rest assured I tried to apologize. The universe can't hold that against me."

The sidewalk is clean, the little rows between sections free from errant weeds or mud. There are neatly trimmed bushes along the front of the blue-gray-sided house with crisp white shutters. There aren't any gnomes or little flags like many homes on this street have, but the mulch is black and looks new. As I take the three little steps onto the wooden porch, I remember what I told my mother about a tidy lawn and laugh.

Before I can talk myself out of it, I rap on the door. There's no dog barking. No feet falling. Nobody on the other side announcing they'll get it. Just silence. I wait a few moments before tapping again.

Just as I turn to head back to the car, relief filling my veins, the door opens.

Standing only a few feet away is a just-out-of-the-shower Dane. His cheeks are smooth and freshly shaven, a pair of red gym shorts showing off a set of toned calves. The gray T-shirt is unnecessary, but I do appreciate the slight clinginess of the fabric to the lines of his body.

His brows are raised, clearly in surprise, as he reaches above his head and grabs the top of the door. There's no tilt of his lips, no outward expression that he's happy to see me.

Talk fast. Get it over with.

"Hey," I say, fidgeting with the hem of my tank top. "I hope you don't mind me coming by so late, but I didn't want to say this over the phone. Not that I had your number but . . ." I look down. "I'm rambling."

I wait a few moments for him to say something. Nothing comes. Holding my breath, I look back up at him. He's *almost* grinning.

"You've always been kind of cute when you ramble." His shoulders rise and fall. "Might be your saving grace tonight."

"I just wanted to say I'm sorry."

He blanches. "That beer couldn't have been that expired," he mutters.

"What?"

"Nothing." He steps onto the porch and pulls the door closed behind him. There are two rocking chairs to my right, and he heads that way. "You want to apologize, huh?" he asks, sinking into one of the chairs. "I better sit down for this."

"You aren't cute when you're being a dick," I tell him, sitting in the other rocker.

"That's not a good way to start an apology."

"I haven't started yet."

He finally smiles a wide grin that shows off his pearly-white teeth. "So? Let's hear it."

"You're enjoying this way too much."

We sit in silence, rocking back and forth in the old-fashioned chairs. The motion is relaxing, and coupled with the sweet scent from the rosebushes planted at the end of the porch, my shoulders sink into the chair.

"I bet Mia tumbles across there, huh?" Motioning toward the front yard, I look at Dane. "It's the perfect length for a tumbling pass."

"She does. It makes me crazy. I'm afraid she'll fall on her head."

Laughing at the tortured look on his face, I shake my head. "It's good to fall on your head sometimes. It teaches you to keep your hands up."

His rocking slows. "Is that why you're here? You fell on your head, and now you're trying to get your hands up?"

"No. I'm here because I'm a guilt-stricken person who doesn't want to go home without at least trying to apologize for things I said that I didn't mean."

"Here's the thing, Neely—I think you did mean them."

"That's not true."

"You sure about that?" He rocks faster again, setting his sights somewhere across the street. "I know you have feelings about Mia, and—"

"I adore her," I cut in. "She's a great little girl."

"I know that," he says quietly.

Most people wouldn't hear the pain in his voice, but it's obvious to me. The notes buried in the language have me wanting to reach out. To touch his arm. To make him look at me so he can witness the genuineness in my eyes.

But I don't. Instead, I fight the constriction in my chest as I search for words. He beats me to it.

"I regret a lot of things." He flexes his jaw back and forth. "I regret thinking I knew what was best for you and breaking up with you so you'd go to college."

"What?" I sit up in the chair. "What are you talking about?"

"I didn't want to go to New York. I'd just started at the mill and figured it would suit me better than some metropolitan city I had no interest in. The mill suited me, Neely. But New York suited you."

Someone might as well be trying to explain to me the earth is flat, because none of this makes sense. I stare at him in the moonlight and wonder if I'm hearing things. "I had no idea that's why you broke up with me."

"I know. I felt like it was easier having you be mad at me and just going. You needed to take that scholarship, Neely. You were so damn talented, and all you ever talked about was this life of doing all this stuff." He looks at the ground. "I didn't want that life, and it wasn't fair to make you pick between the two."

My heart sits at the base of my throat. "It wasn't fair for you to pick for me either."

His eyes lift to mine, and we rock back and forth, searching each other's gaze for understanding.

"I loved you," he says, his voice so soft it's barely audible over the crickets chirping in the yard. "I figured I'd let you go and you'd come back to me eventually."

"I would've. If we were together, I wouldn't have gone to New York after college. But we weren't, and you had Katie and the baby and I couldn't stomach seeing that, Dane."

His face pales. He sucks in a deep, haggard breath before blowing it out slowly. "I've never *truly* apologized to you for that."

"For what?"

"For Katie."

"Dane, I don't want to—" I say, adjusting in my seat. He cuts me off.

"Listen to me. I'm sorry for sleeping with her. I'm sorry for doing that to you. I know those words are the most overused words in the fucking English language, but I don't know what else to say."

Looking away at a tree growing topsy-turvy in a neighboring yard, I fight back the tears in my eyes. This is all I ever wanted to hear.

My heart swells in my chest as I force my lungs to inflate.

"You don't have to accept that," he whispers.

"Of course I do," I say. "But can I ask you why?" I turn to face him. "Why her? Did you really think we would never be together again? Were you trying to move on? I just . . . I can't understand it."

"I don't understand it either, really. I stopped trying to at some point because what difference does it make?" He shrugs. "My dad seems to think it was some form of self-hatred, some kind of 'let's just blow up my entire life now' kind of thing, and as much as I hate to admit he's right about anything, maybe he is."

"He's always right."

We exchange a small grin.

"I regret not coming after you when you left and not trying to find a way to make us work," Dane says. "But I will never regret Mia."

My hand falls to his forearm. We both look at it, my pale skin on top of his tan. "Of course you wouldn't regret her."

His eyes draw away from my hand and to my face before he takes off rocking again. I slip my hand back to my lap and look anywhere but at him.

My thoughts are muddied. A part of me wants to run to the car and flee, taking what's left of my pride with it. Another part wants to say what I came to say and then leave with grace. As the two parts argue, I just sit and wait.

The porch creaks with the motion of the chairs. A car door slams somewhere in the distance. It takes a long time before either of us speaks again.

"I don't know if you know this or not, but Katie left us right after Mia was born," he says.

"I didn't know. I'm sorry."

He shrugs. "I'm sorry for Mia."

My heart pulls as I wonder how she feels about that. "Is she okay with it? I mean, does she miss her?"

"She didn't know her long enough to miss her. That's sad as hell, isn't it?" His eyes are as sober as a judge. "You've heard the stories about my mom. She was mean and awful and could swing a switch with the best of them. I'd hide Matt in my room some days so she'd take her anger out on me and not him."

Squeezing my eyes closed, I bite my tongue. Interrupting him with a full-on rant about how much I loathe his mother won't help anything. Still, it's hard.

"But at least I knew her." He places his hand on my shoulder until I open my eyes. "I knew I wasn't missing anything when it came to her, you know? When my mom died, it was almost a relief. Mia doesn't get that. There will be a day when she feels like she missed out or that she wasn't enough to keep Katie around, and that'll be a day that I can't handle."

I think about Katie and how she always struggled to really fit in anywhere. She went overboard on everything in hopes that she would feel like she belonged. I kind of feel sorry for her.

"What happened to Katie?" I ask.

"What? Do you hope she got eaten by a shark?"

"No. Maybe a piranha," I joke. "Honestly, I hope she's okay somewhere. For Mia's sake."

Dane smiles. "I really don't know. But I hope the same. I hope she's done something with herself and comes back someday sober and happy and wants to get to know our daughter."

"Did things end badly between you?" I ask, not sure if I really even want to know.

"No." He shrugs. "She just said she wasn't into this anymore and was going to leave. And she left. Her attorney sent papers giving me full rights, and that was the end of it. I was suddenly a nineteen-year-old kid with a baby girl. Talk about a learning curve."

Laughing, I decide to lighten the mood. "How'd you do with diapers and onesies?"

"I'm a champ."

Our laughter blends together in the easiest way. It's like the notes just know where to go to be harmonious and we hit them together automatically.

After our chuckles fade, he turns to me again. "I wonder sometimes if Katie just didn't want me. And if somehow I'm to blame for her not wanting Mia."

"Dane, no. That's not fair."

"Life isn't fair. If it was . . ." He looks around the porch before coming back to me. "If it was fair, you and I would've ended up together."

My insides turn to mush as his words hit me straight in the heart. I've told myself for years it never would've worked out between us. That Dane was a bad guy. But none of that is true, and down deep, I knew it. Hearing him say that is a vindication of sorts.

"I guess everything happens for a reason, right?" I ask, using his words from the other night.

"Do you believe that?"

"Not really. I think we can justify things if we look hard enough. And besides, once enough time has passed, you can usually find something good in a situation. Maybe that's the 'reason' everyone talks about."

He slides me a half smile. "Mia's certainly my reason right now and for the next decade or so."

"She'll always be your reason," I correct. "I saw your face today when she ran toward you."

"I'm a sucker. What can I say?" He chuckles. "I worry by the time she has to move out, she'll be so used to all my attention she won't be able to hack the real world. But on the other hand, that might help deter a relationship if she ever thinks about having a boyfriend."

"Oh, she'll have a boyfriend," I tease. "Have you seen those green eyes?"

He rubs his palm on his forehead, making me laugh. "Between Haley and me, she's being flooded with 'boys are bad' rhetoric."

"So," I say, clearing my throat. "Who is Haley, anyway?"

As he stretches his arms over his head, his features fill with amusement. "I forgot about your little jealousy over her."

"I'm not jealous. I have no reason to be jealous. Clearly."

"Fine. I'm fucking her."

"Fine."

I look off into the distance, jealousy burning through me. Just as I'm ready to shove off the chair and head to my car, he bursts out laughing.

"She's my first cousin," he admits. "My dad's brother came to town right after Katie left. Haley and I kind of hit it off in a non-incest kind of way." He lets that sink in. "She had just graduated and didn't have a plan, so I hired her to stay and help with Mia. She does that and works at the library. It's a win-win." He watches me sag against the rocker. "Does that help your jealousy?"

"I'm not jealous."

"Sure. For the record, I find it kind of adorable that you're still jealous to think I'm sleeping with someone else."

"Of course you are," I say. "Do you think I think either of us has been celibate in the last however many years?"

A shadow falls across his eyes, sending a chill up my spine.

"Besides," I rush, "maybe you'll find someone whom Mia loves and you love and you can create a family."

"If there's one thing I know," he says, getting to his feet, "it's that I won't be falling in love. My track record with women is shit. I messed

109

up with you. Something happened to Katie. I tried one more serious relationship with a girl named Sara, and she left. Mia was heartbroken."

I stand too. Dane's bodywash rolls through the air as he leans against the house. I fight hard to stay focused on the topic at hand and not on the sliver of skin showing right above his waistline.

"I get it," I say. "I won't be falling in love either."

"Why?"

"You broke my heart. One other guy I was kind of serious about almost cost me my job. He hated that I worked with mostly men. Hated how many hours I worked. Hated that I was a terrible cook, because his mom was a chef with dinner on the table every night at six."

"So I'm a dick and he was an ass. How's that stopping you now?"

I think about that. "I'm not where I want to go yet. There are a hundred things I want to accomplish before I settle down and let someone else influence that," I admit. "I told myself when I was a little girl that I'd get out of Dogwood Lane and prove that I could be something, and I don't feel like I've proven that yet."

His eyes twinkle with golden flecks as he watches me. "I think you're something all right."

Swatting him in the chest, I head toward the stairs. I stop short of descending. "I am sorry for what I said to you. I was sorry before I knew your child was Mia. I just didn't know how to tell you or if I should. If it mattered."

He shoves off the wall and saunters toward me. Towering over me, he gazes down. "It always matters. You always matter." Scratching the back of his head, he sighs. "Mia thinks an awful lot of you. Thank you for helping her."

"It was really my pleasure."

An innuendo that has nothing to do with the topic at hand is on the tip of my tongue. When Dane smirks, I know it's on his too. I also know I need to go. Now.

"Have a good night," I say, heading down the steps.

"Hey, Neely."

I stop in the middle of the sidewalk and turn around. He's leaning against a post, his arms crossed over his chest.

"Yeah?" I ask.

"You made Mia really happy today. Thank you."

"You're welcome."

"And . . ." He rolls his eyes for my benefit while trying not to crack a smile. "You might've, you know, made me happy with your apology. Even though I still think you need a communications class."

"I'll make a note of that." I get to my car, my heart fluttering away, and open the door. Before climbing in, I look at him one final time. "Good night."

"'Night."

With a final grin that turns me to goo, he enters the house. I slip into my car and turn on the ignition and crank on the air-conditioning full blast. Still, I don't move. Instead, I think about what he's doing inside. Which room is his. What Mia is doing right now.

Grabbing my phone from the cup holder, I pull up my email and find the drafts folder.

Dear Mr. Snow,

Thank you very much for the invitation to interview. I can be available for an interview any day next week from the hours of 10 a.m. to 2 p.m. EST. Please respond with what fits your schedule best.

Sincerely,
Neely Kimber

I hit "Send," put the car in drive, and head down the street, looking back only once.

CHAPTER THIRTEEN

NEELY

So anyway, he has a brother." Grace chomps on a carrot in my ear. "And I might've perused his social media last night, and let me just go ahead and let you know you're welcome."

"Let me guess: Dark hair. Blue eyes. Between six foot and six foot four? White-collar job with at least a master's degree. Briefs, not boxers."

She gasps. "How'd you know?"

I laugh. "Because you always pick out that type for me."

"It's what you like."

A blue truck rolls up to the front of Aerial's and parks a few spots away from me. Dane gives me a little wave as his boots hit the asphalt.

I switch the phone between my hands so Grace doesn't hear if I suck in a breath or otherwise make note of the way my heart is racing. I don't need that conversation.

"That's not my type at all," I tell her, taking in the way Dane's jeans hug his thighs. "You got me all wrong, friend."

"I know you better than you know you."

Dane turns from the sidewalk up the walkway. As he nears, I'm less and less inclined to listen to Grace and more apt to watch Dane move.

I haven't been able to stop thinking about him since I left his house last night. Considering the conversation we had, I should be detaching. There's no point in meddling around with ideas about what his house looks like inside or if I'd still feel like I'm floating if he kisses me behind my ear. Nope. None of that is helpful.

But all of that is true.

"Hey," Dane says, giving me a lopsided grin as he breezes by.

"Hi."

"Who was that?" Grace barks. "Come back here. Talk to me."

"Will you hush?" I hiss into the phone.

"Who was that? Was it Dane?"

I take a few steps away from the entrance as a couple of mothers and daughters exit. "Yes. It was."

"Well, not to be creepy or anything, but I looked him up online. I don't know how to say this, Neely, but he's freaking hot."

"I know." I moan. "I hate him for it."

"Don't hate him for it. Fuck him for it."

I kick at a pebble, my lower stomach clenching at the mere suggestion. "It's not like that."

"Why?" she deadpans. "Explain to me why it's not like that. From here, it looks *very* like that."

"Because."

"Words, Neely. Use them."

I switch the phone between my hands again, catching it as it slips off my sweaty palms in the transfer. Once it's nestled between my ear and shoulder, I sigh. "Look, he and I have a history together that isn't . . . wonderful. I've told you that. But I was talking to him last night, and—"

"Like you ran into him in a cornfield or like you had dinner?"

"I went to his house. Uninvited," I add as she begins howling through the line. "I went to say I was sorry for being rude. That's it."

"Do you know how many men's houses or apartments I've just showed up to randomly? None. The answer is none."

"Because you date men who are unavailable."

"So you're dating Dane?" she goads.

"No. Ugh." I blow out a breath. "He isn't dating because he doesn't want his daughter to get hurt."

"That's so sexy."

"I know."

I kick at another pebble. It rolls down the sidewalk and into a pile of dirt near a dandelion. *It had a softer landing than I'm going to have.*

Another mother and daughter exit the gym, and I find myself waiting to see if Dane and Mia come out next. They don't. My shoulders sag.

"Any chance you'll be back before the weekend?" Grace asks. "I have an extra ticket to a show on Broadway."

"No, but I forgot to tell you. I scored an interview with Archon Sports."

"I love it," she chirps. "That would be a good fit for you, I think. They're really cutting-edge on a lot of things industry-wise. I bet you could work your way in and make a name for yourself."

"I hope so."

"Me too. But, dude, I gotta go. I have an article due in the morning, and I'm about twenty percent done."

"I'm jealous."

"Only you would be jealous of work." She laughs. "I'm off to order takeout and get some words down. Call me later and tell me what happens with Archon. And Dane. Really Dane. That's what I want to know."

"Nothing is happening with Dane," I insist. "I'm leaving here by next weekend. What would be the point?"

"You are lame. Lame, lame, lame."

"Goodbye, Grace."

"Bye."

I tuck my phone back in my pocket and spin on my heel to see Dane and Mia coming out of the gym. Wide smiles split their cheeks, and I wonder if it's their grins making me grin or vice versa.

"Why didn't we get you as our coach?" Mia asks.

"Aerial said she wanted to see that back tuck."

"But she could've come over for a minute. The minis got you. No fair."

"Well, I'll tell you what," I say, coming to a stop in front of them. "I'll ask Aerial if I can get you next time. How's that?"

"Awesome, because we told Aerial tonight we wanted you. No offense to her."

"You better have been nice," Dane warns, his touch of a southern drawl prominent. "I better not hear you were disrespectful."

Mia looks up at him. "Have you ever heard that?"

Dane laughs. "Well, it better not start now."

"It won't." Mia turns to me. "What are you doing now?"

I glance at her father. He has a hand jammed in a pocket of his work jeans as he studies me.

"I'm going to grab some food and do some work," I tell Mia. "Adult stuff. Yuck."

"Come feed the fish with us." She bounces on her heels like she's just cured cancer. "It'll be fun. There is one huge one—Grandpa calls it a koi fish."

"They're all koi fish," Dane says.

"Anyway, there's one huge one I call Shamu. You have to see it."

She takes my hand and tries to pull me toward Dane's truck. I don't move despite her best efforts. Instead, I take in Dane's reaction. It changes the longer I watch. The corner of his lip turns upward. His brows follow suit. The lines on his face smooth as he bites the inside of his cheek.

"You scared of fish?" he asks.

"What? No." I laugh.

115

"I'm going to say goodbye to Madison. You two get in the truck." Mia runs down the sidewalk toward her friend, leaving her father and me alone.

We watch her little ponytail swish behind her as if we aren't sure how to proceed. I run my palms down my shorts and hope they don't leave sweat marks in their wake.

Finally, Dane turns to me. "So you going or what?"

"Yeah. I need to prepare for an interview this week, and I haven't checked the news in so long." I make a face. "I'm a news junkie. I have it on in some capacity a hundred times a day. I don't think I've even turned it on today."

"That's what happens when you have breakfast with Penn." The words are tossed out there as if he's just continuing with our conversation, but the way his jaw tics proves it's more.

I snicker to myself at the touch of annoyance in his tone. "Penn was in the café when I came in to pick up breakfast for me and Mom. We chatted over coffee for about five minutes."

Dane shrugs, but the relief is evident. "You're lucky you just talked to him over coffee. Otherwise, he would've thought you were getting married."

Mia dashes by. "Let's go, people!"

"You guys have fun," I say. Wishing for a split second I was going with them, I glance at Mia. There's a feeling in my chest I can't explain, but I'm not sure I can fill it with any amount of cheesecake when I get home.

I start toward my mom's house when Dane grabs my arm. His fingertips warm my skin, sending shock waves through me. "Go with us," he says.

"I thought you didn't do things with women?"

He considers this. "I don't take women home, because they always leave. You're different."

"How's that?"

"We aren't going home, and you're already leaving. That won't be a shocker when it happens, will it?"

"Come on!" Mia shouts.

Dane lets go of my arm, my skin immediately cooling. It's only temporary. He shoots me a smirk that sends my body temperature bolting upward.

"Let's go," he says, motioning for me to follow.

I do. Maybe because I want to spend time with them, even though I shouldn't. And maybe because I want to watch his butt in those jeans.

⁊৭৯

"Isn't it cool?" Mia asks. Another handful of cereal straight from the box goes into the water. The fish come to the surface, their colors spectacular against the dark water. Oranges, reds, even blues and whites pop against water as they go crazy for the breakfast food. "I don't see Shamu yet. Wait until you see him. He makes these look like babies."

The pond is much bigger than I imagined. Dane told me on the way that his dad moved into a smaller place on more land shortly after I left and inherited an established koi pond in the process.

When we pulled up to the little ranch-style brick home, I fell in love. It's warm and inviting with its deep-red brick and large chimney right up the middle. A few miles outside of town, it's also serene. There were three deer in the front yard when we arrived.

"I'm going to the shed to see if there's more cereal," Mia says.

She jets off toward a little outbuilding, singing a song from the radio as she goes. I can't remember ever being that happy and carefree.

"What?" Dane comes up behind me, making me jump.

"I was just thinking how happy she is." I turn to face him. "It's really a testament to your parenting."

"Better be careful or you'll give me a big head."

I pause. "What? No pun? No punch line?"

His grin splits his cheeks in two. "If your brain goes there when I say 'big head,' I win. No punch line needed."

"Not what I meant."

"It *is* what you meant. You said so yourself."

Rolling my eyes, I turn away and change the subject. "If I ever lived here again, I'd want something like this. Smell that?" Inhaling a lungful of fresh air, I close my eyes and blow it out. "It's so clean."

"It smells like manure. I think Dad's neighbor just fertilized his fields."

I laugh. "It smells better than New York City."

"Can I ask you something?" He steps around me so we're shoulder to shoulder. "I never had you pegged as a city girl. What changed?"

We walk across the grass toward the field behind the house. Trees loom overhead, their leaves rustling in the breeze as I ponder his question.

As we come to a stop, Dane leans against the trunk of an old oak tree. "Even after the whole Katie thing, I still didn't think you'd stay away this long."

"I probably wouldn't have. At first, I just didn't want to see the two of you. I didn't let Mom talk about you at all—or about anything here, for that matter. I just didn't want to know."

"Why?"

I shrug. "I didn't want to miss you all, I guess. And I had a bunch of anger, and that sort of filled a spot inside me for a while. Then I filled it with work and deadlines, and . . . it was easier pretending this place didn't exist."

Gazing across the meadow, I think back to the years I spent inside my apartment or an office building. Most of them were spent alone or with Grace. It felt fine at the time, but now I'm not sure I'll be able to get back to that place again mentally.

I glance at Dane.

I'm not sure I'll be able to forget him again.

"But you're back now," he says, a grit to his tone. "Maybe you'll stay?"

My laugh is weak. "If I came home now, it would feel like I failed. And like I wasted the last decade of my life."

"Even if it were your choice?"

"Yeah. Think about it," I say, picking at a piece of bark on the tree. "How many people actually leave here? And out of that small number, how many come back? Almost all of them." I swat at a bug swarming my head. "Remember when Colin Jenkins left to play football in Wisconsin and then came home as soon as he graduated? Everyone said he couldn't hack it in the real world. He couldn't be a little fish in a big pond."

"So? Who cares what people say?"

"So I don't want that said about me, *and* I want to make it in a place where there are a million people after my job. It's incredibly gratifying." I shrug. "Besides, what would I do here? My degree would be useless."

"I guess." He roughs a hand over his jaw.

"What about you? Would you ever leave here and move to the city?"

"Hell no. Not for all the money in the world."

"Why not?"

"And send Mia to a school full of kids I don't know? No, thank you. I'm just fine with her having most of the same teachers I did and being in class with kids of people I know."

"Think of all the opportunities for her."

He flinches. "Of getting mugged? Shot? Hit by a subway train?"

"No one gets hit by a subway train."

"Not when they're safe in Dogwood Lane, they don't." He shoves off the tree and stands in front of me. He peers down, his eyes full of an emotion that wrecks into me like a cannonball. "Aren't you ever scared something will happen to you?"

"Not really." My throat burns as I do my best to manage the chaos inside me. "I've had a few little skirmishes, but nothing that really scared me that much."

His eyes narrow. "Like what?"

"Nothing. It's no big deal." I look over my shoulder at Mia coming out of the shed and decide to change the subject. "Is she okay around the water?"

Dane doesn't even look that way. "My dad is standing on the back porch. She's fine."

My gaze flicks around until I spy Nick leaning against a post. He gives me a little wave before heading toward Mia and helping her open another cereal box.

"How much of that can she feed those fish?" I ask, turning back to Dane.

"How much is she supposed to, or how much does Dad let her?"

I grin. "So he's easier on her than he was you and Matt?"

He rubs a hand down his face. "It's like he's not even the same person. With Matt and me, yeah. Still an asshole. But with Mia he's a pussy. She gets whatever she wants."

"That's the way it should be with a grandpa." I giggle. "I knew he'd be a good one. I thought one day . . ." My voice trails off. Something I can't put my finger on flits through Dane's eyes, but I look away. "Anyway, I knew he'd be a good one."

"Let's go say hi to Dad before we get out of here." His voice is so low that I almost don't hear him. He turns toward the house and begins his trek back.

I keep a few steps behind him, getting the feeling Dane needs a bit of space. Maybe I need some too. Mentally kicking myself for getting too comfortable, I look up to see Nick watching us.

"Well, if that ain't a sight for sore eyes. Come here and give me a hug," he says.

The lines on Nick's face show his age, proof of a life that hasn't always been easy. Still, he's as handsome as ever. His eyes still shine the same green as Dane's, and his strong jawline is hidden by a neatly trimmed beard.

"How are you?" I let him pull me into his arms. He squeezes me, scents of tobacco and cherries whisking me back to another time and place. "You look good," I tell him.

"Ah, hell. You don't have to sweet-talk me."

"Who said I'm sweet-talking anyone?" I wink. "Seriously. You look good, Nick."

"Well, thank ya. You look like you're doing great, kiddo."

I laugh at his term of endearment. "I'm doing good. Working hard, staying out of trouble. Isn't that what you drilled into us?"

He gives Dane the side-eye. "Glad someone listened to me."

"You know Dane. Always the hardhead," I say, trying not to laugh.

"Me?" Dane looks from me to his dad, then back to me. "You two are full of it."

"I'm just saying, son. If you would've listened to me, you would've put a ring on this girl's finger ages ago."

Dane glares at Nick as I slide out from between the two of them. Mia thankfully chooses this time to squeal from the pond that Shamu has been located.

"You two better behave," I tell the men on either side of me.

"Neely! Come on!" Mia yelps again.

I feel their gazes on my back as I head toward the pond. "Let me see," I say. Standing next to Mia, I take in the blue-and-white fish that's double the size of the others. "Oh, that is a big one."

"I know. He's my favorite." She blows a lock of hair out of her eyes.

"Come here. Let me fix that." I unfasten her elastic and pull her hair into a high ponytail. All the times my mother used to do this to me come flooding back, and as I swipe the band over her hair, I grin. "There you go. All better."

"Thanks," she says, looking at me over her shoulder.

"You two ready?" Dane's voice sweeps across the water.

I turn around. Nick has his hand on Dane's shoulder, saying something to him I can't hear. Dane nods but doesn't look convinced. He just watches me with a trepidation in his eyes that throws me off. Our gazes lock for a split second before I pull mine away.

"You ready, Mia?" I ask her.

"Can we get ice cream?"

"You're gonna turn into ice cream," Dane warns her.

Mia scoops up the cereal boxes and gives them to her grandfather. He gives her a kiss on her cheek before she follows her father through the gate. It bangs shut behind her. I stop by the old man.

"It was good seeing you, Nick."

"It was good seeing you. Come see me more often. Say hello. I practically raised you, and you took off and forgot all about me."

"I'm sorry," I tell him. "I'll keep in touch."

"You do that." He kisses my cheek and opens the gate. Before I'm all the way out, he speaks again. "Neely?"

"Yeah?"

"Keep in touch with that boy of mine too. I know he can be a pain in the ass, but you're good for him. And I think he's good for you too."

I don't confirm or deny, partially because I'm unsure. Instead, I give him a smile and head to the truck.

CHAPTER FOURTEEN

DANE

B owl or plate?" I ask.
"Do we have garlic bread?" Mia asks, surveying the kitchen.
"Do I ever make spaghetti without garlic bread?"

She eyes me. "When you forget to buy it. But I'm not judging you because I can't feed myself."

"Yes, smarty-pants. We have garlic bread. So, bowl or plate?"

"Bowl. I like to dip the bread in the sauce, and the bowl lets me dip better."

"So scientific," I mutter. Putting on the oven mitts, I retrieve the bread from the oven and pop it on top of the stove. The air is filled with a garlicky scent that's one of my favorite kitchen smells. Much better than that damn lavender soap.

While I serve up two bowls of spaghetti, Mia fills two glasses with ice water. Just as I'm carrying the food to the table, the doorbell rings.

"I'll get it," Mia calls, hustling toward the door.

"Look out the window and see who it is before you . . ." I don't get to finish the sentence before I hear Haley's voice. In a few moments she and Mia come around the corner. "We were just going to eat. Want some?"

"What are we having?" she asks, looking at the table and wrinkling her nose. "Did you use jarred sauce again?"

"I'm out of your frozen fancy homemade stuff."

"So that's a yes to the jarred?"

I take my seat across from Mia and give my cousin a look. "Take it or leave it. I don't care either way. But now you can make your own plate."

"Fine, fine." She serves herself while Mia gets her a drink, and a few seconds later, we're finally in our seats. "Who is saying grace?"

Mia smiles. "Me." She rattles off a simple prayer she's used since she could pray. "Amen."

"Amen," we say.

The breakfast nook fills with the sound of silverware clattering against ceramic. We eat in peace for a while before I catch Haley looking at me out of the corner of her eye.

"What?" I ask, dipping my bread in the sauce.

"If you said to someone you needed a break, what would that mean?"

I look at my daughter. She's busy making sure her spaghetti and garlic bread don't touch. "You're just going to dip it anyway. Why are you wasting your time?"

"Because it'll be soggy if it sits there." She looks at me like I'm stupid. "If *I* dip it, the bread is still nice and crunchy."

A glimpse of the upcoming teenage years brushes through my mind, and I have a hard time not just taking her to her room and locking the door now. Before I can get too far with that line of thought, Haley speaks.

"So?" she asks. "What would it mean?"

"It would mean I didn't want to see them for a while," I say.

"Why?"

"That would depend." I take a sip of water. "I'm guessing someone said that to you?"

"John, and I liked him." She moans. "I thought he was The One—"

"No offense," Mia interrupts. "But you thought Harry was The One too. And before him it was Noah."

I tip my fork toward Mia. "And who was the hippie? What was his name?"

"Joel," Mia says through a mouthful of spaghetti.

Haley winces. "Don't talk with your mouth full, Mia. And don't remember everything either. You're like an elephant."

Mia giggles, stabbing her fork in the middle of the pile of spaghetti in her bowl. "Can I be excused? Remembering Joel the Hippie made me lose my appetite."

"What are you talking about? You liked him." Haley laughs.

Mia holds her hand so I can't see her lips. "I know," she whispers loud enough for me to hear. "But I really want to go watch TV." She drops her hand and looks at me. "Please, Dad?"

I survey her bowl. "You can be excused, but get a shower before you do anything else. You smell like cereal from the fish."

"Got it," she says, scooting her chair back. "Thanks, Dad. Bye, Haley."

"Bye, rascal. See you at church in the morning."

Mia's footsteps ascend the stairs as I take another bite of dinner. Haley pushes her food around her plate.

I shouldn't ask her what's wrong—it'll devolve into a therapy session, and I really don't want to figure out her problems. I have my hands full with mine. It's strange how having a smile on your face as you cook dinner can be construed as a problem, but that's reality for you.

I've worked my ass off to create a safe, happy life for Mia. She eats all the colors of a rainbow on most days. I took the bumper out of her crib when she was a baby because I read an article that said kids can get their faces into the padding and suffocate. She's had swim lessons, and I don't bring people in her life who aren't good for her. Except Penn, of course, but he's a good guy at heart.

The only thing I can't get around is my Achilles' heel. The chink in my armor. The one thing that screws me all up every time: Neely.

The day I accompanied Matt to her house to apologize was the start of a connection that's never waned. Sure, it wasn't romantic when it started—we were kids. And now we haven't seen each other for years. But the same feeling, a sense of balance, came rushing back as soon as I saw her.

I've always been a little rough around the edges. Reserved in a lot of ways. I always wonder what people want out of me, but I've never had that thought with Neely. When she's around, I feel like *me*. Like it's okay to be me. That she understands it and, whether she likes it or not, accepts it. No one else has ever made me feel that way. Not even my parents.

Quite frankly, I love Neely. I always have. I probably always will, and that really sucks.

Dropping my fork, I start to get up when Haley sighs.

"Why do I always get my heart broken?" she asks.

My butt hits the chair again. I take in her forlorn face, the slight frown on her lips, and the way her forehead wrinkles. "This isn't a broken heart, Hay. It's just disappointment. You'll survive."

"How can you tell me if my heart is broken or not? Asshole."

"You came to this asshole for advice. Just pointing that out."

She puts her head in her hands. "You're all I got, okay? If there was another option, trust me, I'd go to them."

"Gee, thanks."

I lift my fork and take another bite. The sauce is just fine, despite the way Haley licks at it before taking the smallest bites known to man. Reaching for my glass, I notice the way tears are welling up in the corners of her eyes.

Why do I have to care?

"Fine," I say, putting my glass back on the table. "Coming from someone who has seen you with a broken heart, this is not one. Okay?"

"Who do you think broke mine?"

"The hippie. You really liked him, I think. I don't know why you did, but you did." I shrug. "Watching you tonight, I'd venture to say you'll have moved on in a week. Back happily in love with some other unsuspecting soul."

She loads her fork with spaghetti and pretends to launch it across the table. "I should shoot this at your face for being a jerk."

"How am I a jerk?" I laugh. "I just call it like I see it, and you are 'in love' with someone new every two months. I don't even try to learn their names anymore. It's pointless."

She sits back in her seat and sighs. "Enough about me. What did you do today? You're more chipper than usual."

"I did have an eventful evening." That damn smile that I wore on the ride home, while Mia and I pulled weeds out front, and then while I made dinner comes back. Haley doesn't miss a beat.

She leans forward, resting her chin on her hands. "I'm waiting."

There's no doubt this is going to backfire. If I tell Miss Romantic here that I spent time with Neely, she'll be planning our wedding before the spaghetti gets cold. I should make up some story and play it off, but for some reason I don't understand, I want to tell her. I want to tell someone.

I brace myself for her reaction. "Neely went with Mia and me to Dad's."

Haley gasps. Her hands hit the table so hard the plates rattle. "You're joking. Dane! This is amazing."

"This is not *amazing*." I scoff despite the grin plastered on my lips. "But it was nice, and Mia enjoyed it, I think."

"And you," she says, poking a finger my way. "*You* enjoyed it. I know you did, so don't even try to lie to me."

"Very funny."

She wads up the napkin from her lap and places it next to her plate. "You know, ever since I found that picture of the two of you in your closet, I had a feeling this would come full circle."

"Slow down," I warn. "First of all, that picture was of me, her, Matt, and Claire. Second of all—"

"Her head was on your shoulder."

"And Claire's hand was on my ass. You just couldn't see it," I lie. "Second of all, she's just visiting her mom. She'll be back in New York by the end of the week."

"You must think there's the potential for something there."

I shake my head. "I don't. There is no potential for anything."

"I'm going out on a limb and saying that's a lie."

I pick up my bowl and glass and flip her a warning look. Heading to the sink, I try to put some space between us, but it doesn't work. Like a puppy that doesn't get it, she follows on my heels. The way I swing the dishwasher open doesn't dissuade her either.

"This is none of my business," she starts, "but let me just point out that this is the first woman you've brought around since Sara."

I don't turn around. I rinse my plate and empty the remaining water from the glass and shove them in the dishwasher.

"That has to mean something." Her voice is soft, and something about the way she says those words hits me. "You've never really talked about her before, but I've always gotten the impression she was special to you."

Taking a deep breath, I turn around and lean against the counter. My stomach is a pit of acid, churning violently as I look at my friend. Talking about Neely, saying things out loud, is something I've avoided for the most part for a very long time. It makes me uncomfortable. It feels like a guard has been taken down and I'm exposed. Yet the longer I stand there exposed to Haley's insights, the more comfortable it becomes.

"She was special to me," I say slowly, testing the waters. "She's a special person."

"And so are you in your own way." She flinches. "I can't believe I just said that. Anyway, I love this love story."

I reach down and yank up the dishwasher door. It latches with a pop, making Haley jump.

"It's not a love story," I say.

"Maybe I'm a hopeless romantic, but I have hope."

"You do that."

She jabbers on while I clean off the rest of the table, telling me how second chances happen and she has a good feeling about Neely and me.

I can't tell her I want to have a good feeling about us too. That would put the guard a little too far down to be safe. And would be stupid. It would be really stupid since she's leaving us again anyway.

CHAPTER FIFTEEN

NEELY

You're awfully quiet this morning." Mom glances at me from the passenger's seat. "Everything all right?"

"I'm fine. Just sleepy."

The sun beats through the windshield as I pilot us to Calvary Church. Usually, the sunlight wakes me up and energizes me; I count on that as I head into the office every day. I'm too far gone for any rays to help me today.

Once I finally fell asleep, somewhere around two in the morning, my dreams were loaded with koi fish and green eyes and memories of sitting on the bluff and talking until our curfew hit. Images of dinners with smiling faces and visions of Mia tumbling along grass lawns invaded my dreams too. It was a compilation of the past, the present, and things that will never be. Each time I woke up, once an hour or so, the reality would hit me that none of those things were true, and it was tough getting back to sleep.

I slow the car and make a wide circle around Blue. He doesn't bother to lift his head.

"It's amazing no one has hit him," I note.

"I said the same thing last week. The town ought to get a sign or something that warns people. Like a 'Child Crossing' sign or something."

"Yeah, but really—how many people come down this street who don't know to look for him? There's nothing down here but a few houses, and all the families have lived here forever."

"That's true."

I hit the brakes at the end of the street, and the dishes laid carefully on towels in the back jangle together.

"How many things are we taking to the potluck?" I look in the rearview mirror. "It smells like a kitchen in here."

"It's a carry-in, so I had to bring a covered dish."

"You brought four? Five?"

"Well, I made green beans with bacon because no one ever brings vegetables to things like this. And everyone loves my green beans."

I laugh. "Of course they do. You cook all the vitamins out and flavor them with bacon fat."

"I don't hear any complaints," she says. "I whipped together a Seven Layer Salad and found the prettiest strawberries at Graber's, so I made a strawberry pie for the kids."

"Screw the kids. That's mine."

She shakes her head as we make the turn toward the church. "I also made a raisin pie."

"Who likes raisin pie?" I curl my nose. "That's old-people pie."

Mom looks smug. "Mr. Rambis likes it."

"Ooooh," I tease. "Mr. Rambis likes it. What else does Mr. Rambis like, Mom?"

She swats my shoulder as I pull into the parking lot. "You knock it off. We're at church, missy."

"Like God doesn't know all the unholy things you're doing with Mr. Rambis. Ouch!" I say as she smacks me with her purse. "Kidding. I was kidding."

We step into the parking lot. The large tree in the front still has the tire swing that my youth group put up forever ago hanging off a bottom limb. The front window has been changed, and a plain sheet of glass sits in place of the gorgeous stained glass I remember.

Mom catches me looking at it. "A limb fell off the tree a few summers back and went right through that window. Such a shame."

"It is. It was so pretty," I lament. "I used to sit through the sermons and count the different colors."

It's such a small thing, really, a tiny change in the grand scheme of things. But as I peer up to the spot that used to be so colorful and is now a sheet of plain old glass, I wonder what else I missed. The things I can't see so easily.

There's a part of me that suddenly feels vacant, like there's an empty space that should've been filled with all this knowledge and these experiences—as silly as they are. I stand on the sidewalk trying to make sense of this until the church bell rings.

"Hey!" I call after Mom. "What are we doing with the food?"

"Leave the car unlocked, and someone will come out and get it in a bit."

I stop in my tracks. "Leave it unlocked? Seriously? What if someone steals it?"

She's unfazed, just laughs at my serious questions and heads up the stairs without me. Throwing my hands in the air, muttering that it's her car, I follow.

The entry is full of parishioners. Everyone I pass stops to say hello, many asking how I'm doing and asking me to visit more often. I don't expect the outpouring of love, and it catches me a little off guard.

I enter the sanctuary and spy my mother talking to Mr. Rambis and Lorene, the woman who's played the piano here my entire life, near the front. Scanning the rest of the quaint little country church, my eyes fall on Dane and Mia near the piano. Gripping the end of a pew, I try to look away but can't.

He's in a pair of gray dress pants and a crisp white button-down. Mia is adorable in a yellow dress with pink lace at the edges. Matt stands next to them. He bends down and whispers something to Mia, making her laugh. I laugh, too, even though I have no idea what's transpired.

"He cleans up pretty well, huh?" Claire comes up beside me.

"He's not bad." I can't stop myself from smiling.

"Not bad? I don't know what they look like up in New York, but around here, that's the top of the food chain."

"Food chain?" I laugh, shaking my head. "Oh, Claire."

She shrugs. "You sticking around for the potluck?"

"I'm with Mom and she made forty million things, so apparently. Are you?"

"No. A girl I'm going to school with is having a baby shower this afternoon, so I'm cutting out after the service. Wanna go?"

My gaze drifts back to Dane. He's found me in the crowd and gives me a little wave. I wave back in the most "I haven't been thinking about you all night" kind of way I can.

"I better stay with Mom," I say, turning my attention back to Claire.

"Can I just say she and Mr. Rambis are adorable?"

"How long has this been going on? I mean, I'm happy she's dating or whatever it is, but I can't tell if it's serious."

"Well, they sit together every week. Have for a while now. Since Christmas, I'd say."

"Wow."

"He mows her lawn a lot. I know that. My brother used to do it, but she didn't need help this year."

I look at Claire. "She's baking him pie."

"Is that an innuendo, or she's actually baking him dessert?"

Laughing, I try to cover my mouth with my hand. "Actual pie, Claire."

"Well, we are in the South. You get a casserole for everything. I can't help but think a pie might be some kind of moral woman's subtle cue.

Like, 'Here, sir. Try my pie.'" Claire bursts into a fit of giggles. "I need to go find a seat before I buy myself a ticket to Hell."

"Good to see you, Claire."

"Back at ya."

I start down the aisle toward my mother, my cheeks flushed as I think of her using dessert as a sexual invitation, when Mia runs up to me. "Hi, Neely! I didn't know you would be here."

"Hey," I say. "You look pretty today."

"Thanks. So do you." She smiles sweetly. "Want to sit with me and Dad?"

"Well . . ." I look up at her father. He and Matt are still talking, but both are watching me. There's a pull across the church that draws me to the other side. I give in. "Let's go say hello and then I'll see. Sound good?"

"Yup." She leads the way across the front of the church, past the piano, and to her family.

Matt whistles softly. "You look pretty this morning."

"Why, thank you," I tell him. "It's my mother's dress." I pick at the oversize belt around my waist that's partially an accessory and partially to make the thing fit. "How are you guys doing this morning?"

Before they can answer, Mia chimes in. "I'm going to go say hi to Keyarah and Madison. I'll be back before the piano starts playing." She darts to the back of the church, where her friends have just arrived.

Matt pulls at the collar of his shirt. "It's hot in here. I'm going to get some water."

Dane leans against the windowsill that looks over the back of the church. The view over his shoulder is almost as wonderful as he is. Foliage extends forever, dipping and rising with the hills. It's the kind of view that's inspired paintings for thousands of years.

"I didn't know you'd be here today," Dane says just loud enough for me to hear.

I pull my gaze away from the trees to him. "Mom didn't give me much choice," I admit. "But I probably would've come anyway. I've always liked this place."

"Yeah. Me too. It's why we don't let Penn come. We don't want it to burst into flames."

Laughing, I feel my shoulders relax. "Are you staying for the potluck?"

"Are you kidding me? It's the best Sunday in the month. These ladies know how to cook."

The piano starts playing, alerting us to take our seats. Dane moves toward me. He hesitates, biting his lip before blowing out a breath. "Do you want to sit with us?"

My heart leaps in my chest as a clear indication I do. I want to sit with them. I want to sit with them so badly it actually hurts.

I want to hear them sing. Pass Mia a stick of gum when her daddy isn't looking. Gaze around the church with Dane at my side and feel the peace this place gives me all at the same time.

But if I do, it will be one more memory I'll have to deal with when I get back to New York.

"I better sit with Mom," I say. "Thanks, though."

His nod is subtle. So is the way his face falls.

The way my heart pulls isn't so easy.

"See you after," he says, turning toward his seat.

I watch him go and almost follow. As the pianist hits the second chorus, I get my bearings and head across the room toward my mom and Mr. Rambis.

"I can't eat another bite." I wave Lorene and her scoop of cobbler away. "It was amazing, but I'm going to pop if I eat any more."

"You sure?" The ninety-year-old pianist's hand shakes as she holds out another piece of dessert. "It's the last one."

"I'll take it if she doesn't want it." Mr. Rambis comes up beside me. Lorene dumps the cobbler on his plate with a sigh of relief. "Thank you," he says.

"You're welcome." She teeters off toward a picnic table with a giant umbrella overhead.

The air is filled with scents of food and children's laughter. The kids play a game of kickball in the field a few feet away. Amazingly, only one ball has intruded on the eating area, and I think Matt had something to do with that.

A woman walks by and asks to take my empty plate. I give it to her before turning back to my mother's friend. "How's the cobbler?" I ask before taking a sip of my sweet tea.

"Not as good as your mother's pie."

Choking so hard tea comes out of my nose, I cough in an attempt to clear my airways. Mr. Rambis pats me on the back.

"Are you all right?" he asks as I settle down.

"Yeah," I say weakly. "I'll be fine." My eyes sting from the dramatics, and I blot them with the back of my hand. "Just got a little choked."

"I was hoping we could have dinner one night before you leave," he says. "I remember you as a child, but I'd like the chance to get to know you as an adult."

I take another drink. This time, it goes down without any complications. "Are you serious about Mom?"

He considers this for a long time. By the fourth shifting of his weight from foot to foot, I start to worry. Finally, he speaks. "I've known your mother for years. It wasn't until one day last fall, right before Thanksgiving, when I ran into her at the post office. She was mailing you a box of things because you couldn't come home for the holiday, and I was sending the same kind of thing to my boy out in Idaho. We struck up a conversation, and I realized I never really knew her."

"I remember that box. She sent me one of my grandmother's quilts," I tell him. A touch of guilt strikes through me. I spent that Thanksgiving alone in my apartment, eating takeout and working on a holiday piece for the magazine. It all made sense then, and I get why I did it even now. But for the first time, there's a ball of pain in my soul that I wasn't here. That I can never redo those things with my mom, with my friends, and I missed them for what?

"Getting back to your question," he says, clearing his throat. "I am serious when I tell you I really enjoy spending time with her. I think she's wonderful. And I really, really like her pie."

All I can do is nod.

Someone motions for him across the lawn and he holds up a finger. Turning back to me, he places a hand on my shoulder. "If we can have dinner, the three of us, before you go, I'd love that."

"I'll try," I say.

"That's good enough for me." With a final smile, he weaves through the tables to a group of men.

My hand glistens with the melted ice from my plastic cup. I have half a notion to rub it across my forehead to cool myself down but manage to remember my manners. I'm searching for my mom to see if she's ready when I spy Mia running through the tables toward me.

"Neely! Come with us," she shouts.

"Where are you going?" I laugh.

"To the creek. Dad is taking me, Keyarah, and Madison. Come with us."

I look up to see Dane watching me from the lawn, holding the kickball. He grins.

"You sure?" I ask her, my heart fluttering like crazy.

"Uh, yeah." She opens her palm. A little green-and-yellow bracelet, just like Dane's, lies in her hand. "This is for you."

"Mia," I gasp. I look at her. Her eyes are sparkling, filled with such a pure kindness and affection it brings tears to my eyes. "Did you make this?"

"I did. I made Daddy one a long time ago, and he wears it all the time. Says it's his lucky charm. And I have a pink one and so do Keyarah and Madison, but we don't wear them always because of gymnastics."

I lift the delicate strands from her hand. "Thank you."

She helps me tie it in place and then inspects her work. With a bright smile, she takes my hand. "Come on." She pulls me the way she came, through the tables and over a patch of sand. Once we're almost to her friends, she drops my hand. "Let's go!"

The girls traipse off toward the tree line that hides a little creek. Their dresses float behind them, their giggles swishing through the air.

"Don't get near the water until I get there," Dane warns them.

"Okay," they shout in unison.

"To be young again." I laugh, falling in step with Dane. We head down the slope toward the trees. Dandelions create little pops of yellow against the green, the sky a vivid blue with billowy white clouds overhead. "It's so beautiful out here."

"You look beautiful today."

"Thanks." My cheeks flush, and it has nothing to do with the sun. "You clean up pretty nice yourself."

"I don't love shirts like this. I feel like I'm getting strangled." He picks at his collar.

"I don't love dresses either. I wear them to work when I have to, but it's much easier navigating New York in pants, I think."

"What's it like there? If you were walking around on a Sunday afternoon, what would it be like?"

I take in the lush green foliage in front of us, the high grass sprinkled with beautiful flowers, and laugh. "I'm not used to seeing pretty things when I walk outside. I usually get a bunch of buildings, a couple of rats, and a man telling me I have to get a new route because a movie is filming in front of me."

He makes a face. "I don't know how you live like that."

"You get used to it."

We get to the tree line. Dane goes first down the path to the creek. It doesn't look as worn as it did when I was little, but it's still clearly marked. The girls' laughter echoes through the valley.

Birds call overhead and gnats buzz my face. It's weirdly refreshing.

"Watch your step," he says. "There's a big hole up here, and I know you don't look where you're stepping." He hops over a trench.

"That's not a hole." I laugh. "A hole is a dip. That's a . . . cut."

"Give me your hand."

"I can make it."

"Give me your hand," he says again. His hand stretches toward me. Instinctively, my hand falls into his. "Oh, you got your bracelet."

"I did." I think I beam, but I don't care. "I love it."

"She worked on that for three nights." He squeezes my hand. "Now jump."

"You realize three little girls just did this without help, right?" I ask, enjoying the warmth of his palm.

"Country girls. You're a city slicker now."

"I am not."

He wrinkles his face at the defiance in my tone. It takes me aback too. I don't know why I took that as an almost-insult, but I did.

"Jump," Dane says.

Determined to show him I'm not a city slicker, I leap across the trench with gusto. My toe catches on a tree root, and I crash into Dane's arms.

We both gasp as his arms wrap around my waist and my chest hits his. It takes a second to get my head together. I can feel his heart beat against my cheek. His cologne hangs in the air, but being so close, I can smell *him*—the oils on his skin. The sweetness of his breath. The scent that's strongest in the crook of his neck.

He grins as I look up, trying to catch my breath.

"Good thing I warned you," he teases.

"Yeah," I pant. "Good thing."

His palms lie flat against the small of my back. His fingers flex against my shirt. Our eyes stay locked together, a grin tickling the corner of his lips.

Whether it's too much contact or the sweet summer air, all my sense of reality is lost. I fall happily into his gaze. My lungs fill, my heart skips as he begins to lower his head to mine.

He pulls me closer to him. I lock my hands around his waist. We fit together like a puzzle in the middle of this little forest.

Just as his lips dip toward mine, his eyes sparkling like a million stars in the sky, Mia shouts, "Dad! Are you coming or what?"

I sag, unable to catch myself from laughing. A deflated balloon, I blow out the rest of the air I've been holding.

"Damn kid." He chuckles, flexing his fingers against me. "Coming, Mia, darling."

"Hurry up. We want to play in the water," she calls back.

He holds me for a moment longer. I soak up the sturdiness of his body and the way his arms feel around me. I breathe him in one final time before planting my hands on his chest and pressing gently away.

His head bows as he turns toward the creek.

The rest of the walk is quiet. The logical part of my brain chastises me for caving. The human side declares it's only that—human. How was I to resist being in his arms when it feels like I was just there? Like, somehow, being nestled against him is as natural as being on a balance beam?

The girls see us coming and waste no time getting closer to the water. They toss in rocks and limbs and find a frog on the other bank, but Dane won't let them that far out to grab it.

I pick out a spot of grass beneath a tree and plop down. Dane teaches the girls how to skip rocks across the water. He doesn't get frustrated when they ask the same questions over and over, nor does he become irritated when they do exactly the opposite of what he tells them. He just smiles and repeats himself or shows them again.

They play at the water's edge for a long time. I join them as they attempt to build a dam. When it washes out, so does their excitement.

"Can we head back to the church now?" Keyarah asks. "I'm thirsty."

"Me too," Madison agrees.

"Yeah. Go on," Dane says. "Stay on the path. We'll be behind you shortly."

"Can I ask you a question?" Keyarah giggles. "Are you boyfriend and girlfriend?"

My eyes whip to Mia. She's biting her bottom lip just like her dad does when he's nervous. She looks at me for an answer.

"No," I say as cheerily as I can. "Dane and I are friends. We grew up together."

"My mom said you two used to be boyfriend and girlfriend," Keyarah says. "We were looking through her old yearbooks, and I saw a picture of you together."

"Like I said, we grew up together." I look at Dane for support. "That's all it is."

"That's all it is." He casts a somber look at me before turning back to the girls. "Stay together and go straight to the church. Got it?"

"Got it," Mia says. She flashes us a peace sign before they trample off the way we came.

Dane sits next to me. He stretches out, propping up on his elbows. He joins me in glancing across the water.

We don't say anything for a long time. I wonder if he's replaying the trip down here like I am. Just as I get to the part where he almost kisses me, he chuckles.

"What?" I ask.

"I don't remember being their age and knowing what a girlfriend and boyfriend even were. Girls were gross."

"I wasn't a fan of boys until a green-eyed brother of a little punk in my class showed up at my front door," I say. "That sort of changed things for me."

He laughs, looking up at the clouds. "I remember going home that night and trying to get all the information I could about you from Matt. Of course, being the idiot he is, he knew nothing. He was like, 'Uh, I think she brings her lunch and doesn't get a tray in the cafeteria.'"

"Well, that was true." I laugh. "You were the first boy I ever had a crush on. My first kiss. My first . . . everything."

The clouds shift overhead, allowing the sun to break free. It glimmers off the trickling water below us.

"I don't regret dating you anymore," I say softly.

"You mean you used to?"

"Yeah. I mean, I've spent a lot of nights in a shitty apartment in the city wondering what your little family life was like down here. I felt shafted, to be honest."

"And I spent a lot of nights home alone with a baby, wondering what you were doing in the big city. I felt, like, jealous sometimes, to be honest." He moves his neck back and forth. "This shirt is killing me."

My fingers dig into the grass in a futile attempt to keep from reaching over to him. But the longer I look at the way the sun kisses his skin, noticing the way my heart feels full as he looks at me and smiles, the more the resistance wanes.

"Here. Let me help you," I say. Stretching across the space between us, I unfasten a button. My fingers tremble as they brush against his skin, freeing the top two spots.

He watches me closely, the warmth of his body washing over me. I wonder if he's thinking about the possibilities of undoing all the buttons, of shedding his shirt. Of removing my dress.

Before I pull away, he sits up. We're inches apart. My heart races as my mouth goes dry.

His eyes shine, the gold flecks brighter than even the greens. "For the record," he whispers, "I haven't regretted kissing you once."

"For the record," I say, forcing a swallow, "if I lived around here, I'd have a hard time not kissing you more."

That's all it takes. My stomach whirls like a banshee as he leans up and touches his lips to mine. I don't close my eyes; I want to see and feel everything.

His lips are soft, his breath hot against my mouth. His lashes full as they lie splayed against his cheeks. Just as we pull apart, a flurry of giggles rings out from behind a shrub above us.

I cover my face with my hands and try to quiet the racket in my body. I want to shriek, to fist pump, to call Grace and tell her right freaking now like a juvenile that Dane kissed me. But none of those options are appropriate for a woman nearing thirty—especially a woman nearing thirty who will most likely be regretting this decision shortly.

"Get back to the church," he shouts, although it's laced with a laugh. He gets to his feet, offering me a hand. "We better get back before those three start telling people all kinds of stories."

He helps me up, and I follow him along the trail toward the church. We stop at the trench and he turns to me. "For the record, I don't regret that kiss either." He then flashes me the widest smile and hops to the other side.

I take his hand and make it across more gracefully this time. "For the record," I say, looking at his handsome face, "I don't either."

I leave him standing behind me.

CHAPTER SIXTEEN
DANE

A drill rips through the air behind me. Close. Too close. I jump a mile. "Damn it, Penn," I say. The set of plans in my hand ripple as I wipe my brow. "It's too early for your bullshit."

"It's almost noon," he cracks. "Besides, when did you get so jumpy?"

I ignore his question, mostly because I don't have an answer, and lay the plans out on the floor instead. "Come here," I say, motioning for him to crouch with me. "We can't finish this trim until the concrete guy comes in and works his magic on the floors."

Penn lowers himself. "Yeah, but that's the general contractor's problem. Not ours."

"We're ahead of schedule. I called the contractor, and they're going to see if the concrete guy can get up here in the next week or so. In the meantime, let's jump to the pergola in the back tomorrow and see if we can wrap up what we can."

"Sounds good."

The rumble of tires on gravel catches our attention. We stand and wait for the car to appear. Penn's face lights up when he sees it's Haley.

"Can you not hump her leg?" I mutter.

"Her leg isn't what I want to hump."

Sighing in exasperation, I head across the grass. Haley is out of the car, and Mia's right behind her.

"Hey, Dad!" My daughter heads toward me with a book tucked under her arm. She beams. "We've been to the library today. I know you're over the whole bedtime story thing—"

"Because you're old enough to read to me at this point."

"You'll miss it one day." She shrugs as if she's challenging me to argue that. I can't. "Anyway, I got a couple of new books. I think you're going to love them."

I look at Haley. "Did you have her get something about baseball? Grilling? Camping?"

"No," Mia says. "But I did have to check out one about a boy that gets lost in the woods. He lives in a tree or something. That's right up your alley. Not really mine, but . . ."

"It's called expanding your horizons," Haley insists, coming up next to us. "I'm all for princesses, but it's time for a change."

"Uncle Matt!" Mia abandons us in favor of my brother. Once she's out of earshot, I know I'm in trouble. Haley's shit-eating grin is legendary.

"So . . . ," she says.

"So, what?"

"So a little birdie told me you were caught kissing a certain someone at church yesterday."

"A little birdie, huh?" I look at the sky. "That's interesting."

"I think it's very interesting. And exciting," she almost squeals. "And I'm kind of annoyed I'm getting information from a child. I thought we were better friends than that."

"Do you call me every time you kiss a guy? Wait. Don't answer that."

She laughs. "Yes, I do. Or I at least tell you the next time I see you."

"And this is the next time I'm seeing you," I point out.

"You were going to tell me?"

"No."

She goes on a mini rant about how I should've told her, how she feels like she basically wished us together, and how I'm now holding out. I head to my truck, hoping she'll get distracted by Penn.

Things never happen when you want them to.

She chases me down the slope and continues to rail me.

I've fought this very topic for the last almost twenty-four hours. There's no way to deny the excitement in my stomach or how perfectly Neely still fits in my arms. Forgetting the sweetness of her breath, the softness of her lips, is impossible, and I've replayed the moments with her since Mia and I pulled away from the church.

My initial worry was Mia. She seems to be taking it better than I am.

"What does this mean?" Haley asks.

I open the driver's-side door of my truck and sit in the cab. She leans against the door, basically blocking me in.

"This means you're trying to trap me in here and shake me down for information," I say.

"Of course that's what this means. I meant, what does the kiss mean?"

"You look into things too much."

"I won't deny that. But when you slip up and kiss a woman in front of Mia, a woman I know you have feelings for, that means something."

I could argue this. Tell her Mia got it wrong or that it was a friendly sort of thing. I could lie to her until I'm blue in the face, and it wouldn't matter. She'll press on until she gets what she wants. The trouble is— what do I want?

I lay in bed all night and mulled over that question. What do I want? What *can* I want? I've been with a few women since Sara, but those relationships have been a hookup here and there. Nothing that had a stickiness to last more than a few months. They were flings, moments in time, and the women knew it.

It's not that way with Neely. I don't think of her and wonder where I can meet her for a quickie. I don't forget about her while I'm hanging trim and remember her only when she calls my phone. I sure as hell don't think of other women since she came back.

She fit right back into that spot—*her spot*—in my life. I think of her when I'm brushing my teeth. I wonder what it would be like to wake up with her in the morning and how it would feel to have her sitting with Mia and me at the dinner table. All the things that will only set me up for pain later because she has no interest in sticking around.

I'm eaten up with this shit. I'm no better than the teenage version of myself who overthought everything. Neely isn't someone I can gamble with. There's no kissing and forgetting. There's only wanting more. Needing more. Desiring more.

And not being able to have it.

I don't know what to do with that.

"You ignoring me?" Penn comes up to the truck, his gaze set on Haley. "My feelings are hurt."

"How are you, Penn?" She gives him a quick once-over. "You look hot."

Penn's jaw drops. "I've waited for this moment for years."

"No, really. Make sure you drink enough so you don't dehydrate."

He bites back a smile as I laugh. Haley laughs, too, but I can see she feels a little bad about teasing him.

"Seriously," she says. "How are you, Penn?"

"You're here. I'd say I'm more than decent right about now."

"I'd say you were more than decent a few hours ago." She points at his neck. "Was she blonde?"

"Was who blonde?"

"Whoever left that lipstick on your neck. It's a bluish red, so I figured she's probably fair headed."

I burst out laughing as Penn clamps a hand on his neck. Haley holds her hands up by her sides and shrugs.

"You're so predictable," she says.

"That wasn't lipstick. It was paint."

"It wasn't Claire's night off last night, was it?" I ask. "She wears a lot of red lipstick."

Penn plays it off like the playboy he is. "Don't listen to him, Haley. I'm all about you right now."

"I know you are. And in a few minutes, when you realize this is going nowhere, you'll be about someone else. That's the beauty of you, Penn."

Penn looks at me. "Was that a compliment? Should I take it like one?"

"No." I laugh. "No to both."

"Fine, but the option is there. You need someone to keep you warm at night, I'm your man."

Haley takes a step toward me, wagging her finger in the air. "About that . . ."

Penn's head sweeps from her to me, to her, back to me. "You aren't sleeping with Haley, are you? Damn it. I called dibs on her."

"First of all—" I start before Haley chimes in.

"You can't call dibs on a person. I'm not something you can put a stake in."

"Wrong choice of words," I mutter.

Penn smirks. "Oh, baby. I could put a stake in it all right."

Haley's eye roll is long and deliberate. "You're disgusting."

"Yeah, yeah, yeah." Penn heads back up to the house. "I'm taking lunch in twenty."

"Okay," I call after him. Turning my attention back to Haley, I sigh. "As you were saying?"

"I made a decision. I'm going cold turkey. I'm not dating anyone for six months."

Draping my arm over the steering wheel, I raise a brow. "You think you can pull that off?"

"I don't know, but I have to do something. My track record is broken heart, broken heart, broken heart. Even if you think they don't qualify." She looks over her shoulder as Matt and Mia start down the slope. "I fall in love too easily. So, new rule: no talking to, dating, having dinner with, having sex with anyone for six months. Starting now."

"I want to be all supportive, but I don't think you can do it." I chuckle. "You aren't without a guy for three days at a time, Hay. How do you think you'll make it six months?"

She sticks her hand out toward me. "Bet me."

"What are we betting?"

"If I win, I get to name your baby with Neely."

"What?" I ask, laughing hard. "You're outta your mind."

She shrugs. "And if you win, you get to pick the next three guys I date."

Rubbing my hands together, I watch her confidence wane. "Deal." I snatch her hand in mine and shake before she can reconsider.

"That looks like serious business," Matt says as he and Mia approach. "Do I even want to know?"

I glance quickly at Mia. "Not right now. So what are you doing today, rascal?"

"We did the library this morning, and now we're going for shaved ice."

"News to me," Haley says. "I thought we were going to your house and cleaning out your closet."

Mia twists her face. "Maybe shaved ice and then the closet?"

"I think we can make that work," Haley says. "Dane, I need ten bucks."

Fishing in my back pocket for my wallet, I pull out the soft leather. A twenty goes from my palm to Haley's.

"Dad, I was wondering something," Mia says.

The wallet goes back in my pocket at a snail's pace as I absorb the inkling of something behind Mia's words. "What's that?"

"Can we see Neely tonight?"

Just mentioning her sends a zing of excitement through my body. Mia catches this and starts a little dance, and I realize I have to catch myself, and her, before this gets any further out of control.

"I bet she has things to do," I say. Mia stops moving. "She's going home soon. You know that, right?"

Matt takes a step back. Then another. Then makes his way back up the slope, not wanting a part of this conversation. Haley, on the other hand, stands behind Mia with her hands on my daughter's shoulders.

"I heard her tell Aerial that. I know she doesn't live here. But . . . but that was before you kissed her, Dad."

Blowing out a breath, I climb out of the truck. I kneel in front of her so we're eye to eye. "That was a friendly kiss. I told you she and I are friends," I say gently. "Neely is a nice person, and I like her very much. But that's all. She's going home soon and that's that."

The words taste awful coming out of my mouth. It's hard not to cringe at the way my stomach twists admitting that. Haley watches me, putting me on the spot, and I try to remain as unaffected as I can. For Mia. For Haley. And for me.

Mia's head cocks to the side, her cheeks rosy from the sun. "I don't know a lot about kisses, but I know I don't kiss my friends like that."

I laugh as I stand straight again. "And you better never kiss anyone at all. Got it?"

She just grins. "I think Neely thinks she's your girlfriend."

That's enough. I pick up my daughter and toss her over my shoulder. She squeals in delight as I twirl her around and head toward Haley's car.

"What do you know about girlfriends, anyway?" I ask. "You're a baby."

She kicks her sandal-clad feet in the air. "I'm not a baby."

Haley's laughter fills the air as she steps in front of me and opens the back door. I plop Mia in her seat.

"You behave today," I tell her. Bending down, I kiss her cheek.

"Now that's a friendly kiss," she says. When I groan in response, she shrugs. "What? See the difference?"

I swing the door closed and turn to Haley. "Good luck with that today."

"I'm kind of on her side," Haley teases, climbing in the front seat of her car. She talks to Mia as they get buckled in and then backs down the driveway.

I stand there for a long time once they're out of sight. I've wondered if a day would come where Mia misses having a woman in her life besides Haley. So far, I've been able to be all the things. But is that time almost up?

My eyes squeeze closed. Immediately, images of Neely pulling Mia's hair into a ponytail at Dad's stream through my mind. It was one of the purest, sweetest things I've ever seen. They get along so naturally with their spunk and gymnastics and hearts of gold.

Blowing out a breath, I open my eyes. My boots scrape over the gravel as I turn to go back to work. On my way up the hill, I make a deal with myself: if I can ever find a woman as perfect for Mia and me as Neely, I'll scoop her up in a second. Because despite everything my heart is telling me to do, I don't have a choice with Neely. I have to let her go.

CHAPTER SEVENTEEN

NEELY

M r. Rambis is coming over to fix the ice maker, right?" I take a
sip of coffee.

"He said he'll be over this morning. He's an early riser, so I expect
he'll be by relatively soon." She fills a thermos with decaf and adds a
splash of milk. "I just didn't want you to be spooked if you walk in here
and see him."

"Um, good call. Seeing a man in my mom's kitchen would be rather
shocking."

She throws her purse over her shoulder and then stops in her tracks.
"It doesn't bother you, does it?"

"What? Mr. Rambis?"

"Yes. Does it bother you that he comes by and that I spend time
with him?"

Putting my cup down, I lean against the counter. "You're a grown
woman, Mom. I'm fairly certain you can make your own decisions
about who you spend time with."

"I haven't spent time with someone in a really long time. I keep
thinking I'm missing something or wondering if I'm being objective."

"I don't think liking someone has anything to do with objectivity. You don't want a guy who just checks the objective boxes. You want someone who makes you feel good."

Her shoulders sag like a weight has been removed. "I enjoy spending time with him. So that's good."

"Super good. It'll not be so super good if you're late," I say, nodding toward the clock on the oven.

"Oh, crap. You're right. I gotta go." She heads for the door. "See you this evening."

"Bye, Mom."

The door shuts and everything goes quiet. I wait for a siren to wail or someone to shout outside, but nothing happens. I smile.

After grabbing my coffee, I mosey down the hallway. My computer is on my bed, and I lift the lid and settle in front of it. One email from Archon Sports shines above all else.

I click it.

> Dear Ms. Kimber,
>
> Thank you for your reply.
>
> I have scheduled you for a call this afternoon at one o'clock Eastern. I'll call the number on your résumé.
>
> Looking forward to meeting you,
> James Snow
> Managing Editor, Archon Sports

"Ah," I say, falling back into the pillows. It takes a second to catch my breath. I didn't expect the interview to happen so quickly; I thought I'd have more time to prepare.

I go over the job description and realize it's about two levels below what I did for years. It should be a fairly simple, routine interview about things I could talk about in my sleep. And if it works out, I could be in New York in a couple of days, working.

Springing to my feet, I gather my things to get a shower. For the first time since I got here, it feels like I have something to do. That there's a point to waking up and going on about my day.

Heading into the hallway, I let out a shriek. "Mr. Rambis. You scared the crap out of me."

"I'm sorry," he says, rubbing a hand over the top of his dark hair. "I thought your mom told you I was coming by."

"She did. I just forgot." I toss my things in the bathroom and then head to the kitchen. "How are things going?"

"I think this water line is clogged," he says, shining a flashlight behind the refrigerator. "Other than that, pretty good." The light flickers off. "How are things with you?"

"I just got an interview, so I'm pretty happy today," I say.

"Here? In town? Or in New York?"

"New York."

He nods. "Congratulations, Neely. That's great."

"Thanks." I pick up the paper plate from Mom's toast this morning and toss it in the garbage. As the trash hits the bottom of the can, my spirits seem to sink a little with it. "Can I ask you something?"

"Sure."

"What's the scariest thing you've done?"

He laughs, setting his flashlight on the table. "The scariest thing I've done? You mean one of those houses at Halloween or becoming a parent? Two different categories of fear."

Mia's giggle echoes through my mind. The smell of Dane's skin warms me from the inside. The hollowness at realizing I won't see them again, not like I'm seeing them now, is almost crushing.

"More like becoming a parent, I guess," I say.

"Nothing is as scary as that." He pulls out a chair and sits. "People say falling in love is hard, but it's not. It's not a choice if it's done right. And some people say getting married is paralyzing, but when I married my wife, I wasn't scared at all."

"May I ask what happened to her?"

"Car accident. Christmas Eve," he says. "She swerved to miss a deer, we think, and hit a tree." His face falls. "She shouldn't have been out driving that night. It's a burden I'll live with forever."

I cross the room and place a hand on his shoulder. "I'm sorry. That's terrible. But you can't blame yourself for a decision she made, Mr. Rambis."

He looks at me with a set of deep-brown eyes. "You can call me Gary. If it's easier for you. Or Mr. Rambis is fine if that works better." He takes off his glasses and polishes them on the edge of his shirt. "I'll be honest in saying I don't know how to work this really well. I don't have a lot of experience dealing with . . . things like this."

"Me either," I say. I watch him for a long moment before pulling out a chair across from him. "I think I'll go with Gary. It seems less teacher-y."

"May I ask what prompted the question about fear?"

"I've always known exactly what I want out of life. There was no question. I even have a little check-off box in my apartment in the city of things I want to achieve by the time I'm thirty, and believe it or not, I have most of them already done."

"That's great."

"Yeah." My voice trails off as I think of how to put the rest of this. "I guess I'm having a mini pre-midlife crisis."

Gary laughs. "How so?"

"I'm just second-guessing some things. Is that normal?"

"Absolutely." He nods. "I think we all have a few times in our lives where we sort of sit back and reevaluate what we've done, what we're doing, and where we're going. At least the intelligent people do." He leans forward. "Think about it. If you continue on the same path your whole life without thinking, just plod through the day-to-day activities because it's on the schedule, do you even want to be where you end up?"

"See? That's my problem," I tell him. "I know where I want to be. That hasn't changed. But maybe now . . . maybe now . . ." I blow out a breath and look at him. The understanding in his eyes, devoid of judgment, almost brings tears to my eyes.

"You don't have to explain anything else. I get it. Just know one thing. There is more than one way to cook an egg, if you know what I'm saying."

He hasn't said anything, really, that fixes any of the anxiety in my gut. Still, I can't help but feel a little more settled.

I stand. "Thanks, Gary. I appreciate you taking the time to talk to me."

"Anytime."

With a lump in my throat, I head to the bathroom and jump in the shower. The warm water usually releases tension in my muscles, and I work through a lot of things mentally while standing under showerheads. I try to focus on the interview, on the questions he might ask and the responses I should give, but my brain keeps going back to Dane and Mia.

I massage shampoo and conditioner into my hair. Working the suds around, I splash some on the back of my neck and rub the knot that's forming at the base of my skull.

I don't have time for this. I have an interview to focus on so I can get back to my life.

Still, even as I remind myself of this, I think of Dane's smile. My back hits the shower wall.

Might as well get used to it. That's all he has been and all he's going to be—a memory.

The water turns off with a quick yank of the handle. I step inside the foggy bathroom and dry off.

Lifting the jeans I brought into the room, I wonder why in the world I chose them.

Because that was twenty minutes ago. You were full of hope back then.

The fabric roughs across my skin as I make quick work of dressing. Going full speed keeps me occupied, and when my mind starts to wander, I pull it back to the next task.

Leave the bathroom.

Wave goodbye to Gary.

Go into my room.

Make sure the phone is charged.

Brush my hair and add some straightening balm. Brush it again.

Open the computer and do a quick scan of the Archon Sports website.

By the time the phone rings, my nerves are a little more even-keeled. I answer it. "Hello?"

"Is this Ms. Kimber?"

I settle into my desk chair. "It is. Is this Mr. Snow?"

"How are you today?"

My breathing evens out, and I fall right back into the role of professional and try to get myself back on track.

CHAPTER EIGHTEEN

NEELY

D o you think you got the job?" Grace asks. "I need you back here. I've learned over the past week that you are the only person I really like."

A flock of birds take off as I pass their little perch on the top of the slide. The park is empty except for one child and their mother over on the swings.

"I think it went well. He said he'd get back to me soon, so we'll see."

"Let me know as soon as you know. A bunch of concert dates were just posted in Cooper Square, and tickets go on sale on Friday. I'll grab us some if you'll be back."

"Sounds good."

The sun filters through the old trees in the center of the park. I walk the circular drive that encompasses the play area. From my mom's house to the park, around the drive, and back is one mile even. I've probably coursed this circle five times now, but my brain is too tired to compute how far that is.

"Hang on," I tell Grace. A rumble sneaks up behind me. An engine revs, making me dash off the asphalt and onto the grass. "Why don't you . . ." I turn to see Dane's truck pulling up beside me. "Hey."

He stops. Arm resting on the window, hat on backward, he grins. "What are you up to?"

"Just walking. Needed some activity and fresh air today."

"Could've come to the jobsite. I'd have hired you in place of Penn."

"I'm not good with a hammer."

"I could teach you." He plucks the truck into park. "Want to grab some dinner?"

"Can you hang on one second?" I hold up a finger and lift the phone to my ear. "Hey, Grace. I'm gonna call you back later, okay?"

"I love his voice. In my mind, he's wearing red-and-black flannel with a big wad of chew in his bottom lip. That's so gross—I hate spit. But it's also hot in a weird southern-boy kind of way."

Laughing, I look at Dane. He's looking at his own phone.

"Well, it's too hot for flannel and tobacco causes cancer. Your vision is all wrong."

"Wanna paint me a picture?"

"No," I say. "I'll call you tonight."

"Fine. Bye."

"Bye." Shoving the phone in my pocket, I walk up to the truck. He puts his phone on the console.

"So, dinner?" he asks again.

My stomach flutters. There's nothing I want more than to hop in his truck and drive back roads with him until the sun sets. But then I think of the interview today, and I know it's not a good idea. For any of us.

"How'd Mia take seeing us kiss yesterday?" Saying the words out loud causes my thighs to clench. "Was she okay with it?"

Dane laughs. "Oh, she was okay with it. She's told everyone she knows and now thinks we're boyfriend and girlfriend."

"Really? That's adorable."

"I've tried to explain that it was a friendship kiss, but she didn't buy it."

"A friendship kiss, huh?" I grin. "Well, I'm glad we've cleared that up."

He reaches out of the truck and almost touches me but stops a few inches short. "How did you classify it?"

"Total friendship kiss. That's exactly what it felt like."

Dane shakes his head. "I didn't say that's what it felt like."

We laugh together. I grip the doorframe as we exchange a heated look.

"Come on. Have dinner with me," he says. "Or go for a ride. Whatever you want to do."

"I don't want to confuse Mia any more, Dane. She's so sweet, and I don't want her to think I'm another woman coming in and leaving."

A slow, infectious smile slides across his face. "Well, Mia isn't here, is she?"

There's nothing about that I can say no to.

⁊৫

"I haven't been here for years." Climbing out of Dane's pickup, I breathe in the water-infused air.

Dogwood Lake sits right below us. From our vantage point on the bluff, we can see the changes in blues as the depths vary. A few boats remain as the sun begins to set against the prettiest backdrop of tall pines and rippling water. Purples and pinks streak across the sky as a farewell to the day.

"I bring Mia up here sometimes," Dane says. He joins me at the front of the truck. "She likes to bring a little portable grill and have picnics. It's fun."

"It sounds fun."

"Are you going to miss this when you leave?" He doesn't look at me when he says it. His gaze remains focused on the lake in front of us. There's something about the way he asks the question that makes me think it's less about if I'll miss things and more about whether I am really leaving.

I take a couple of steps ahead of him so he can't see my face. "Yes. I'll miss this." I force a swallow. "I had an interview today." When he doesn't respond after a few seconds, I look over my shoulder.

He's standing still, his hands stuffed in his pockets, his face sober. It makes my heart twist.

"How'd it go?" he asks carefully.

"Good, I think. It's a few notches down the totem pole from where I was, but there's a lot of room to move and grow there."

"Can I ask why you're looking for a new job?"

I blow out a hasty breath. "To keep it simple, I was passed over for a promotion that was mine. I hate when people say that, but it really was. My bosses created a whole new department based on my idea, and they didn't give me an opportunity to get in there and see it come to fruition. So I quit."

He gauges my reaction before reacting himself. Finally, he chuckles. "I'm not surprised."

"Why do you say that?"

"Because. Look at you. You're . . ." His voice trails off and is replaced with a laugh. "You're a woman who knows what she wants, and you go get it. You're strong, Neely. You're smart. You trust your gut and don't let anything get you off track. Hell, you were leaving Dogwood Lane before I slept with Katie. Before you hated me. I respected the hell out of that then, and I respect the hell out of you now for this."

I gulp, not sure what to say.

His features soften. "You're what I want Mia to be."

My lips part. I can barely make him out through the tears in my eyes. "That's the nicest thing anyone has ever said to me." I feel like a baby. I turn away so he doesn't see me dabbing my eyes with the end of my shirt. Just as I'm bringing the fabric to my face, a set of strong arms wraps around me from behind.

"I shouldn't be doing this," he mutters against the back of my head. "But fuck it if I can help it."

There's no stopping myself from relaxing into him. It's comfort at its best. My body fills with a tingling warmth that I would harness and keep forever if I could. I close my eyes, breathe Dane in, and appreciate the moment where nothing matters but this.

"I've tried to avoid this with you," I tell him.

"Yeah. Me too." He rests his chin on the top of my head. "But for what it's worth, you didn't put up too much of a fight."

My chest shakes as I laugh. "Yeah, well, what can I say? I'm a sucker for pain."

He twists me around in his arms. A hint of perspiration dots his forehead as he watches me with a cautious glance. "I don't want there to be any more pain between us. I know you're leaving. I got that. I'm aware. But I'd like to enjoy however long you're here, if we can. If that's okay?"

My brain buzzes with confusion and excitement. Alarms also buzz in my ears, warning me that the potential to get destroyed is very real. If this were a business decision, I'd take some time to ponder it. But it's not. It's Dane. "I'd like that too."

He takes my hand and leads me to the edge of the bluff. The colors are fading, the sun barely bridged over the horizon.

"I was afraid of your reaction to Mia," he admits. "I didn't know if you knew she was my child or if you'd dislike her on principle."

I force a swallow, trying to shove the guilt of my feelings on this topic back down. It doesn't work. My throat constricts instead.

"I spent a lot of nights hating the idea of her." My head whips to his as I lay this out there, knowing I can't take it back. "I would just lie in

162

my bed in the dorm or in my apartment and think how her life ended a part of mine." I look at the ground. "That makes me sound terrible."

"I don't blame you for feeling that way." He takes my hand again and gives it a squeeze. "It's true in a way. If I hadn't gotten Katie pregnant, who knows what would've happened? But that being said," he says, lifting my chin so I'm looking him in the eye, "I wouldn't change it. I know that sounds like a dick thing to say to you of all people, but I can't imagine my life without that little girl."

His words hurt a part of me that wishes he and I had been able to experience something like having a child together. But the longer I look in his eyes, the longer I really think about it, the wound sort of fills.

He was made to be Mia's dad. Knowing them together now, I can't imagine him without her or her without him. It's a weird thing to consider, especially knowing how much I'd wished she didn't exist for so long, but it's still true.

"I can't imagine your life without her either. And I feel terrible for having felt that way."

"I'm not judging you for anything, Neely. I've seen you with her, knowing who she is. She adores you. You've been nothing but kind to her. Besides," he says, "although it's not really the same, I spent a lot of years hating gymnastics. That's what took you away from me."

"Yeah, well, I spent some time hating it too. Competitions are tough on the brain and body."

He takes a step back, biting his lip. "Well, from where I stand, your body looks like it fared just fine."

"Thank you." I try to be serious but end up laughing. "I think you've been spending too much time with Penn."

"That *was* a Penn-like thing to say." He cringes. "What's happening to me?"

"I don't know but you better watch it. You'll ruin your reputation."

"I don't think I have a reputation." He seems to consider this. "I think I'm just Mia's dad. I've lost all parts of Dane the Person."

I saunter toward him and fight a smile. "Is that so?"

He reaches for me, digging his fingers in my hips. I gasp as he drags me into his chest.

"I take that back," he says, his eyes burning a hole in me. "I still have some parts."

If he weren't holding me, I think I might fall to the ground. My legs wobble. My hands tremble as I bring them to his face and cup his cheeks. I hesitate, not sure if I should back away or go forward, but the choice is made when he squeezes my hips again.

"I'm not sure I believe you," I whisper.

"Let me show you."

His lips fall to mine in a lazy, unhurried way. They brush over my mouth, capturing the moan that emits from my throat.

As if on autopilot, my lips part, and he wastes no time licking through the inside of my mouth. My knees buckle. My blood goes so hot I think I'm going to pass out.

He brushes a hand up my spine. His fingers work through my hair, touching me as if his life depends on it.

I can't breathe. I can't think. I can only absorb the growing intensity of his soft lips and firm hands. When I begin to shudder under his touch, he breaks the kiss.

His eyes are wild, his breath panting, as he searches my eyes. I want to lift his shirt over his head. My fingers itch to dance across his bare skin and feel him against me. But as I'm assessing the potential pleasure versus pain in this situation, he takes a step back.

"We have two choices," he says, still catching his breath.

I shake my head. "No. We only have one."

My shoulders fall, my bottom lip trembling, because as much as I want this with him, I can't have it. There's no reason to continue this. It'll only make everything harder. He isn't just a one-night stand, even though I suck at those too. He's Dane. He's the only guy I've ever considered being with for a very long time. He's the only man with whom I have a hard time forgetting the way it is.

He nods, bowing his head. "We better get out of here then."

"Yeah. I think so."

He opens my door and I climb in. He gives me a long, sorrowful look that cuts me to the core before shutting the door.

CHAPTER NINETEEN

NEELY

Where's Mia tonight, anyway?" I ask as the truck hits a dirt road. "She's staying with Madison and Keyarah. They were all supposed to stay at our house, but their mom offered to take them to a movie and I got out of it."

"I see."

The sky is dark, trees thick on either side of the road. The only light comes from the headlights shining down the country road. I settle against the seat and try to let the sound of the engine's purr relax me.

I would have no problem reaching over and taking Dane's hand. I'd not even have a problem leaning over the console and planting a kiss on his cheek. It would be the most natural thing in the world.

Whoever said to do what's right, not what's easy, is an asshole. Right, but an asshole anyway.

"Hey," I say, leaning forward. A security light shines up ahead a good way off the road. "Is that Malone's Farm?"

"Yup."

"I used to love it out there. I'd volunteer to clean the horse barns just to get to spend the day with them."

The light gets brighter. I plant myself sideways in my seat and watch the complex of farm buildings grow closer.

"If you want to stop by, we can probably get away with it," Dane says. "I come out here sometimes when they're clearing land. Things like that."

I whip around. "Really? We won't get arrested or anything? And you wouldn't mind?"

He pretends to think about it. The truck almost passes the turnoff before he swerves right and hits the driveway. "Of course I don't mind," he scoffs. "I'll warn you, though. He doesn't have horses anymore. Got too old to take good care of them."

"That's sad."

"Yeah, well, we live, and unless we die, we get older. Right?"

"I guess."

The truck slows as we approach two buildings on the right and the horse barn on the left. An old farmhouse that looks like it hasn't been inhabited for years sits at the end of the driveway.

"I'm guessing no one lives here?" I ask as the lights scan across the acreage.

"Nope. He moved in with his daughter in Fairbanks. He has a guy manage the place for him, but to be honest, there's nothing here to manage anymore."

Dane parks the car in front of the horse barn. "You wanna go in?"

"Can we?" I hold my hands together in front of my chin. "Please?"

"The things you talk me into." He winks as he shuts off the engine. "Let's go."

I slide out of the truck and slam the door behind me. Crickets chirp from all angles, and lightning bugs flicker in the distance. I take a long, deep breath.

"I'm starting to worry about you and the smell of manure," Dane says. He motions for me to come along.

We make our way through the darkness under a sea of silver stars. Memories of running through the fields and chasing lightning bugs come cascading back to me.

Dane digs a key out of an old lantern hanging near the door and pops it in the lock, which opens with a creak. I stand in the doorway, unable and unwilling to descend into the dark barn until Dane flips on the lights.

A buzzing sound comes from the bulbs at the top of the barn as they light up the space. Five stalls line the area to my right, and three stand in a row on my left. At the end is an office that the Malones used to run their farm.

"Wow," I say, spinning in a circle. "This is even more beautiful than I remembered."

The tops of the stalls have hand-carved details in the wood. The beams are thick and rustic, and I could imagine this place selling for a million dollars in New York. Yet somehow, the thought of this place in the city seems wrong. Like the preciousness of it would be spoiled.

I start down the long corridor, noticing all the little things about the place the younger version of me didn't appreciate.

"Thunder used to be in here," I say, resting my arms on top of a stall door. "He was my favorite. He was a butterscotch color and a creamy white. He was so gentle."

"I remember him." Dane comes up beside me and peers into the empty stall. "I think Lucy was beside him."

"Yes. I used to think they were the horse version of husband and wife." I laugh. "They used to stick their heads out of the stalls and neigh at each other."

The glow of the lights overhead creates the calmest ambience. All the stress from my interview, the anxiety from kissing Dane, the nervousness about all the decisions I need to make seem to have vanished.

"It's really sad to see this place like this," I say. "It was always so busy. So chaotic. So full of life."

"Farming isn't what it used to be. With government subsidies and people moving to the suburbs, there isn't a big market for a hundred-year-old farmhouse that needs work on a bunch of land that needs to be maintained." Dane shrugs. "It's sad, I agree. Blame it on technology. That's what I do. It's ruining everything."

I lean against the stall door. "I guess Mia won't be texting me anytime soon."

"When she's sixteen and gets a car, she can have a cell phone. I can justify that."

I bite the inside of my cheek. "Let's see how things go the next few years."

"We sure will."

"She'll be the only person in middle school without a phone. What are you going to do when Keyarah and Madison have one?"

"Take them when they come to my house." He shrugs. "I'll be the mean dad. I don't give a shit. She's not getting warped by all this crap online."

His passion is adorable. My shoulders shake as I quietly laugh.

"What?" he asks.

"Nothing."

He cocks his head to the side. Shadows fall across his face, making it hard to concentrate. "You think this is funny?" He tugs at his bottom lip with his top teeth. "Because I promise you, there's nothing funny about it."

I clear my throat, trying hard not to laugh again. "Absolutely. You're right. Nothing funny at all."

As we settle, my heartbeat picks up the pace. Dane draws his gaze down my body. A trail of fire is left in its wake as his eyes hood. The greens darken, the gold flecks all but gone. He takes a step toward me.

"Dane . . ." I take a step backward.

"Neely." He moves toward me again.

My breathing becomes ragged as the air heats between us. A spot in the center of my stomach begins to wind tighter and tighter, causing my blood to pulse faster and faster.

I keep moving backward until I hit the wall. The wood doesn't give. There's nowhere to go. Dane stalks toward me like a man on a mission, and I'm the treasure at the end.

Pressing up on the balls of my feet, my hands fisting at my sides, I have about two seconds to decide what to do. The closer he gets, the more damp my skin becomes and the more my lips part, wanting to be kissed.

He plants his hands on either side of my head. I can smell his testosterone, feel the energy rippling off his body. He looks at me with a bridled lust on the brink of breaking.

Screw it.

I lift my chin. "Are you going to kiss me or not?"

He starts to smile but stops himself. "Are you sure?"

"Seriously?"

"I'm warning you—I think my self-restraint when it comes to you is tapped out."

My hands shake as I bring them to his face. "Well, that's good because I don't have any more either."

I get a blip of my favorite grin before he kisses me so hard my head rocks back against the wood. My hands run down his chest, over the length of his sides, and on to the small of his back.

His lips taste sweet, his mouth as hot as fire. Every lick of his tongue makes me moan a little louder. Each press of his hips into my belly makes me ache deeper.

He roams his palms over my body. Across my swollen breasts and down to the top of my groin, he brushes his touch everywhere he can without breaking our kiss.

"Damn. You," he groans.

I nip his bottom lip and am rewarded with a deep, throaty growl. Every insecurity and possible thought about stopping this is gone.

I'm all in.

Digging at the waistband of his jeans, I fumble with the button. His eyes fly open as he realizes what I'm doing.

"You sure?" he asks as he plants kisses over the side of my face.

"Does it seem like I'm sure?" I laugh, tilting my head to the side.

He kisses from my ear to the hollow of my throat. My fingers fly against the button and work the zipper down. He gasps as I dip my fingers into the front of his boxers and feel his hardened shaft against my hand.

His eyes shine as he pulls away.

"When did you become a little minx?" He laughs, lifting the hem of my shirt. The material goes over my head and sails into the darkness.

"It's hard to pinpoint a specific time," I tease. I shove his pants down to his ankles. "Although this one night in the Bronx, on top of the—"

He swallows the words from my lips, halting my story. "I don't want to hear about it. Now take off your pants." He removes his shirt, his chest and abs on full display. They're hard and defined but not overdone by hours in the gym. They're cut from lifting wood and hammering nails all day. It's perfect.

Kicking off my flip-flops, I shimmy out of my shorts. "You asked. I was wrong, though. It wasn't the night in the Bronx." My shorts end up in a pile next to his pants on the floor. "It was in Manhattan."

"My goal tonight," he says, grabbing my ass, "is to make you forget about Manhattan."

I lick my lips. "You have your work cut out for you, buddy."

He peels my panties down my legs and then pins me to the door. He lifts me up. My legs lock around his waist. The door scratches at my back, the wood rough against my skin.

His cock presses against my opening. I can feel the heat between our bodies and my wetness coating the inside of my thighs. His hands, rough and gritty from the wood he works with all day, free my breasts from my bra so they sit on top of the underwire.

"Good lord, Neely," he grumbles.

He takes one nipple in his mouth, sucking it gently between his teeth. The other is rolled between thick fingers. Each sensation is another douse of gasoline on the already flaming inferno in my gut.

My head falls back, my back arching in order to tilt my pelvis. His cock plays with my opening like a tease.

"This is great," I say. "But this is not making me forget Manhattan." I shove my opening toward him to drive home the point.

"If Manhattan was that great, you wouldn't be here."

"Fair enough."

He starts to say something else. But as his lips part, the words don't come. Instead, a softness washes over the greens of his eyes, and I feel my chest tighten in a way it never has with a man in this position.

The air between us shifts, an intimacy that would make me ill with someone else, thick as it lingers around our bodies. But I'm not ill. Not with him. Instead, I find myself falling into the sweet, crooked grin he casts my way.

He lowers his lips slowly, his gaze never breaking mine. He kisses me softly, passionately, with something more than a need for an orgasm. I kiss him back and lose myself in the warmth of him.

All too soon, he drops me to my feet.

"What the heck are you doing?" I ask.

"Condom." He digs through the pocket of his pants and finds a wrapper. He rips the plastic with his teeth and rolls it over his length, never taking his eyes from mine. "Ready?"

"I've been ready for ten freaking minutes." I lay my palms on his hard biceps, my fingers digging into his skin.

He lifts me again. This time, his cock parts my pussy and sits heavily in my opening. "Feel that?"

My chest heaves. "Yup."

"Want more?"

"Yup—ah!" He splits me open, filling me with his length. The end of his cock hits the wall of my pussy. The pressure is incredible. "You could've warned a girl."

"A girl that's run her mouth as much as you should've expected it." He regrips my hips. "I can barely move inside you."

"Well, Manhattan . . ."

He slides out. There's a moment of relief as he exits me, but it lasts only a moment. He presses back in hard. My back slams against the wood. The contact stings on both sides.

My head starts to spin.

His head buried in the crook of my neck, he slides in and out in a steady motion. Our bodies become slick with sweat. The door behind me bites into my skin, but it doesn't actually hurt. It just adds to the pressure building in my stomach.

With each movement, he fills me to completion. There's no performance anxiety like I have with other men—does my hair look right? Is my stomach pouching? I think of nothing other than the pleasure he's delivering one thrust at a time.

"I can't get enough of you," he groans. Cupping my breasts, he massages the heavy globes. "I just want to get my hands all over you. Touch you everywhere."

I suck in a breath. "If you keep rubbing my clit like that, I'm going to come all over you."

He chuckles. "I love when you talk like that."

"Frankly?" I ask, brushing a lock of sweat-soaked hair off my forehead. "Fine. I'll be frank. Make me come, Dane."

His jaw sets. His hands find my hips again. He looks me dead in the eye as he shoves into me. Over and over again, he finds the sweet spot in the deepest part of my body. My breasts vibrate on my chest, my head knocking against the wood. It's a bedlam of sensation, a cacophony of noise that builds me up so high there's only one choice: to fall.

And fall I do.

"Dane," I scream into the night. The world bursts before my eyes as the top of my head threatens to explode. I grip his ass, the muscles flexing under my fingers, as I urge him on.

He doesn't stop. Doesn't slow. Just milks every last ounce of pleasure from my body as only he can. As the colors slow and the final jolts of orgasm roll through my legs, he pushes into me one final time.

My body tenses around him as his cock swells. He closes his eyes and groans the sweetest, sexiest sound I've ever heard.

The muscles in his neck flex as he works out his orgasm. His body trembles against mine. I bury my head in his chest and listen to his heartbeat patter wildly inside.

By the time he pulls out and lowers me back to my feet, I can barely stand. Keeping my eyes open is a challenge.

I lean against the wood, letting my eyes close, as he pulls on his pants. Before I know it, he's lifting me in his arms and carrying me through the barn. My head rests on his shoulder.

A door creaks open before I'm laid gently on a blanket. I want to ask where I am or what he's doing, but it's too soft and I'm too sleepy. Another blanket is placed over my body before I feel Dane curl up against me.

He kisses me on the top of the head. "Sweet dreams, Neely."

"Mm-hmm . . . ," I say before slipping off to sleep.

CHAPTER TWENTY

NEELY

S hould I walk you to the door? I feel like that's the gentlemanly thing to do." Dane looks at me from across the truck with a shit-eating grin. "It's less of a walk of shame if I do that, right?"

"I'm a mess." I look down at my clothes. We dusted them off the best we could and picked all the hay we could find from my hair. Still, every time I move, I find more evidence of the night spent in the horse barn, besides the fact that I smell like it. "I don't think now is the time to start behaving like a gentleman."

"Here's the question—did it make you forget Manhattan?"

The dull ache between my legs flares. "Yes."

He smiles like he's won a prize.

"Thanks for last night . . ." I cringe. "Did that sound like I was thanking you for sex?"

"Weren't you?"

"No," I say, nudging him with my shoulder. "I was just thanking you for spending time with me. Or something."

He leans over the console, his eyes shining. "I'd rather like to believe you were thanking me for sex."

I press a kiss to his lips in a move that shouldn't be as thoughtless as it was. "I gotta go. My mom is probably watching out the window and gearing up to play Twenty Questions."

"She is."

"Huh?"

He nods over my shoulder. "She is watching. Look."

By the time I turn around, the curtains are fluttering closed. "She really was." I gasp. "I was just being facetious."

I grab the door handle but am stopped by Dane's palm on my forearm. "Neely?"

"Yeah?"

"I hope this doesn't make things hard between us. I know what we've both said about relationships and you leaving and all that, but I'd like to think we're both adults who can handle this without screwing everything up."

He's too handsome for that. Too sexy. Too kind and considerate and too good of a man to have sex with and walk away. But that's what I have to do.

"Of course we are," I say. "We knew what it was when it happened. Right?"

"Right." The words lack the assuredness I hoped to hear. "Better get in there and talk to your mom. Tell her I said hi."

"Will do." I hop out of the truck, and with a final wave, I make my way up the sidewalk. I no more than get inside the house before Mom rounds the corner, acting surprised.

"Well, good morning to you."

"Cut it," I say. "I know you were looking out the window."

"I heard a truck pull up. What do you expect?" She leans over and plucks a piece of hay out of my hair. "This is a good sign," she says, waving it in front of me.

I laugh. "Will you stop it?" I work my way around her, avoiding eye contact. I learned as a child she has a hard time asking questions if you don't look at her. "I'm going to grab a shower."

"Good, because you smell like a barn."

"Fitting."

I hear her quick intake of breath behind me but continue looking forward. Once in my room, I find my phone just as it starts to ring.

"Hello?" I ask, not recognizing the number.

"Is this Neely Kimber?"

"It is," I say, grabbing a set of clean clothes from my suitcase.

"This is James Snow. I wanted to call and let you know personally that we were highly impressed with your résumé and interview. We'd like to offer you the editorial position, contingent upon a face-to-face interview."

I sit on my bed and stare blankly at the wall. "Oh. That's great," I say, hoping he takes my tone more enthusiastically than it sounds to me.

"I've sent you an email that goes over our proposal of employment. If you find it acceptable, we'd want you to get in here by the end of the week. You have lots of ideas and so do we. We believe that, together, we can make a great team and have a wonderful impact in our industry."

He continues on, rattling off their distribution statistics and plans for expansion. I nod, even though he can't see me. It's all I've got. My emotions are tied up in a man in a truck heading to pick up a sweet little girl from a sleepover.

"How does that sound?" James asks.

"Great," I say, despite not having heard anything he said. "I'll take a look at your proposal and get back to you."

"Wonderful. I hope this is the start of a successful relationship."

"Me too. Talk soon."

"Goodbye, Miss Kimber."

The phone falls from my hands and lands on the bed. My heart falls, too, but I'm not sure where it lands quite yet.

DANE

"You've got to be kidding me." I pull my truck into my driveway and park next to my dad's.

He's sitting on the porch, reclined back in a chair, drinking a bottle of water I'm sure came from my refrigerator. Inside the house.

I sigh.

"Hey," I say, climbing out of the truck. "What's happening?"

"Not much."

"Must be pretty bored to be coming by here this early."

"Nah. Just thought I'd check in and see how you were doing."

I take the steps toward him. He has one leg bent, his ankle resting on his knee. The worrying part is he doesn't quite look pissed. I'm not sure how to deal with him when he isn't half-pissed about something.

With a curious look, I sit in the chair beside him.

"You smell like shit," he says.

"Ah, there you are. I was starting to get worried you were getting soft on me."

He looks at me over the top of his glasses. "Where's Mia? I thought maybe she'd want to take a ride with me over to get a couple new koi."

"I gotta pick her up in a few. She's over at Madison and Keyarah's. You know the Tiptons."

"I saw their granddad in the feedstore the other day. I didn't realize that's who they belong to. They're good people."

"I told you that." I sigh. "If you want to pick her up, I can call over and let their mom know."

Please say yes and go.

He takes a little tube from his pocket. The toothpicks inside rattle as he shakes it until one is free in his palm. Studying me intently, he squeezes a little wooden stick between his lips and works it around.

"Can you just tell me why you're really here so I can go get a shower?" I ask. "Not that seeing you first thing isn't a fine way to start the day. I just have things I need to do."

"I'm worried about you, Dane."

"Here we go." I groan.

His foot drops to the floor with a thud. He sits upright and takes the toothpick from his mouth. "I was watching you with Neely the other night, and I've about worried myself sick you're gonna let her go again."

"That's not your business, is it?" I chew on the inside of my cheek to keep from saying anything more. Everything inside me tells me to rip his ass and ask him where he gets off giving anyone relationship advice when he let my mother get into a drunken rage and whack me and Matt with a belt a few times a week.

"If it were just you? No. I don't give a damn who you hole up with if it's just you. But you have a little girl who needs a mama and—"

"Hold your horses, Pops."

"I'm not holding anything except you by the scruff if you don't start listening to me, kid." He shakes his head. "I'm not taking anything away from you by saying that. You're a hell of a father, Dane. Better than I was with you and Matt. But Mia deserves to have a mother, and as much as I like Haley, she doesn't fit those shoes."

He has a point. He knows he does, and he knows I know he does. That's why he doesn't flinch when I start to stand.

"Mia deserves a good life. Whether that's with a mother or it's not. But I'm not about to ask some woman, let alone Neely, to step into that role."

"Why not Neely?" he asks.

"Because she doesn't want it," I say through gritted teeth. "She has a life somewhere else. She's happy there. She's made it crystal clear she's not staying here for her mother. For me. And definitely not to take care of a kid that's not hers." I head toward the door but stop before I push it open. "Who would I be to even ask her to do that? It's Neely, Dad."

With the bliss of last night replaced with a somber illustration of the future, I head inside and go straight for the shower.

CHAPTER TWENTY-ONE

NEELY

"Let's take the routine from the top," Aerial says over the chatter. "Places, please."

I wait for the cue. Mia's team takes their places, and Aerial gives me a thumbs-up. I hit "Play."

The music comes on, an old song from the fifties that has the girls performing a little dance. They're adorable as they swing their arms and booties around the gym floor. Out of nowhere, a boom thunders from the speakers, and the girls all fall to the floor.

"Five, six, seven, eight." Aerial counts as the music changes to something more mainstream.

The girls get into new positions as the tumbling passes start. Mia darts across the front of the mat, connecting three back handsprings together. She pops a little pose before jogging to the back. They perform a few stunts and another dance and end it with an epic set of tumbling passes before the final notes are hit.

"That's amazing!" I tell them, coming onto the mat. The girls run to me, their eyes as big as saucers.

"Do you really think so, Miss Neely?" they ask in different variations.

"I do. Just remember to smile and sell it to the crowd, and you got this."

Mia falls into my side, wrapping her arms around my waist. "You're the best, Neely."

"Me?" I ask, laughing. "You were the rock stars out there."

She grins up at me. "You're still the best."

My heart overflows with feelings for this child. Is it fondness? Do I adore her? Probably both. But the way my insides swell up when I look at her little face seems more than that.

"Practice is over," Aerial says. "You girls did super tonight. Make sure you grab a flyer off the table in the locker room and take it home to your mothers."

"Is it Manicure Day?" Keyarah asks, bouncing on her toes.

"It is," Aerial agrees.

The room erupts in a wild cheer as they race to the locker room. I notice Mia is the last one instead of being in the middle of Keyarah and Madison.

"What's Manicure Day?" I ask Aerial as Mia disappears into the locker room.

"It's a tradition started right after you left." She bends over and picks up a few wrist wraps from the mats. "The mothers get together with their daughters and do a mani-pedi day before the Summer Show. Remember how you used to get together and make your hair bows?"

"That was my favorite day. How tying off the fabric around the elastics was fun I have no idea, but I loved it. Every year, I loved it."

"We started buying the bows online, so Manicure Day took its place." She shrugs. "New generation, new traditions. Although if you ask me, the hair bows were more about team building. I think the manis are really for the moms."

The girls file out of the locker area. Mia is, once again, last. In her hand is a red sheet of paper she shoves into her bag on her way out the door.

"I'll see you tomorrow, Aerial," I call out. Jogging across the gym, I meet up with my girl. "Hey, you. You did great today."

She doesn't look up. "Thanks." She presses on the doors and doesn't hold them open for me like she usually does.

I step into the sun and see Dane walking toward us. His smile falters as he takes in Mia's demeanor. "Hey, rascal. How was practice?"

"Good." She stops in front of her dad.

"Everything all right?" he asks.

"Yup." She takes her dad's hand and then looks at me. "Can we go get a hamburger at Mucker's?"

Dane and I swap glances. I wish we could click over into the playful mode I see hidden beneath his concern for Mia. I wish even more I could stand next to him and feel him at my side. But just as I wish for those things, Mr. Snow's offer pops up like an annoying online ad.

"Sure," Dane tells Mia. "We can go get a burger. Sounds good to me."

"Will you come with us, Neely?"

I want to say yes. I need to say no. All I can do is look at the adorable little girl with a sad streak in her eyes, and I can't find the guts to answer either way.

Dane does it for me. "She better go or we'll kidnap her."

This puts a piece of the sparkle back on Mia's face. That, in turn, trumps the best solution of starting to wean myself from them.

"Let's go, ladies," Dane says.

Mia offers me her free hand.

I take it.

"And then a cab pulls up to the curb, right? I'm thinking my luck has finally changed, and I start running down the sidewalk, waving my arms like a lunatic." I demonstrate, with a little exaggeration, my arms flailing around in the air.

Mia giggles before taking a bite of her burger.

"I almost get there. I'm this close," I say. "And my heel gets caught in one of New York's famous sidewalk cracks, and I go face-first into a pile of snow."

"I bet that was cold," Mia notes. "How'd you get up?"

"Luckily, this man was walking by and helped me up. That's not common in the city. Most people would just watch you walk out into the middle of traffic and not blink an eye." I take a drink of my vanilla milkshake and shrug. "The man hailed me a cab, and I got back to my apartment. It was a heck of a day."

Dane sits next to me, not saying a word. We're early for dinner at Mucker's and are the only people in the actual dining area. There are a few groups on the patio.

"I need to go to the bathroom," Mia says, wiggling in her chair. "May I be excused?"

"Go ahead," Dane tells her.

She skips off, her spirits seemingly better than they were when we got here. I watch her ponytail disappear into the bathroom before I turn my attention back to her father.

"What do you think was wrong with her?" I ask.

"I don't know."

"It came out of nowhere. She was hugging me and happy as a lark, and then she wasn't." I take another drink. "She's too young for hormones. Or is she? What age do girls start their periods these days?"

Dane goes pale. "I have no idea. Surely not at her age."

"I wouldn't think so. It seems so young."

The waitress comes up to the table and clears away our empty plates and the giant bowl of ranch dressing we shared for our fries. Dane requests the check and a box for the rest of Mia's burger.

He leans to the side to retrieve his wallet from his back pocket, and I catch him grinning at me.

"What?" I ask.

"Just thinking you smell better than the last time I saw you."

"You should've seen my mom." I groan. "She picked out a piece of hay right away and was like, 'This looks like a good sign.'"

Dane laughs, handing his credit card to the waitress as she reappears.

"I'll be right back," she says.

My jaw drops. "You didn't even look at the bill."

"So?"

"So? She could charge you for ten burgers, Dane," I say, flabbergasted. "You always check the bill before you pay."

"I'll get to see it again before I sign the receipt. And come on, Neely. It's Mucker's. If they overcharged me, I'd get free food for life."

I twirl my straw around my glass. "I forget things like that are different here. You don't check in New York and your bill goes up one hundred percent."

The corner of his lip curls. I hold my breath as he moves his hand. He lays it on the inner corner of my thigh, his fingers pressing roughly against my skin. "I can tell you something else that goes up one hundred percent," he says. "At least it does when you're around."

I slip my hand on top of his and bring it higher until our entwined fingers sit between my legs. "Are you talking about the temperature around here?" I tease.

"Well, it is awfully hot." He nudges his hand against me. "But I was talking more about how erect certain things get."

"What's 'erect' mean?" Mia hops into her seat and grabs her milkshake. She looks from me to Dane. "Is 'erect' like a barrette? For my hair?"

"Yup." Dane swallows. He jerks his hand from me like it is on fire. "Just like that."

"That's not true." I roll my eyes. "'Erect' means something is stiff or straight. Like when you're in a pyramid. Your legs should be erect because it's easier for your bases to hold you. Get it?"

"Erect. I like that word." She slurps the final drink from her glass.

"Really?" Dane mutters under his breath.

"Do you want her to have a bad vocabulary?" I ask just as softly.

He leans toward me, his lips glancing my ear. "I'd like her to have a censored vocabulary, if you don't mind."

"Let me clue you in on something, big boy," I whisper. Glancing at Mia, I ensure she's preoccupied with the television hanging near the bathroom door. "When a guy comes on to her one day, and he will whether you like it or not, you don't want her shocked at words he throws around. Understanding things like the word 'erect' will give her confidence. Trust me."

He throws his hands up in the air and settles back in his seat.

"Look at me, sitting erect," Mia says with a hint of pride.

"That's it." Dane scoots his chair back and stands. "I'll pay and then be in the truck."

I can't help but giggle as he walks to the cash register and asks for the receipt to sign. He doesn't check the price, just scribbles his name, takes the card, and walks out.

"What's wrong with him?" Mia asks.

"Oh, he's just being a baby today. You ready to go?"

"Yes." She hops off her chair and follows me to the door.

We mosey through the parking lot side by side, neither of us saying a word. Once we get to the truck, I hold the door open while Mia climbs into the back, and then I get settled in the front beside Dane.

"Everyone ready?" he asks. "Buckle up back there, rascal."

The sound of the buckle clicking into the clasp rings through the air. "Don't worry. I'm buckled in and sitting erect."

I snort so hard I almost choke.

"You owe me for this one, Kimber," Dane says.

I glance over my shoulder to see a wickedly sexy smile gracing his lips. My legs pull together.

"I look forward to it."

CHAPTER TWENTY-TWO

NEELY

The couch in Dane's living room is perfectly worn. Each cushion is broken down to the point where you sink in like you're in a soft cloud as soon as your behind touches it.

Curled up in the corner, I listen to Dane and Mia laugh upstairs. Every now and then, he makes a weird voice, and she bursts out laughing.

The inside of their house isn't at all what I expected. Everything has a place, and everyone has a job. It's a mishmash of styles and decorations that seem to work together somehow. There's even a cookie jar on the center of the island in the kitchen filled with peanut butter cookies.

You can feel the joy when you walk in, sense the loyalty in the walls as you stroll down the hallway decorated with pictures of Mia at different stages of her life. I've never felt so comfortable in someone else's house before.

My phone vibrates on my lap. A text from Grace pops up on the screen. I look at it like it might bite me—not because of the text, but because of the email that needs responding to.

I've reread Mr. Snow's offer a few times. It isn't groundbreaking, but it isn't bad. It's certainly better than nothing. I should take it. I know I should. But every time I have my finger on the "Reply" button, I chicken out.

I tell myself it's because I know I'm worth more. I made almost double that at my old job and had half again more leave time. But something wrestles inside my chest, and I know it isn't all about leave *time*. It's about leaving *them*.

Dane's footsteps echo down the hall, and it isn't long before he comes around the corner. He's changed into a white T-shirt and a pair of gray sweatpants, and all I want to do is bury my face in the soft cloth and have him hold me.

"You're being beckoned," he says. A hand on his hip, he sighs. "Apparently she needs to talk to you now. I wouldn't let her get out of bed because if she does that, we'll never get her back in there."

Unfolding my legs, I stand. "What's she want?"

He shrugs. "I already read her bedtime story, which is ridiculous at her age, but I can't tell her no."

"I think it's adorable." I start by him, but he pulls me toward him.

"I think you're adorable."

"You do, huh?"

"I do." He plants a loud, wet kiss on my lips. "Now go figure out what she wants so we can move on with our night."

I take the stairs two at a time. "I like the sound of that."

Dane's footsteps fall behind me. "It's the door with the glitter. Make it snappy." He pats me on the behind as I enter Mia's room.

"Hey, you," I say. "Ready for bed?"

She's snuggled under the covers. "Yeah."

"What's going on?" I ask, sitting on the edge.

"Well . . ." She looks at Dane standing at the door. "There's this Manicure Day at the gym."

"I saw the flyer. It looks like fun." I brush her hair out of her face with my hand. "Are you excited about it?"

She throws the blanket over her head.

"Mia." I laugh. "What are you doing?" I tug the blanket down so I can look at her. "What's up?"

She chews her bottom lip. "I . . . You . . ." She takes a deep breath. "Will you go with me?"

My heart melts. "Yes, I'll go with you. Of course. Why would you think I wouldn't?"

"It's for mothers and daughters." She looks at Dane. "It's okay if I ask Neely, right?"

I twist around. He's propped against the doorjamb, looking at us in disbelief. "Yeah. It's okay with me."

"You'll go?" Mia shimmies from under the covers. "It's in the afternoon, and the girls say it's so much fun. They do their fingernails and toenails, and they bring them little cookies and stuff."

"Haven't you gone before?"

She shakes her head. "I didn't have anyone to take me."

"Honey, Haley would've gone with you," Dane says, coming into the room. "Or I would've gone. I don't know how good my feet would look all polished up, but maybe I'd like it."

Mia laughs. "You can't go. You're a boy. And Haley could've, but . . . she's not my mom."

"Mia," I say, resting my hand on her lap. "I'm not your mom either. I'm your friend. Your dad's friend. You know that, right?"

"Yeah." She grins like she's playing along to some game and curls back up under her blankets. "So you'll go?"

"Yes. I'll go." I lean forward and press a kiss to her forehead. "Now get some sleep."

She yawns, waving at her dad as he turns off the light. "Love you, Dad."

"Love you, rascal."

I step out of the room when she calls out again. "Love you, Neely."

I look up at Dane. He touches my cheek, as if that somehow will tell me what to do. "Good night, Mia."

He pulls the door closed. "That wasn't what I expected," he whispers.

"Me either."

"Are you okay with all that?" He searches my face. "If not, I'll work it out."

I take a quick inventory of how I feel in this moment. I have no regrets. I don't wish anything were different. In fact, I'm happy. I reach up and kiss his cheek. "I'm very okay with it."

He takes my hand. "Let's go to my room."

"I need to do something first. Go on without me, and I'll be there in a second, all right?"

"I don't want to go without you." He pouts.

"Give me five minutes." I laugh. "I'll be there. Promise."

"You have five minutes and your time starts now."

Rolling my eyes, I head across the hall to the bathroom. Once locked inside, I sit on the toilet seat and pull out my phone. My heart beats a little quicker with every second that passes.

I unlock the screen and pull up my email. Mr. Snow's offer is at the top. I open the message and hit the "Reply" button.

Mr. Snow,

Thank you for the generous offer. However, after much thought and consideration, I don't feel this position would be a good fit for me. I appreciate your vote of confidence and wish you the best of luck going forward.

Sincerely,
Neely Kimber

As soon as it's sent, my shoulders completely fall in relief.

I make my way to Dane's room and find him lying across his bed. He props up on his elbows when he hears me walk in.

"I have something to tell you," I say, shutting the door behind me.

"What's that?"

I walk to the side of the bed near his feet. "I got a job offer yesterday."

"In New York?" he asks carefully.

"Yeah." Sitting on the edge of the bed, my hand squeezing his thigh, I look back at him. I give myself a moment to panic, to wish I had taken the job. Those things never come. Instead, the longer I sit beside him, the better I feel. "I just turned it down."

"You did?"

"I did."

In one swift movement, he sits up and grabs me around the waist. I'm beside him on his white comforter before I know what's happening. He strokes my cheek with the pad of his thumb and gazes into my eyes.

"Can I say I'm glad you didn't take it?" he asks.

"You can. I'm glad I didn't take it too."

"Can I ask why you didn't take it?"

"They offered me five sick days." I snort. "And it's another six blocks from my apartment."

He grins, but it's not wide or joyful. "Everyone needs more than five sick days."

"That's what I was thinking." I link my leg over his.

"Are you still job hunting?"

"Yeah. I mean, I have bills to pay. I just can't find anything that checks all the boxes I need checked."

He nods. "Until you find something, I hope you'll let me check some of your boxes, if you catch my drift."

Laughing, I scoot closer to him. "I thought you owed me one?"

"No, *you* owe *me* one."

He rolls me over onto my back and smothers me with kisses. Thoughts of New York float away as I fall under Dane's spell.

CHAPTER TWENTY-THREE

DANE

"My usual, please, Claire." I turn away from the counter and head to a little table by the door. Grabbing a seat next to Haley, I let out a yawn.

"Tired?" she prods.

"Yeah."

"I heard you had a little slumber party last night. According to my sources, Neely stayed all night."

"Your source is nine years old and unreliable," I say, taking a cup of coffee from Claire. "She left really late, so it wasn't technically all night."

Haley rolls her eyes. "Semantics."

"Facts." I take a sip of the hot beverage, hoping it wakes me up. I haven't woken up this happy and delirious in a long damn time.

Claire bends forward. "Neely stayed all night with you?"

"No, eavesdropper. She came over. She left. If you're gonna spy on people's conversations, at least get them right."

Claire laughs, shoving a pen back in the apron around her waist. "I'm a waitress. Eavesdropping is part of the job description."

"So give us the details," Haley suggests. "What happened? Is she moving in yet?"

My finger drags around the brim of my cup. I wish she were. I wish I could tell them she was never leaving me again, but that's not true. Although after last night, it might be more of a possibility than I'd imagined.

"She's not moving in, but she did turn down a job offer," I say with a hint of smugness.

"Yes!" Haley fist pumps. "I'm so invested in this."

Claire shakes her head. "This is the way things should be. Neely back home, living with you. Pregnant, but I'll give you some time on that."

"Gee, thanks," I croak.

Claire laughs and goes back to the front of the restaurant.

"Forget babies, although I can't wait to have another little Mia to watch. Wait," Haley says, holding up a hand. "That needs to be a deal breaker for you."

"I'm not following along."

"Neely has to agree I can watch your babies. Some women come in and shove out the poor nanny, especially if the nanny was hired before she came around. Let her know I'm not, in any way, shape, or form wanting her job. I just want to watch the babies."

I laugh, but secretly my balls are tightening. The thought of having a baby with Neely is foreplay. The idea of her swollen with my child feels so good it aches.

"I'll put that in the deal," I promise. "No cock unless Haley gets to watch the results."

"That's a gross way to put it, but it gets the point across. I think," she says, clearly confused. "Anyway, how do you feel about things?"

"You know what? I'm feeling pretty damn good."

"I love seeing you in love." She sighs, cupping her cheeks with her hands. "It's so beautiful."

"I didn't say I was in love. I just said I was feeling good." I try to put in words what I feel without getting too cheesy. "She just fits right into my life. Mia loves her. She seems to really love Mia too." I shrug. "It feels right."

"Sounds like my kind of conversation," Penn says. He drops into a seat by Haley. "So, what feels right? Are we doing a round-robin sort of thing?"

Haley gives him a blank stare. "You have a one-track mind."

"So?"

"So? Don't you think it's time to grow up some, Penn? Maybe focus on investing money or buying a house? Something besides hooking up with the next girl you meet."

"Right now I'm focused on hooking up with you."

"Forget it," she says. "Not happening."

"Our girl Haley here has vowed not to date anyone for six months." I look at Penn and smirk. "Looks like you're out of luck until the new year."

Penn furrows his brow. "I don't see how this affects me at all."

"Me either," Haley agrees.

"I don't want to date you. I want to sleep with you." Penn smiles triumphantly. "Let me know what day works for you."

"The sixth Sunday of the month. I'll sleep with you on the sixth Sunday of the month." Haley rolls her eyes. "Now, back to the person who *is* getting laid."

"I think you misunderstand my enthusiasm for sleeping with you as I'm not getting laid." He leans toward her, smirking. "I promised to be practiced up when you call."

"Penn, I'm not calling. Not now. Not ever."

In typical Penn fashion, he shrugs like he doesn't care. He leans back in his chair and looks at me. "Does all this jabbering mean things are going good with you and Miss New York?"

"There are days I hate you," I tell him. "Today is one of them."

"Why? I just asked a question."

"Why don't you get a coffee or whatever it is you came here for and get to the jobsite before you get fired?" I ask. "And tell Matt to have the lumber taken off the pallets before I get there."

Penn stands up. "Fine. But let me point out this morning that there are days when I think you really are your father's son. Today is one of them."

"Go to hell." I chuckle.

"See ya up there," he tells me. "See ya later, Haley."

"Goodbye."

Once Penn's gone, Claire comes over again. "He drives me insane."

"Penn? He drives us all insane," Haley notes. "What did he do to you?"

"We have this friends-with-benefits thing going on, as you all know. Well, he stood me up last night, and I found out he was with Brittney. Can you believe that?"

"Yes," Haley and I say in unison.

Claire shakes her head. "I'm cutting him off. If I want a booty call, I'll call someone else. He's not that good."

"Don't let him hear you say that," I kid. "He'll feel like he has to prove a point."

She rolls her eyes but watches as he pulls out of the parking lot. "Asshole," she grumbles before turning back to the kitchen.

I sip my coffee while Haley checks her phone. She's not used to having a couple of extra hours in the morning. Dad grabbed Mia early for a day of koi shopping, which thrilled my daughter to no end.

As the hot liquid wakes me up, it becomes clearer how I feel. And what I want. And what I need to consider.

"What are you thinking?" Haley asks, bringing me out of my haze. She points at me. "You have that la-la land look on your face that scares me."

"Do you think Mia is happy?" I ask her.

"Definitely. Happier lately than usual, even. Why?"

All the pieces of my life come together into one cohesive puzzle in my heart. For the first time in my life, I feel like I've identified all the sections of my life and have them all within my grasp. I almost can't believe it.

"Dane . . ."

"Let me ask you a girl question," I say, setting down my drink. "If you didn't want to be serious with a guy, you wouldn't spend a lot of time with them, right?"

Haley grins.

"Like, you wouldn't have dinner with him and his kid. Help tuck the kid in. Fix her hair. That kind of thing. You wouldn't do all that unless you saw a future with them. Does that sound legit?"

"Totally." She lays a hand on mine. "Mia aside, I've never seen *you* this happy. In all the years I've known you, I've never seen you like this. It makes me wonder if the Dane I knew before all this was really just a shell of you."

"I am happier. I wake up and don't just think about Mia and what she needs for the day. For once, there's something there just for me. That probably sounds selfish, but it's true."

"Selfish?" She laughs. "No. It sounds like you're a man with needs and you've found someone that might meet them."

"I just keep thinking what it would be like for us to wake up in the same house. For Mia to have a mother-like figure in her life—no offense, Haley. We love you."

She holds up her hands. "No offense taken. That's a job I don't want. You know that. I will give that girl whatever she needs, but I'd rather not take on the duties of a parent. Besides, she needs someone in her corner. I'm not around all the time."

Nodding, I sip my coffee again. "I need to figure out a way to keep her here."

Haley cheers, then clamps a hand over her mouth. "Yay," she whispers.

"You're nuts." I throw a tip on the table and head to the front. I toss a ten-dollar bill on the counter and take the bag with my name spelled out across the front. "Thanks, Claire," I call out to her in the back.

"See ya, Dane."

As I walk by the round table by the door, I pause. "Thanks for listening, Haley."

"It's why you pay me the big bucks."

With a spring in my step, I head into the warm summer air with a head full of ideas.

CHAPTER TWENTY-FOUR

NEELY

"Madison! Point your toes!" I call out as she lands her tumbling pass. "No. Do it again." Jogging over to her, I put a hand on her shoulder. "You can do better than that. Remember—you perform like you practice. Habits are built here, when you're doing it for yourself and no one is watching." I work my head side to side. "Except I'm watching, and you have to do it again."

She sighs, but smiles. "Okay. I'll try again."

"Good girl."

I get out of her way and watch as she readies herself at the opposite end of the room. She inhales and then sprints a few feet and begins her tumbling pass. This time, as she flips through the air, everything is nearly perfect.

"Great job," I tell her as she looks my way. "Very, very good, Madison. I knew you could do it."

"Thanks, Neely."

The girls work in little groups, each focused on a certain element Aerial feels they could improve on. I love the team-building aspect of the groups. It lets the girls see they aren't the only ones struggling in an area.

After surveying the practice pods, as Aerial calls them, I head to the water fountain for a quick drink and almost run into Aerial herself.

"Hey, you," she says. "I heard you yelling at Madison. I'm glad you did that because that second pass was awesome."

"You've got a great group of kids here. They take criticism well. They work hard. They have positive attitudes, for the most part."

"Come into my office for a second, will you?"

I follow her inside and lean against the wall. "What's up?"

She fights with the words she wants to use. "I know you said your heart isn't here."

I shift my weight back and forth. That was certainly true when I said it at a time that feels like a lifetime ago. My heart was very much rooted in New York then. Now? I'm not so sure.

"If you ever wanted to stick around," Aerial says, "I'd love to talk to you about taking over the gym."

"What?" I ask, shoving off the wall. "What are you saying?"

"I'm getting old. I still love the kids and will always want to be a part of the learning environment here. I don't think I could exist if I didn't. But there are lots of days, Neely, where I don't want to deal with the rest of it." Her shoulders sag. I can see the exhaustion, the years of worry and wear written on her face. "But what do I do? I've spent my entire life building this gym. We have the Summer Show that's basically a tourist attraction for the whole town at this point. We have the competitions in the winter that keep a lot of little girls, and some boys, working hard and staying out of trouble. I don't want to walk away and just shut this place down. I've worked way too hard at it for way too long to do that."

I look at the floor, trying to replay that through my mind. "You want to retire?" I ask. "Is that what you're saying?"

"I'm saying I want to walk away in a large way. But I want to hand this place off to someone who will love it and care for it as much as I do. And honestly, you're the only person who will do that."

"Aerial, I'm flattered," I say, still unsure if I'm hearing this right. "But I can't take over the gym."

"Why?"

"I'm honored, Aerial. Truly. This is your baby, and for you to think I could do it justice, even partially, is one of the nicest things to ever happen to me." I stop talking and look at her again. "I'll think about it. I'll see what I can do. But I still have a lot of irons in the fire up north, and I'm not convinced that's not where I should be."

"But you aren't convinced you should be either."

Glancing around the room, I see the trophies from years gone by. I see the pictures from teams and students and handwritten letters sitting in frames. All of that is nice, but that isn't what Aerial is asking me to take over. She's asking me to take over the heart and soul of the gym.

My mind floats to my apartment in the city and all the things there. If I go back, I'm going back to things. A job. A subway pass. A rack of shoes I can barely afford because rent is so freaking high.

I'm not going back there for the heart and soul of the place. Maybe that means something.

Maybe it means something, too, that when I think of my life there, it feels shallow. There's no color like in Dane's house, no laughter like at the gym. It's a bleak, monotonous life that isn't as appealing to me as it once was.

"I won't keep you waiting long," I promise. "I have a lot to think about."

"Absolutely. I'm honored you'd consider it, Neely."

I pull her into a big hug before letting her go.

"Okay," she says. "Enough about the gym. What's happening with you and Dane?"

I sigh. "I don't know."

"I've been seeing you with him here and there. Mia acts like you're best friends. You should've heard her in here before you got here tonight, telling everyone you were taking her to Manicure Day." Aerial stops. "Do you know how much that means to that little girl?"

"I think so."

"Many women wouldn't have been able to accept her like you have. It shows your grace."

"That's silly," I say, waving her off. "Mia's a great kid. She can't help the circumstances in which she was conceived."

"Again, not everyone would see it like that." She picks up a few papers on her desk and puts them on top of a larger pile. "Based on what you just said, I'm guessing you still might leave town?"

"I'm so torn, Aerial," I admit. "There's a growing part of me that thinks I could be happy here. Mom is here. Heck, I even like Gary. It's so beautiful here, and I love seeing Claire and Matt and Penn . . ."

"And Dane."

"And Dane." I grin. "But if I do that, if I stay here, I fear I'll always feel robbed, because what am I going to do here, Aerial? I can run the gym for you. I could pick up some freelance work somewhere, probably. But how am I going to feed that part of my soul that *needs* to do something . . . else? And does that mean I've wasted my entire life up to this point if I don't go back?"

"Maybe everything you've been through so far was to prepare you for this? Or something else, even if it's not this."

I look at her honestly. "Or maybe I need to realize this is a honeymoon phase and it won't always be like this here. With Dane or the gym or even Mom. It's all new and fun, but it won't always be."

"Sounds like you have a conundrum."

"It feels like it too."

"Let me know what you decide," she says. "But my fingers are crossed you decide to stay home where you belong."

"Thanks." I laugh. My phone buzzes in my pocket and I pull it out. "I need to take this."

She gives me a wave as my spirits sink like a ship. Hustling outside, I wait until I'm alone before I answer. "Hello?"

"Is this Neely?"

"It is."

"This is Frank Selleck. How are you?"

My old boss's boss. His voice rings through the line. It feels like forever since I heard it, but also like we just spoke yesterday. We used to get together about big projects or to brainstorm. There's a warmth to his tone that makes me relax a bit, but I still sit on a picnic table while I gather my wits.

"I'm good, Frank," I say, clearing my throat. "How are you?"

"Been better, been worse."

Mia waves as she trots off with Keyarah and Madison. I wave back.

"I'm calling you for a few reasons," Frank says. "For one, I'd like to apologize."

"For what?"

"When the résumés came across my desk for the new magazine, I assumed incorrectly that you already had a position there. Mark and I had talked extensively about putting you in charge of the Creative Department, so I assumed your résumé was sitting there as a protocol thing, not for actual consideration. Your vision really shaped the entire concept of what we're looking to do, and I felt you, above everyone else, myself included, were the best choice in leading our company into this new sector."

The phone almost slips from my hands. His words are drowned out by the adrenaline coursing through my veins.

"Well, thank you for that vote of confidence," I reply. "It's too bad I wasn't selected to work on the new project at all."

"That's the second reason I'm calling, Neely. Not promoting you was an oversight on our part. On *my* part. I'll take responsibility for it. But I also have to take responsibility for correcting wrongs, and not having you leading that team is definitely a wrong."

"What are you saying?" I ask. I pick out a little pebble on the ground and stare at it.

"I'm saying we want you back. *I* want you back. I don't hold it against you for quitting for one second. I would've quit too. As a matter of fact, if you hadn't, I would've been disappointed."

I hop off the table, unable to sit still any longer. "You want me back. How? In what capacity?"

"I want you to lead the Creatives. I want you to direct our approach to this thing. What types of articles are we publishing? What images are we showing? I want you to be the one to present me with a final version of anything that goes out so I know it's been through you first."

Tears sting my eyes as I realize what he's saying. He's giving me the one thing I've always wanted, the platform I've begged for. Prayed for. Quit for. He's giving me the only thing I've ever set my heart on.

A car backs out of a parking space in front of me and a horn honks. A window rolls down and Mia and Keyarah wave. "Bye, Neely," they shout.

My hand comes up, but it doesn't quite move. I can't move. I can only listen to Frank tell me he wants me back in two days.

Two.

Days.

Before Manicure Day.

Before the Summer Show.

Before I have time to break this to Dane and Mia in a way they deserve.

"I'll give you ten percent more than we were offering for the position you applied for," he says. "You're worth it. This project depends on you."

I watch the car disappear from sight. *But so do they.*

I shake my head to focus. "Can I also point out that Lynne stole my ideas and no one thought anything about that? And that it's taken this long for you to even realize I'm gone?"

"That's not true, Neely. Your resignation came to my desk the day after it was filed."

"And my contributions to the company weren't enough for you to call me before now?" I ask. "I gave everything I had to that company, Frank. I gave it my all for a very long time. And then this happens, and I'll admit, I'm not really feeling valued."

"I'll shoulder the blame for that as well. Your name has been on a sticky note since the day I realized you were gone. I originally thought it was a two-week notice, which would've had you still here or close to it. I didn't realize at the time it was effective immediately." He blows out a breath. "I'm in over my head here, Neely. We're trying to do a lot of things, trying to break down those doors you talk about all the time. But I can't do it without someone who feels as passionately about it as you do. Come back. Help us. Let's make a dent in this industry."

Those words are all I've wanted to hear since I stood in my cap and gown and received my diploma. If I don't go back, if I don't try, I'll always wonder what I could've accomplished—wonder if I could've done all the things I wrote down in my journal with a sunflower on it that's under my pillow in New York.

"Can you be back in two days?" he asks. "I know this is impromptu, but we've committed to the launch dates, and I have to be sure we can pull them off."

A single tear rolls down my face as my mouth says the words my heart can't. "I'll be there, Frank."

CHAPTER TWENTY-FIVE

NEELY

H i, honey!" Mom greets me from the kitchen. The house smells like pie and roast beef. It sours my stomach. "I'm making a raisin pie for Mr. Rambis, but I made you a coconut cream pie too. So no jealousy, all right?" She pokes her head around the corner. "Honey. What's wrong?"

"Mr. Rambis is Gary to me now," I say flatly. "We worked it out."

"That's nice." She watches me walk into the kitchen and get out a glass. "Neely?"

I don't look at her yet. I'm afraid I'll cry. If that happens, she'll probably panic, and her panicking won't help anything.

"I have some great news," I tell her. Ice clinks into the glass before I fill it with water.

"Great news is usually accompanied by a little more enthusiasm than I'm getting from you," she notes. "Are you sure 'great' is the right word?"

On any given day, this news is great. Life-changing, even. It's what I've worked my whole life for. It's not that the word is wrong by any means. It's that I'm having a hard time making peace with it.

I take a sip of the water. The cold rush slips down my throat. Instead of shocking me back to reality, instead of waking me up from the fog I feel like I'm walking around in, it chills me to the bone.

"I got two job offers today." I lead with facts and numbers. I learned to do that in a random college class that I took just to finish my generals. People have a hard time arguing numbers, and if you start a conversation with hard data, they're typically more engaged in your words. You sound smarter. And God knows I need all the wisdom I can get.

"Two?" She lifts a brow. "That's amazing."

"Aerial asked me to take over the gym today. I think that's amazing."

Mom's eyes light up. "I actually think that's wonderful." She turns to the stove and puts on her oven mitts. She pulls two perfectly baked pies out and sets them on a cooling rack. "You're so good with kids, honey. And the fact that Aerial trusts you to take over her namesake really says a lot about your reputation." She plops the gloves down and turns to me. "I'm quite proud of you. You know that?"

I nod. I try to smile. I attempt at finding a twig of excitement somewhere in my system as I make my second declaration. "I also got a call from Frank Selleck."

"He's from your old company, right?"

"Right. He is Mark's boss. I worked with him a few times on special projects *and* in developing the new magazine."

She stills, watching me. It just makes me more nervous.

"Frank basically said they screwed up and want me back. Now. Ten percent more money than the job I applied for plus all creative control, more or less." I wait for a surge of adrenaline that doesn't come. "This isn't just my dream job, Mom—it's the next level. This is the stuff that happens to other people."

I haven't said it out loud until now. I stand by the refrigerator, which is covered in gaudy magnets and old pictures, and hope something I've just spouted off will hit me like a ton of bricks. That maybe this will start to feel less like a move to dread and more like something to feel energized about.

Tick, tock. Tick, tock.

Nothing.

I try again.

"This is everything I've ever wanted."

Mom goes to the sink and rinses off her hands. "I know it is, and I'm happy they realized what they lost."

"Are you?"

"Absolutely. I want you to have what you deserve. You deserve this. You've worked very hard for this opportunity, and if it's what you want, then I'm thrilled for you, honey."

I wait for her to continue. When she doesn't, I look at the ceiling. "But . . ."

"But do you think, possibly, you deserve *more* than they're offering you?"

"They're giving me a huge raise, Mom."

She smiles faintly. "I don't mean financially."

The kettle is in her hand when I open my eyes. She begins to fill it at the sink, then sets it on a hot burner. My chest squeezes so tight I don't know whether to yelp from the constriction or cry from the agony. I just know this isn't what it's supposed to feel like.

"You keep telling yourself all the things you'll gain from this new job," she says. "You list them out like it'll hit critical mass at some point and you'll finally be convinced it's the right choice."

"I don't have to be convinced. It is the right choice."

"Fine," she says. She stands on her tiptoes and pulls a box of tea bags out of the cabinet next to the spice rack. "It's the right choice. But what does this job not give you? What do you have to give up to take it? That's what I was saying when I said what if you deserve more."

My fingernail goes to my mouth, but I stop my finger midair. I turn it over and look at the nail as my heart sinks to my stomach. What will I give up? I cringe at the pain that settles in my chest.

Manicures with Mia. Lazy evenings with Dane. Burgers at Mucker's while Penn tells wild tales of his exploits, and hugs from Matt that feel as natural as breathing.

Weekend drives along dirt roads and quiet mornings on the porch with coffee. Grocery stores that barely qualify and trips that require you to drive around old hound dogs lying in the middle of the road. Sunday potlucks and random conversations with Gary and margarita dates with my mom where she liquors me up to extract information.

I'll give up all of that.

My heart splinters into a hundred jagged pieces as I get exactly what my mom is saying. The list of negatives is just as long or longer, if I'm being honest, than the list of positives. Why did I ever come back home? Why did I open this stupid door to start with?

Mom places two mugs of tea on the table and takes a seat. I follow suit because I don't have a better option.

She lifts her mug to her lips and blows across the water. Steam whispers through the air, looking like a ballerina slipper, and I wonder if Mia would see it too.

"What are you going to do about Dane?" Mom asks. "Have you told him?"

I shake my head. A lump sits at the base of my throat, and I'm not sure I can speak over it. It feels like it's blocking off all my air and if it moves, I'll puke instead of breathe.

"Maybe it's because I'm an old woman, but I was hoping things were working out between you two."

I force the lump to the side and wait for the bile to settle. Finally, when I feel like it's safe, I try to explain it. "Things are working out. That's the problem." I frown. "He's great. Mia is great. I even turned down a job last week because of them."

Mom flinches. "I didn't know that."

"I did. It was a decent offer, but it didn't seem worth it to take. I was sort of mulling it over, and Mia called me to her bedroom and asked me to go . . ." I can't say it. I hiccup the last words and blink back red-hot tears. When I finally am able to look at my mom, there are tears streaming down her cheeks too. "Don't cry," I tell her.

"You're crying." She sniffles. "If you hurt, I hurt."

"I hurt by my own choice. They're going to hurt by it too."

A tear rolls down my cheek and splashes in the tea. I watch the water ripple around the droplet.

"They'll understand. If this job is what you want, then you have to take it, Neely."

"If I don't take this, I'll always regret it. I could stay here, marry Dane, and in ten years, look at him and blame him that I gave up on myself. I can't do that, Mom. I can't do that to me or to him. It's not fair."

"No, it's not. It's not fair to either of you." She puts her mug on the table. "You're a smart girl. You'll do the right thing. I have more faith in you than I've ever had in anyone in my life."

We sit quietly for a long time. Mom gives me space to work through things in my head, but I don't do that. I'm not sure I can. I certainly don't feel the faith in myself that I can get through this.

The thought of telling Dane what's happening is enough to have me running to the bathroom and vomiting in the toilet.

CHAPTER TWENTY-SIX

NEELY

I scan the flights to New York. There are a couple departing late tomorrow that look good and a few the next morning. I close the lid to my computer and rest my head against my pillows.

It's so odd to think I'll be back in my apartment in a matter of hours. As I glance around the room and listen to my mother banging around in the kitchen, I realize how acclimated I've become to this place. To this lifestyle.

Despite the stress on my shoulders, I haven't felt this relaxed in forever. Everything here happens at such a crawling pace compared with the city, and while I thought it would be boring, it's kind of nice. It's fun to wave at the neighbors in the morning, and the constants in life here—Blue in the road, unstable Wi-Fi, and a fish special at the Dogwood Café on Fridays—are much more pleasant than the constants of city life.

A part of me wishes Frank hadn't called. I feel guilty for thinking that, especially after wishing for this job for so long. But if he hadn't, I'd be at Dane's right now doing something with him and Mia.

I don't know how to tell him I'm leaving. I almost don't have the courage to do it face-to-face, even though I know I have to. The thought of him looking sad or lonely slays me, but to think of him angry with me for leaving breaks me apart.

As if he knows I'm thinking about him, his name flashes on my phone. I consider letting it ring but know that's the wrong thing to do. I need to be an adult.

"Hey," I say into the line.

"Want to meet us for ice cream?" Dane asks. "The girl here wants this new flavor where they hide actual bubble gum pieces in the cone. Totally gross, in my opinion, but she's demanding it."

"Come with us!" Mia shouts from what I'm guessing is the back seat.

My stomach twists in a tight, intricate knot—one I know I won't be uncoiling anytime soon.

I hop off the bed and pace my room. "I was going to call you," I say.

"Oh yeah? What about?"

"I wanted to talk to you."

"Well, we'll pick you up and we can talk over ice cream."

"The ice cream cone will be erect!" Mia giggles.

I can't help but smile despite the heavy loneliness that's settling over my heart. "Um, I wanted to talk to you in private, actually. Can I meet you somewhere?"

The line gets quiet. With each passing moment, my anxiety soars higher. I imagine the look on his face, the look on Mia's, the conversations that need to be had and had soon.

I can still taste the bile in my throat from getting sick. That, coupled with the way my stomach is churning now, has me heading back toward the bathroom just in case.

"I can see if Haley can come by and watch Mia, if you need me to." There's more than a dose of caution in his tone.

"Can you?"

"Yeah. Where do you want to meet?"

"The bluff?"

"Give me thirty."

"I'll see you then." I end the call and get sick all over again.

æS

Dane's truck is already parked when I arrive. He's standing by the little stone wall that I've always thought was constructed to keep people from falling over the edge of the hill. He doesn't look back as I pull up and doesn't act like he hears the engine shut off. I don't bother to get out quickly because until I do, this thing between us isn't over.

His back ripples under the green shirt that's stretched across his torso. He moves slightly, slipping a hand in a pocket. I say a silent prayer for strength and guidance before exiting the car.

The air is a few degrees cooler than it has been. The leaves seem a little more yellow too. I bet this place is spectacular in the fall, and the fact that I won't see it with Dane pokes me right in the heart.

"Hey," I say, coming up behind him.

He gives me a small smile. "Hey."

I want to protect him from what I'm about to say, to wrap my arms around him and plant my lips against his chest. But how unfair would that be? To be that close to him in such a caring embrace when I'm about to tell him I'm leaving him. Again.

"You can kind of feel autumn coming, can't you?" I ask. "Some of the leaves look more yellow today than they have, I think."

"I guess."

"It'll be a beautiful backdrop for Mia's barbecues up here."

"Yeah. I'm sure it will." He turns to face me, his jaw flexing. "What's going on, Neely?"

"What do you mean?"

He rolls his eyes as he shrugs. "Oh, I don't know. You had me meet you up here, alone, and I didn't get the feeling it was to hang out. Maybe I'm wrong. I hope to hell I'm wrong."

213

"I just wanted to talk to you without Mia being around." I walk around, kicking at rocks, wishing I could disappear and be done with this. "What's she doing tonight?"

"She and Haley are watching a movie at the house." He flips me a cocked brow. "She's hoping you're coming by later."

I nod, wanting to say I wish that, too, but I look away. "Dane," I say, the words coated with unshed tears. "I have to tell you something."

I wait for him to respond, to say something—anything—but he doesn't. He doesn't move a muscle.

"Aren't you going to say anything?" I ask.

He studies me. "If this is going where I think it's going, I'm not about to help you do it."

"Dane . . ."

His temple pulses, a bead of sweat forming along his brow as he looks at me. "What is it? Just tell me so we can stop playing this game."

"This isn't a game."

"I fucking hope not."

"I got a job offer," I choke out. "In New York."

"And you turned it down. I know."

I shake my head side to side. "I got another one. At my old company."

"So? Like you'd go back to work for a company that treated you like shit."

"It was a misunderstanding," I tell him.

His laugh is anything but amused. His eyes are so cold they almost pierce me. "A misunderstanding, huh? How long did it take them to realize they made a mistake?"

"It's not like that."

"No, you know what? *You're* not like that. The woman I know would stick to what she believes in. Look at us," he says. "I fucked you over, and you didn't come home for almost ten fucking years. You wouldn't work for a company that treated you like that."

"They apologized," I tell him. "You didn't."

He looks away. I wait for him to respond, to somehow open a door and make this easier, but every second that passes shows me he's not about to make this easy.

I take a deep breath. "I took the job, Dane."

His eyes go from ice cold to red hot.

"You what?" He looks at me like I'm speaking Swahili, like he can't understand the words I'm using. "You're leaving?"

"Tomorrow night."

"You've got to be fucking kidding me." He spits the words with an edge of fury that has me flinching.

"I'm not. I'm sorry."

He takes off his beloved Dodgers hat and sends it sailing over the bluff. His hands go straight to his hair, tugging at it with both hands. When he turns to me, his face is beet red, a vein pulsing in his temple.

I want to reach for him, to wrap myself around him and somehow make this better. But I can't because there's no way to make this easier. For either of us.

He paces a circle, his nostrils flaring. "You're leaving us? Now?"

"I have to," I insist. Tears flow down my cheeks as I wish I had a way to make this all stop. To pause time and live forever in this moment, minus the bomb I just dropped. "It's a great opportunity—"

"It's a fucking job, Neely." He glowers.

"It's a job that means something to me."

He throws his head back. "I'm glad you stick to your guns about things that really mean something to you."

"That's not what I mean."

"No." He looks at me with a ferocity that knocks me a few steps back. "You don't get to play that card. You leaving us for a fucking job means it's exactly what you meant."

"Dane . . ." I wipe away the tears with the backs of my hands. "I told you from the beginning I wasn't staying here."

"Maybe. But you led me on. You rejected one job. What was I supposed to think? Huh?"

"Dane . . ."

"Don't 'Dane' me!" His voice echoes over the bluff.

"What was I supposed to do? Stay here and give everything up? For what? You? Mia? Neither of you are mine, Dane."

The fury in his eyes softens just a bit, enough to make me drag in a lungful of air. He stands in front of me, his hair a wild mess and his chest rising and falling at warp speed.

"Believe it or not, I try to do what's right," he says, his tone a few octaves lower than before.

"And so do I. And right now I have to do what's right for me. Is it wrong that I don't want to give up everything I've wanted, everything I've worked for, for a *possibility* with you?"

He fires a look my way that I can't quite read.

"Would you want to come to New York with me?" I offer, knowing damn good and well he won't.

"No."

My shoulders sag. "But you expect me to stay here."

Give me a reason. Just a little bit will be enough. Just something to hold on to.

He shrugs. "You know what? You'd just leave anyway."

"That's not fair. Or true," I say, my voice wobbly.

"You left before—"

"You made me!"

"Fine," he says, his chest shaking with anger. "I made you. Maybe I make all women leave me. You. Katie. Sara. You're better off going, I guess."

My hand trembles as I point a finger at him, my vision blurred by white-hot tears. "You can't lump me in with them. We were different. You are why we didn't work."

"Then. And you are why now." He turns toward his truck but doesn't move his feet. He just watches me over his shoulder as I break.

I crouch down and hold my head in my hands. I cry harder than I've ever cried. I cry so hard I think I might break in half.

"If you cared as much as you're letting on, you wouldn't go," he says. "It's really that simple."

"It's not that simple," I sob. Standing up again, my body still shaking with the force of the tears, I look at the gorgeous man in front of me. "I've wanted this my entire life, Dane. How am I supposed to not take a chance of a lifetime?"

"This," he says, motioning between us, "was what I've wanted my entire life. This was my chance of a lifetime."

"Don't say that."

"You have your truth. I have mine." He turns his back to me and heads toward the truck.

Panic bubbles inside me as I chase after him. The closer he gets to the truck, the sooner he'll be gone—probably forever this time. The thought of it, despite knowing it must happen, has me running faster.

"What's that supposed to mean?" I cry.

He stops at the front of the truck. His lips are twisted as he settles his gaze on me. "You can't even see what really matters anymore. Should Mia have given you some kind of award instead of a bracelet?" He glares at me. "I let you in our life. In our home."

"Well, I let you in my life, too, you know." I rub my thumb over the soft threads of my most cherished piece of jewelry. "I let you both in my life."

"Pardon me. We were clearly a threat," he deadpans. "You know how much of a threat I was to you? I was trying to figure out how to ask you to move in with us, and all the while you're plotting to leave."

My world crumbles around me, my knees threatening to fail altogether. I can't blink the tears back faster than they fall.

Why couldn't he have said this a couple of days ago? Why does this have to happen now?

Memories of Mia's laugh and Dane's smile flash through my brain, and I choke back a sob.

"I'm a fucking idiot. I guess Haley and her romantic ways are rubbing off on me, because I thought you and I were going somewhere. And not to New York," he adds as he walks toward his truck.

"Dane! Wait!" I call after him.

He holds up a hand to signal he's done with the conversation. I chase after him anyway, even though I know it's pointless. I need to let him go and sort this out, but I'm a glutton for punishment.

I catch him right before he makes it to his truck. I grab his bicep, but he shakes me off. "Dane. Wait. Listen to me, please."

"What?" He spins around, almost knocking me over. "What could you possibly have to say now?"

I catch my breath before making my final request. "Can I tell Mia?"

He laughs long and loud, as if he just heard a great one-liner. Then he glares at me and opens the door to the truck.

"Please," I beg. "I want to make sure she knows this had nothing to do with her."

"You know what?" he says, climbing in the cab. "Stay away from my daughter."

"Dane . . ."

He shakes his head as he starts the ignition. "I'll tell Mia. I'll tell her in a way I think won't break her heart since you obviously don't give a fuck."

"You aren't being fair," I cry.

He doesn't respond. Just looks at me with watery eyes before pulling away.

CHAPTER TWENTY-SEVEN

NEELY

I'm pretty sure my face is swollen. I think I can see the bags under my eyes when I look at an angle. My lips hurt, probably from crying until the sun came up, and my heart is in so many pieces I think they're scattered across all of Dogwood Lane.

I thought about staying here. I gave it more than a few moments of consideration over the course of the night, mostly when I thought about picking up the phone to call Dane. Every scenario ended with me being unsure about what I could've done at the magazine, and I don't want to ever hold that against anyone.

Throwing my last pair of jeans into my suitcase, I latch it shut. My bag goes on top, balanced perfectly, before I roll it to the door. I don't leave. Not yet. Instead, I turn around and take in my childhood bedroom, my home for the last couple of weeks. I'm going to miss the warmth of the blankets and the way the sun comes in the windows at a slight angle. That's not to mention all the little things on the walls, in the drawers, and on the shelves that remind me of being younger. More naive. And probably a lot happier.

I make my way through the house, taking in the pictures and mementos of a life well lived. Leftover pie sits on the stove, and I grin at Claire's joke.

The sky is overcast as I make my way to the car. Gary and Mom are standing on the driveway, awaiting my arrival. Mom has a handkerchief in her hand, already blotting her eyes.

"Stop it," I tell her, coming to a stop. I pull her into me and give her the warmest, sturdiest hug I can manage. "I love you. I'll be back to visit. I promise."

"This visit was one of the happiest times of my life," she says. "Having you around, being able to enjoy little things with you, has been a mother's dream."

"I've had a great time too." I kiss her cheek before turning to Gary. "And it's been a pleasure getting to know you."

"I'm going to pretend you meant that much cheerier than it came out."

"I know. I'm sorry." I sigh. "I'm just kind of melancholy today."

"You have every right to be. It's hard, sometimes, to make choices in life when it's not a clear-cut decision. All you can do is make the best choice for you, and I believe you did that. Or, at least, you made the choice that feels the best for you."

"I'm not feeling very good this morning," I admit. "But you're right. I'm sure when I see the Statue of Liberty, I'll come around."

He gives me a one-arm hug. "If you need anything at all, please don't hesitate to reach out."

"Thanks, Gary." I lean in and hug Mom once more while Gary puts my bags in the rental car. "I love you, Mama."

"Oh, Neely . . ." She lays her cheek against mine and holds it there for a long time. "I'm proud of you. I know this decision wasn't easy." She kisses my cheek, her tears wetting my face. "I love you."

With a little wave, I slip into the car and back out of the driveway. I honk three times as I make my way down the road.

I pull to a stop at an intersection and do a quick scan of my gauges. The little orange marker shows I'm definitively on empty. I make a quick right and head to Elmer's Gas Station.

I pick a pump and get out. Swiping my card, I set the nozzle to fill and figure I may as well go inside and get a few snacks for the flight.

The air inside the station is ice cold. I peruse the smoked almonds and beef jerky packages, but none of my usual go-tos look appetizing. Nothing looks good, even the cinnamon breakfast cakes I love but don't let myself have very often.

I turn to leave but almost run into Susan. Keyarah and Madison's mom stops in her tracks. "Neely," she gushes. "How are you?"

"Good," I lie. "How are you?"

"Fine. Picking up some sports drinks for the girls. Aerial said practice tonight is going to be a run-through of the routine until it's perfect, so we better be prepared to stay late."

"That sounds about right. We're getting close to the Summer Show. It's time to start perfecting things now and making the girls really put on the final touches."

"Will you be there?" she asks, picking up a bag of pistachios.

"No, actually. I won't be."

"Well, you've been such good help to the girls. I know they absolutely love to see you in the gym."

"I—"

"And Mia." Susan giggles. "She is beside herself about you. She told me how much time you've been spending with her and Dane. I'm sure it's hard to spend time with him," she says, wiggling her eyebrows.

"I—"

"Don't worry. Your secret is safe with me. If it is a secret, that is. I'm just thrilled to see her really coming out of her shell these days, and it's all thanks to you."

I force a smile that I don't feel. That I don't mean. That takes the place of the terrible sadness that weighs on my soul.

"To tell you the truth, Susan, I'm on my way out of town."

"For the day?" she asks, lifting a perfectly manicured brow.

"For good."

She's obviously taken aback. A hand goes to her throat as her eyes grow wide. "Really?"

"I was never staying forever," I say, going through my well-practiced spiel. "I was waiting on a new position to open, and it has, so I have to go back to New York." Feeling awkward, I grab a bag of peanuts. "I'll miss the girls."

"I guess you're not taking the job at Aerial's?"

"I didn't know anyone knew about that," I admit. "But no, I'm not. I can't. I haven't told Aerial that, though, because this all happened so fast. I'll call her when I land or maybe tomorrow."

Susan nods. "Good luck to you. I hope you find whatever it is you're looking for, Neely."

"I'm not looking for anything." I laugh, confused. "I'm just trying to work and make a difference."

"Honey, with all due respect, that's not true. If all you wanted to do was to make a difference, you would stay right here in Dogwood Lane."

"This community doesn't need me."

"Keep telling yourself that. Keep telling yourself that Mia doesn't need you, if no one else." She heads to the cash register, and like a fool who can't run away from pain, I follow. "Besides, I saw you with them. The only person who runs from what you have with Dane and Mia is someone who's looking for something else." She tosses her nuts on the counter. "I hope you find whatever it is."

Needing air, needing space, I toss my peanuts in a bin with discounted chocolates and head to my car. The pump is finished. I take the nozzle out and hang it back on the hook before realizing who is standing on the other side of my car.

"Matt," I say, unsure as to what he's going to say. My heart thumps in my chest as I take in the guy who used to be one of my closest friends.

"Did you think you were going to leave town without telling me goodbye? Again."

I walk around the back of the car and into his open arms. The contact is enough to make me blink back tears again.

"I hate crying." I laugh, pulling back. "I swear I've cried more in the last twenty-four hours than I have in my life."

"Why is that?"

"Because this time it's all my fault. I have no one to blame for any of this but me."

"I know you didn't mean for this to happen," he says. "I know you aren't a hateful person."

"Thank you. That means a lot to me right now."

He lifts his shoulders up and down. "Look, I don't know how all of this played out, and I don't want to know. I don't care. I just know you're my friend, and I wanted to tell you to be careful and that I love ya before you go."

"Damn you." I blot at my eyes with a tissue I find in my pocket. "I don't have time to get over to your dad's. Will you tell him I said goodbye and I'll see him when I visit?"

"So, ten years from now?" Matt jokes.

"I promise to do better."

"You better or this country boy is coming to the big city. Yeehaw!"

I laugh. "You're such a dork."

"Yeah, I know." He takes his thumb and rubs a small circle on my forehead. "Be safe."

"I will. Be good."

"I'll try." With a simple smile, he starts across the parking lot.

"Goodbye, Matt," I call after him.

"See ya, Neely."

As I climb in my car and start the ignition, I watch Matt pull away. The farther he gets from sight, the worse the pain gets in my chest.

It didn't hurt this bad the last time I left. Why can't I shake it off?

Cranking the air conditioner and the radio, I step on the gas and make my way to the airport. I look back only once.

CHAPTER TWENTY-EIGHT

DANE

She's gone. She's really, truly, actually fucking gone.

I think I'm going crazy. I actually believe I know the minute she left town. I couldn't breathe, and I had this insane need to get in my truck and barrel to the freeway, but I didn't. Because people who do stuff like that are lunatics, and I'm not.

Not really.

I was grateful for Mia's extralong practice tonight. It just gave me a bigger window without having to talk to Mia about why we aren't seeing Neely again. Then Susan offered to let her stay the night, and while she didn't say why, the sad look in her eyes told me she knows Neely's gone.

I hoped she'd change her mind. I hoped she'd start to leave and realize that Mia and I were worth it, that we were worth staying for.

She didn't.

Meandering through my house, the night as dark as coal outside the windows, I feel like I'm coming out of my skin. There was a time not long ago I loved a quiet house. I loved an evening free with nothing to do. That's exactly what I have, and I think I'm losing my damn mind.

I got used to her too fast. I became dependent on her laugh, her stories, her body against mine. Now I'm all fucked up, not knowing what to do with myself, and I have no one to blame but me.

There's a knock at the door, but I don't even get excited. It's not Neely's knock. It's Haley's. I don't tell her to come in either, because I know she will whether she's invited or not.

Sure enough, within a few minutes, she comes walking around the corner in the kitchen. She stops when she sees me.

"You look bad," she says. "Good grief, Dane."

"I've seen better days."

"I believe that just by looking at you." She hops up on a barstool at the island and watches me. "So, she left."

"Yeah."

I can't even get riled up about it anymore. The anger is gone. It's just disappointment and loneliness I can't put into words.

I want to tell Haley *this* is a broken heart. *This* is what devastation feels like. But I don't have the energy to even try.

"I will say," Haley says, swinging her feet back and forth, "I'm surprised she left."

"That makes two of us."

"But I kind of like it." She grins wildly.

My eyes close, then reopen slowly. "I'm sorry. I think I misheard you."

"You didn't. This will make for an epic romantic finale."

My head falls to my hands. "She left me, Haley. There is no epic finale. It's done. Kaput."

"This is why you can't call yourself a romantic."

I pick up an orange and toss it from hand to hand. "Good thing I don't see myself as a romantic then, huh?"

She snatches the orange out of the air. "What's the plan?"

"The plan for what?"

"I don't know. The plan to get her back? To forget her? To pull a Penn and screw so many women you forget who's who?"

"Not that." I hop on the counter, the cold marble kissing my ass. "I knew better than to screw that one, and I went against my rules."

"So why did you?"

I look at her with a blank face. "Is that a serious question, Haley?"

"Yes. Why did you sleep with her if you knew, without a doubt, that it was wrong?" She hops off the chair and rounds the island. Her hands on the counter across from me, she leaps up and takes a seat. "Was she hot? Sexy? Did she come on to you?"

Blowing out a breath, I remember the way Neely felt against my body. The way she looked into my eyes and everything just felt right. Nothing mattered because I had her.

Except I didn't.

"You want to know the truth?" I ask. I grip the corner of the counter and feel a sense of calm run across my skin. "I loved her, Hay. I really did."

"You do love her then."

"I guess I do." I pick up another orange and throw it at her. She catches it with ease. "There. You happy now?"

"No. I won't be happy until you're happy. Well, I'll be a lot happier in six months when I can go looking for my Prince Charming again."

I consider something. "Maybe there are no happy endings. Maybe we're all searching for this fairy tale because mass-market media shoves it in our faces, but maybe it's all a made-up thing that we will never get."

"Ew. Lies. All lies." Haley gasps. "In fairy tales, they find the person they're supposed to be with. It's not two random people who just decide they want to hook up. It's soul mates, finally coming together in the midst of a crazy scene and having to battle the world as a team."

"I still think it's stupid."

"I still think you're stupid," she says. "But let's get back to Neely."

Just hearing her name hurts. It brings back a rush of memories that I don't want to deal with. "Let's not." I get off the counter and lean against it instead. "I have one regret."

"That you haven't gone after her yet?"

"No," I reply. "That I blew up at her. I was pissed."

"Rightfully so."

"I kind of lost it a little. It just set me off because I really believed she wouldn't go, even though she kept telling me she was. How could she leave me? How could she leave Mia? They had plans. Neely was taking her to the Manicure Day with the gym." I look at the ceiling and close my eyes. "I don't even know how to tell her, Haley. She's going to be destroyed."

"Want me to do it? I can make it sound a little better than you, being that my heart isn't broken."

"I think it needs to come from me. As much as I don't want it to, I think it's best." I blow out a breath. "I did this to her. I should be the one to take the brunt of it."

She gets off the counter and stands beside me. She could not say a word and that would be fine. I get what she's saying without the words needed to say them. But it's Haley, and she won't miss an opportunity to speak.

"Remember when you hired me?" she asks.

"Yes. Where's this going?"

"Patience, Dane. Patience." She pats my shoulder as she walks by. "You told me that day we'd have to work together to raise this kid. That we were a team. You wanted it seamless, remember?"

"And I think we nailed it."

"We totally nailed it." She grins. "I know a few things about you. Probably more than I want to, really. But one of those things is that you'd never, ever hurt Mia. Ever. So no more of the 'I did this to her' crap because I'm not going to listen to it. It's not gonna fly with me, bud."

Her words help more than she knows. "You're all right, you know that?"

"Yeah, I know. Now, if you're gonna live, I'm gonna go home and get some sleep. I have a feeling tomorrow is going to be a long day."

"I'm good." I let her grin warm me. "Thanks for coming by, Haley."

"Anytime. Call me if you need me."

And with that, she's gone.

And I'm alone.

And missing Neely like it's my damn job.

CHAPTER TWENTY-NINE

NEELY

E xcuse me," I say, trying to slip by a handful of people on the street. Horns honk so loud around me, sirens wailing in the distance, that I'm not sure anyone even heard my voice. Or maybe they did and didn't care. Either way, I get knocked sideways by only one person as I duck into my favorite coffee shop.

I spent last night strolling around my neighborhood, trying to get the energy of the city in my blood again. For some reason, the smells percolating through the manholes make my stomach crawl in a way that's more violent than ever before.

Spying Grace at a little table in the corner, I make my way through the line.

"You're home," she gushes, giving me a quick hug. "I went ahead and got your coffee so you didn't have to wait."

"Are there always this many people here?" I grumble, sitting across from her.

She slow blinks. "Yes. Have you been gone that long?"

Shaking the cobwebs from my head, I take the coffee across from me. It's rich and aromatic and everything a coffee should be. I bet Claire wouldn't agree.

"So . . . ," Grace prods, flipping a lock of hair off her shoulder. "What happened in the country?"

I open my mouth to tell her something, but it comes out as a tired exhale. Grace sets her cup down. There's a bright-pink lipstick stain along the top.

"Okay. What's going on?" she asks.

"Nothing. We aren't ruining our reunion coffee with tales of my heartache."

"Heartache?" She leans back in her chair, a tiny diamond stud glistening in her nose. "We need to get to the bottom of this."

"There's nothing to get to the bottom of," I tell her. "I saw Dane a few times, as you know, and spent some days with him and his little girl."

"The little girl who is a product of the reason you left in the first place?"

I ignore that. It's not important. "Mia is adorable and a gymnast like me. What's the chance of that happening?"

"You do realize you're all gooey-eyed over a man and a little girl, right? I mean, if you're cool with it, I'm cool with it, but I am worried about you." She looks bewildered. "Out of all the potential things I saw happening with you going back there, this was not one of them. I'll say that."

I take a drink of my perfectly brewed coffee. It's so spot-on, it's almost annoying. "It doesn't matter. I came back here."

"Which thrills me because I was going nuts without you." She throws up her hands. "When I got your text, I lost my cool in the middle of the salon. No one has any sense in this city, Neely. No one."

"Well, I lost it in the middle of my apartment last night. You should've come over. We could've flipped out together."

She furrows a brow. "What was wrong with you?"

"Oh, the people who live above me were pounding around all night. More car alarms went off than I thought possible. The hot water took ten years to warm. Need more?"

Grace laughs, her bangles clamoring together on her wrist. "You spent way too much time in the boonies."

"No joke. It's definitely going to take some time to readjust."

To readjust. What a nice way to put it. I don't need to adjust again to life here. What I need is to figure out why I feel like something is missing. Or wrong. I didn't leave on the oven or a curling wand, and I picked up all my mail at the post office. So why on earth do I feel like something needs to be done?

"Neely?"

"Yeah," I say, coming out of my daze. A dull throb taps away at my temple. I just want to close my eyes and go to sleep.

"Tell me about Dane."

My eyes snap to my friend's. She's drinking her caffeine, watching me carefully.

I don't want to talk about him. I don't want to go there at all. But knowing Grace, this conversation will have to happen, so I might as well get it over with.

"He's gentle and kind, but fierce and loyal," I say, the words coming easier as I go. "Watching him with Mia will melt you in your shoes. He reads her bedtime stories and spoils the crap out of her, but she has chores to do and he makes her do them."

I get settled in my chair.

"Mia has him wrapped around her little finger, but how could you not be? She's the cutest little girl ever. A little sassy but all sorts of sweet, and she loves tumbling, so that's right up my alley. And she has a thing for koi fish, which is random, but that's her grandfather's fault."

"I'm with her on the koi," Grace says. "They're gorgeous."

"Right? And Dane's brother, Matt, is like a giant teddy bear. I actually think you'd like him a lot, Grace. But stay away from Penn. He's . . ."

"What?"

I laugh. "I can't decide if you two would get along or hate each other."

Her eyes light up as she leans forward. "Ooh. What's he look like?"

"He's muscly in a carpenter kind of way. Dark hair. Blue eyes. Tattoos probably everywhere, but I don't know that to be a fact," I say.

"Sounds cute."

"You would totally think he's cute. Trust me."

She nods, a satisfied grin on her face. "How's your mom?"

"Good. She has a boyfriend now, which is weird, but he's a nice guy. Claire made a joke about my mom making him pie—I'm sure you can imagine what it is—and now I can't think of pie or him without that line in my head." I laugh at the memory. "You should go down there with me sometime, Grace."

The glow from talking about Dogwood Lane flickers away. The chill that's been inside my soul for a day now comes back. I shiver, lifting the coffee to my chest and holding it with both hands.

"Are you sure this is what you want?" She leans forward on the rickety pub table and looks at me with a seriousness that startles me.

"Is what what I want?"

"This." She holds her arms to her sides, her bangles catching the light from overhead. When they drop to the table, they jingle. "Don't get me wrong. I want you here. But do *you* want you here?"

I sit, stunned. My jaw hangs open as I look at my best friend. "What are you talking about? Of course I want to be here."

She sips her coffee, eyeing me over the cup. Her question leaves me irritated, and rather than call her out, I take a drink of my overpriced coffee.

Finally, right before I'm ready to lose my mind, she sighs. "Look, Neely. All I'm saying is that I've never seen you as animated as you were a little while ago. You've been excited about articles and opportunities, but I think you just went ten sentences and didn't even breathe."

I look at her like she's lost her mind. Still, her stupid words cause my mind to drift back to Dogwood Lane. My heart pangs for the smell of fertilizer, the taste of Mom's pie. I'd do almost anything to see Dane's smile and hear his voice whispering at the shell of my ear.

"That. Right there," she says, pointing a pink-painted finger at me. "That's what I'm talking about."

My stomach rolls as I look at the manicure and think of Mia. "Enough, Grace."

"I can't let this go. Trust me, I'd like to. I'd like to tell you what concert tickets I bought us and fill you in on my dating life. But none of that is important, and this is. And as your friend, I have to be honest with you even when I'll lose in the end. You need to go home, Neely."

"I can't. I go to see Frank tomorrow."

"I get that. And you deserve that job. But if anything in the world made me smile like you do when you talk about Tennessee, I'd never leave it."

I lean forward and look at her earnestly. "But this is the only thing I've ever wanted. To be at the helm of something big. I've waited my whole life for this moment."

"You don't think I understand that?" She arches a brow. "I kill myself for the same thing you do. I bust balls every day so I can feel like my life means something. But you know what?"

"What?"

"I don't have anything else." The light in her eyes dims as she glances down at her cup. "I don't have a Tennessee. I don't have a mom who bakes pies or a Dane who adores me. Or a Mia, but I'm kind of happy about that." She makes a face. "But if I did have them, I'd walk away from all this."

My throat squeezes shut as I think of all the things she's just said. There's a pull on my heart I almost can't bear.

"You have waited your whole life for this," Grace says, standing. It takes a second to get her balance on her two-inch heels. "But which moment do you mean?" She grabs her purse and coffee and kisses my cheek. "Call me later. I'm late for a meeting."

I watch my best friend exit the café and hail a cab. I won't see her again until the weekend because there won't be time. There never is here.

I get to my sneaker-clad feet, happy not to be wearing heels today, and take my phone out of my pocket. A picture of Dane, Mia, and me at Mucker's is my screen saver, and as much as it kills my heart to look at it, I can't change it. It's my last thread to a few days of my life that will always feel like some of the best.

Before I tuck my phone back in my purse, it lights up. I don't know the number, just that the area code is Tennessee. With bated breath I answer. "Hello?"

"I heard ya left." Penn's voice glides through the line. "Is that true?"

"Yes."

"You kind of piss me off with this shit." He tries to say it like he's joking, but the grit on the back end proves he's not. Not entirely, anyway.

"Penn, I'm sorry. It was a last-minute decision, and I didn't have time to make the rounds."

"Yeah, I know. You never have time for us peons down here in the sticks."

My heart splinters. "It wasn't like that."

"Maybe not. I mean, I know you like me even if you don't like the rest of them. Can't say I blame you," he jokes.

"I will come back and see you. Maybe for Thanksgiving? We could rent out Mucker's and have our own holiday. All of us."

"Yeah, we'll see." He sighs. "I have a lot of shit to do today. But I thought I'd call you and make sure you had my number. Don't take it personally, though. I always make sure women have my number."

My eyes water as I laugh at his very Penn-like way of being nice. A woman with a bag as big as a truck bumps me, and I don't even care. I don't even look at her. I just stare at the dirty window in front of the coffee shop and wish it were the Dogwood Café.

"I'll call. I promise." I sniffle.

"Do that. Not too much, though. That might be weird. But if you need something, give me a holler. I'd like to know you're alive every now and then."

"Okay."

"Good. Now I gotta go because this guy I work for is a complete fucking asshole today, and he left Matt with a list of shit for me to do, and I have to figure out how to get out of it."

Laughing, I grab a napkin off a table and dab at my eyes. "Take care of yourself."

"I will. You too."

"Bye."

The line goes dead. Somehow, it feels like my connection to anything that makes me smile is also terminated.

CHAPTER THIRTY

DANE

It's a hand-wash-the-dishes kind of night.

Rinsing the last few cups and setting them on a towel, I look out the window. It's a beautiful summer evening. Although the sun isn't quite set yet, there are lightning bugs going to town in the field outside. Neely would love it.

I flip off the water, irritated with myself, and grab a towel to dry my hands. All day, I've tried to retrain myself to not think of her. To not associate things with her. To not let my mind wander to a place where she exists.

There's a chance I'll have to buy a new truck. And burn most of my clothes. And sell the house.

Shaking my head at my own stupidity, I toss the towel back on the counter.

It hurts worse this time. Before, when she left, I was already prepared for it. She was leaving for school even before the whole Katie mess, and we had a rough plan for us to stay connected while she was gone. The key was this: She was coming home. That, and she wasn't leaving me specifically.

Both keys are lost now. She's not coming back, and it feels like a total rejection of a life I could've offered her, a life I live and wanted her to share with me. But that was my mistake. I hoped too much and I knew better.

Mia's feet hit the floor above me. I listen to her rummage around the bathroom. Each moment that goes by tightens the knot a little harder in my stomach. She's asked for Neely a few times tonight, and I wouldn't humor Haley by listening to how many times she asked for her today. I have to tell her the truth, some version of the truth, and I don't know how to do that.

If she cries, and I bet she will, I'll probably break. This is my doing once again. This wound I'm getting ready to inflict was done at my hands even though I promised myself I'd never do it again.

I guess you can't trust anyone. Not even yourself.

I wait for her feet to hit the hallway and for the mad dash to her bedroom. I wait and wait and wait, but it never comes. Heading for the stairs, I look up toward the hallway. Just as I put my hand on the banister, trying to decide whether I should check on her, her little voice calls out my name.

"Dad." She says it in a way that's not a shout and not a normal talking voice either.

I'm to the bathroom door in a half a second. "You okay, rascal?"

The door opens. Her eyes are filled with trepidation as she looks up at me, her hair wet from the shower. "Will you walk me to bed?"

"What's this about?" I ask.

She shrugs. We make our way silently down the hall and to her room. She wastes no time climbing into her bed and getting buried under the blankets. Once she's settled, I take my perch on the edge of the mattress.

Smoothing her hair off her forehead, I search her little eyes. "What's going on?"

"Where's Neely, Dad?"

"Home, I guess. I'm not sure."

"Is she coming back?"

Emotion swallows me, sitting right across the bridge of my nose. I blink rapidly. I pray faster. I will myself to stay strong even though I want to go to my own room and fall face first into the mattress.

"She always told us she was going back to New York," I say carefully. "We were expecting this, right?"

"No," she says, the words padded with unshed tears. "She has to come back, Daddy. We have the Manicure Day."

"And she really wanted to do that with you," I tell her. "I know she did. She was really looking forward to it. But her boss called and needed her back soon, so she had to go."

A solitary tear trickles down her freckled face. "She didn't say goodbye?"

"She didn't have time, baby girl. She told me to tell you she would miss you and she hated going, but she had to. She didn't have a choice."

I grip a handful of sheets and squeeze it with everything I have. Sitting here and answering her questions, *lying to her*, breaks my heart. I fight back tears of my own, both from watching her pain and acknowledging my own.

"Can't you go get her?" Mia asks.

"I can't. It's not my place."

"Why isn't it? You'd go find me if I ran away, wouldn't you?"

I take a deep breath. "I would find you in a second because you're my child. It's my job to find you."

"Well, Neely is our family. Doesn't that mean it's our job to find her?"

"I know you love her. Heck, I do too," I admit. "But she's not really our family. It doesn't work the same."

Mia sits up in bed. Her pajamas, a gift from Haley decorated with little girls doing various gymnastics events, remind me of Neely too.

"But she is our family," Mia insists. "I feel it in my heart."

I give up. Batting back tears, I watch her eyes fill with her own. I want to tell her I feel it too. That I love her unlike any way I've loved someone before. That if I could go to New York and throw her over my shoulder like a caveman and carry her home, I would.

"You should find her, Daddy. *Please.*"

"It doesn't work that way."

"Yes, it does," she insists, her voice beginning to break. "If you love somebody, you look for them. You look and look and look until you find them. And I know you love her just like she loves you."

My nose burns as I fight my emotions from getting the best of me. Instead, I pull Mia into my arms. She climbs on my lap and puts her arms around my neck. Her tears dampen my T-shirt, and I just want to hit a button and rewind some of this crap. Make it not happen. Unbreak our hearts.

I hold her like I used to, back when I had to walk her from the bathroom every night. Seeing my strong, sassy preteen hurting like this, so unsure, rips at the fibers of my soul.

"Madison ran away," she sniffles. "She hid in the doghouse outside because her brother was being mean to her."

"Running away is never good. You always talk to me if you have a problem. Got it?"

She nods. "Madison said she just wanted her brother to find her. That's why she hid where she did, because she knew if he looked he'd find her there. He said he hated her and wished she wasn't alive. It hurt Madison's feelings. So maybe this is Neely's way of doing that. Maybe we hurt her feelings."

"No." I pull her back so I can look her in the face. "We didn't hurt her feelings. Her leaving isn't about that." I want to shake her, drive this point into her so deep she doesn't forget it. "This has nothing to do with you. Nothing."

I exhale, the weight of our world embedded in the sound. I hold Mia tight, as though if I squeeze her enough, it'll put our hearts back together again.

We sit in the silence for a while, each of us lost in thought. I don't know how to replace Neely in our lives. Certainly not with another woman. But there is a void that I don't know how to fill, and I know Mia feels it too.

"Are you sad, Dad?"

"Yeah," I say, my voice husky. "I'm pretty sad."

"How sad are you?"

"I don't know." I chuckle. "How do you measure how sad you are?"

She shrugs. "I don't know. I don't think I've ever been this sad before."

Squeezing my eyes shut, I kick myself for opening us up to this. Was it worth it? Were a few days of fun worth this?

"I liked having her here," she says. "I liked knowing she was downstairs with you when I went to sleep. It felt like you were happy then. Like I didn't need to worry about you anymore because she was worrying too."

"You don't have to worry about me, Mia. I'm a grown-up."

"Sometimes you have to worry about grown-ups too. You clearly don't have it all figured out."

My chest shakes as I laugh. I pull Mia closer. "Thanks for the vote of confidence."

She pries herself from my arms and crawls across her bed. Sitting with her knees pulled to her chest, she wrinkles her nose. "If it helps, I'm not as sad as you," she says.

"I'm glad to hear that."

"Wanna know why?"

"I'd love to know why," I say, twisting around to face her.

"I know she'll come home."

"She isn't a puppy, Mia. And I do love your optimism, but I really want you to understand that she's not coming back." I stand up. "I know it's hard to accept that. It's hard for me too. But we have to."

"She won't come back with that attitude." Haley's voice rings out behind me.

Mia giggles as I roll my eyes and turn to face our nanny.

"Please, Haley, join our conversation," I mutter.

"I don't mind if I do." She trots over to the bed and sits by Mia. "Just so you know, I agree with the kid."

"Because you are a kid," I say.

"No. Because I told you, this is the perfect moment for you to go find the girl." She clutches her chest and looks at Mia. "Every good love story has a moment that makes you swoon."

Mia wrinkles her nose. "I just want Neely back."

"How do we do that?" Haley asks. "What do we need to do?"

"Face reality," I tell them, getting annoyed. "We can't make her come back."

"No, but we can try to persuade her to." Haley kisses my daughter on the top of her head and then stands. "Do you love her?" she asks me.

"Yes."

"Do you want her to come back?"

"Yes."

"Do you feel like your life will never be the same if she doesn't?"

"Yes." I sigh.

"Then go get the damn girl. At least try. Have you ever even tried before?"

It's the last question that sparks something deep inside me. It's the question that resonates through my mind, plants a seed that maybe, just maybe, Haley and her antics are onto something.

"Just try, Dad. If she doesn't come back, at least we know you tried." Mia waits for me to respond. "Try for me."

I feel my resignation waning. It slips through my fingers despite how hard I try to keep a grip on it.

What can it hurt? All she can do is say no.

"Is your schedule clear for a few days?" I ask Haley.

Mia jumps to her feet on her bed and cheers. Haley picks her up, and they do a little dance around the room, making me laugh. But when they dance over to me and I wrap my arms around the two crazy girls, I think they might be onto something.

"I'm going to check flights," I say, a bubble of panic erupting in my core. "What else do I need?"

"Give me your credit card, and I'll take care of the logistics," Haley says, setting Mia on the bed. "You go pack your stuff and figure out what award-winning speech you're going to use to win her back."

"My wallet is in the kitchen," I call out over my shoulder. "It'll take me an hour and a half to get to the airport."

"Go, Dad, go!" Mia shouts.

This is probably a ridiculous idea. But as I grab my travel bag out of the closet and imagine seeing Neely on her turf, I realize that, ridiculous or not, this has to happen.

She's family, whether she knows it or not.

CHAPTER THIRTY-ONE
NEELY

Another night of no sleep. Another morning of perfectly frustrating coffee. Another day of keeping my phone in my hand just in case Dane calls.

He won't. There's no chance and I don't blame him.

The thing I love about him most, something I was able to identify somewhere between the thirtieth and fiftieth siren last night, is how much he loves Mia. Everything he does centers around her. How many men do that? Not many.

That being said, I hit him right where it hurt. Whether I meant to doesn't matter. His greatest fear was having someone come into their lives and leave, and I did that. I didn't even tell Frank to let me think about it. I didn't even ask for a couple of weeks to help break the news to Mia. I just left, and that's really what's keeping me up at night, not the sirens.

When I looked in the mirror this morning and put on a coat of lipstick for my meeting with Frank, I hardly recognized myself. My dress was one I've worn before, and the lipstick was my daily go-to just a few weeks ago. But when I look at my reflection, all I see is a person I don't know.

When did I become the person who's so hedonistic I just run off on a whim? I spout off all these mantras, say all this stuff about empowering others, when in reality, I'm just as focused on myself as anyone else.

At least that's how it is here. That's how *I* am here. As I push open the doors to my old company and take the elevator to the twentieth floor, I wonder if I'll ever be able to flip a switch back to the old me. The one who's up before dawn, champing at the bit to get here. The one who's still here after dark, finishing projects that could wait until the next day.

This was my life for so long. It was as much a part of me as Dogwood Lane or my love of gymnastics. *Why do I feel like an outsider walking up to the receptionist's desk?*

"Neely," Georgia says, her headset perfectly in place. "It's such a pleasure to see you today."

"It's good to see you too." I rest my briefcase on the stone ledge and sign in. "How have things been around here?"

"Stressed. Everyone's been running around like crazy. I know with this new launch, things are being leveraged and it's doubled Frank's load, but now that you're here, maybe that will ease up some. For me, anyway."

"Sounds fun." I grab my things and head over to the row of leather chairs lining the wall. I take a seat. I fiddle with my green-and-yellow bracelet—it absolutely does not match my attire, but I couldn't make myself take it off. It reminds me of green eyes and sunshine, and both make me smile, even if I don't feel like it.

A few familiar faces stroll by, stopping to say hello. They tell me how much I was missed and congratulate me on coming back. I smile and thank them and wonder why in the heck it doesn't feel like something to celebrate.

The floor-to-ceiling windows look over the street below. There are cars and buildings and people occupying every square inch of space. There's not a green speck anywhere to be seen. I'm wondering if it's possible for the air to be used up without any trees close by to create more when the door to Georgia's right opens up and Frank walks out.

"Good morning, Neely," he says, his baritone voice ringing through the reception area.

"Good morning, Frank." Chin held high, I pick up my briefcase and follow him into his office.

Three empty coffee cups line the side of his desk. A roll of antacid tabs sits next to his nameplate. The room is stale and dank, and as I sit across from his desk, I wonder how he works like this.

But you did.

Shoving that out of my brain, I focus on Frank. He smooths out his tie as he sits, hiding a spilled coffee stain on his mustard-colored shirt.

"Thank God you're here," he says. "I'm about to lose my mind."

"Rough morning?"

"Rough morning. Rough week. Rough week before. This launch is going to be the death of me." He shuffles around a stack of papers and pulls out a haphazardly put-together grouping of files with a rubber band around the middle. He plops it in front of me, shaking the coffee cups. "This is yours."

"That looks like a mess, Frank."

He nods. "I told you things were a mess when I called. You're the only person I know who can iron them out."

His praise settles over me. It feels good to have him acknowledge my abilities. It feels good to have his respect. Good, but not great. That messes with me a little.

"I've called a meeting for this afternoon," he says. "I'll let everyone know then that you're in charge. Whatever you want, consider it done." He leans back in his seat, the casters rolling a bit as his body moves. "You've earned this, Neely."

"Thanks." I breathe in deeply and almost choke on the stagnant air. "I'm excited to start."

"There aren't many people with your work ethic," he says. "People willing to give up their private lives to make something work. You're impressive."

Or stupid.

"I cleared out the office down the hall," he says. "You can get your things situated in there as soon as we're done here. May I suggest ordering something you can sleep on?"

His laugh fills the room, as if I'm now a part of some club that gets to give up sleep for work. I'm okay with that, really. But as his laughter settles and I realize there are no pictures of anyone in his life on his desk, I realize what else he's had to give up.

Frank goes on, rattling about all the benefits of the job, the little perks I'll get for being in upper-level management. All I can hear are the things I'm giving up.

"You get a tab at Gulliver's, for lunch."

It won't be as good as Mom's taco salad.

"You can get tickets to any sporting event in the city you want. We just need a little notice."

Can you get me tickets to the Summer Show?

"You get to watch the sunset behind the building from your office window." He laughs heartily as he moves on to the next topic.

Running my hand over my face, not even caring I'm probably smudging my foundation, I remind myself to breathe. The walls feel like they're caving in on me. Crushing me. Pushing me out of the room.

I look out the window and try to imagine the sun setting behind the buildings. I don't know that I ever noticed it before one way or the other, although I have doubts you can see it at all. Even if you can, it wouldn't compare with the spectacular sunsets on the bluff.

With Dane.

I'm so far from him, so disconnected from reality. Nothing about being here is right. It's like being dropped into a story you should know like the back of your hand, but you forgot to read the ending.

I imagine years of coming into this building. The things I can accomplish. The little plaques that will line my walls someday, just like they line Frank's. Awards. Recognitions of achievement. Industry accolades.

But what would they replace? Pictures of a husband? Of children? Macaroni art from elementary-school craft days? Memories outside these four walls?

The question my mom asked me suddenly makes sense. What do you have to give up to get what you want?

The answer is everything.

Maybe I didn't get it before when I lived and breathed this place. But now that I've had a taste of more, of early-morning kisses and cherry-flavored kids' drinks, I realize what I didn't then: I can hope for more for me. I can need more for me. I can expect more. And as I listen to Frank, I know I want more. Not just for me but for Dane and Mia too. For us.

My chest constricts as I try to rationalize with myself. *Think of all the things you can do from this position. Think of all the good you can do.*

Maybe.

The one place I know I can make a difference is in a little blue-gray-sided house on the edge of town. They need me, and even more, I need them.

I matter there. My heart is there. And if I leave here soon enough, maybe I can convince them to take me back.

"Frank," I say, interrupting him. "I'm sorry. I'm really, truly sorry." I grab my briefcase and calculate how long it will take me to get to the airport. "I can't take this job."

"What?"

"I can't take this job." The words come out freely, releasing the monkey on my back. "It's just not for me."

He leans forward, his tie hanging askew. He removes his glasses and looks at me. "May I ask what changed your mind?"

Tears dot my eyes as I look at his tired face. "A man I owe a new Dodgers cap. A little girl who needs me to take her for a manicure." I hiccup a sob.

"This is disappointing. I thought you wanted this?"

"I thought I did too. I thought this was the key to everything. I realized while sitting here this morning that everything I ever wanted is in a little town in Tennessee."

"I hate to hear that." He moves in his seat, the cracked leather creaking under his weight.

"I hate to hear it too. I'm just . . . I'm not the person I was a few weeks ago."

He looks unconvinced as he sits back in his chair. "Care to explain? I'm having a hard time accepting this, Neely."

I lug in a breath of stale, fast-food-scented air. "I feel as passionately as I ever have about empowering girls and giving women a voice in a field where they oftentimes go unnoticed. That hasn't changed."

"Then what has? Neely, quite frankly, you're turning down something most people work their whole lives for. *You've* done that—worked for this. And now you're giving it up? I don't understand."

"I know, and I'm sorry to let you down. I've always felt there was more out there for me, that if I kept pushing, I would wake up one morning and find it. But really, I think what I was looking for was inside me all along."

Aerial's speech comes swirling back, bringing with it another round of tears.

Dabbing at my eyes, I shrug. "I don't need a worldwide platform to make a difference. I don't need a title to validate who I am or what I believe." I look out the floor-to-ceiling windows and beyond the sky-scrapers filling the sky. "And I don't need a big old city to shield me from my fears."

I think he's going to be angry. I straighten my shoulders and wait for him to tell me not to use him for a reference when I come to my senses. I prepare for him to tell me I'm wasting the biggest chance of my life.

Instead, he smiles. "You know, sometimes the best changes happen at the grassroots level."

I pass a hot swallow down my throat. "I didn't expect you to say that."

He grabs a tissue from the box on his desk and dabs it on the back of his neck. "If you want this job, Neely, I want you to have it. But I'll say I'm almost relieved you don't."

"Why?"

"Look at me," he scoffs. "My wife left me twenty years ago and took our son with her. I see him when he's in town on work, maybe twice a year. I missed being with my parents when they were on their last legs. I don't even know what fresh air smells like anymore."

"Why do you do it then?"

"Same reasons you wanted to. I just didn't wise up soon enough. You did." He gets to his feet and shoves his glasses back on his nose. "You have an excellent gut for doing the right thing. Your instincts are spot-on. Always trust them. It'll get you further than anything else in your life."

I stand, too, and shrug. "Now what?"

"It looks to me like you need to catch a flight."

The magnitude of the situation slams against me. I almost drop my suitcase. "I do."

"Why aren't you skipping out of here, then?"

"What if he doesn't take me back?" I look at him and he laughs. "I'm not kidding, Frank. What if he hates me?"

"He won't."

The anger in Dane's eyes the last time I saw him flickers through my mind. My heart squeezes so hard I'm afraid it's going to stop pumping. "I don't know. He's pretty mad at me."

"I'd be mad, too, if you were my girl and you left me for a stupid job in New York. But let me tell you something about men."

"Okay," I say as we head to the door.

"Men get angry and loud and bristle because we don't know how to be vulnerable. We're so afraid of losing position and getting hurt that we try to make ourselves seem invincible, even if it's only ourselves we're kidding." He pulls the door open. "Go to him, Neely. Be honest. Lay it out there, and I promise you, he'll take you back."

"I hope so, Frank." I step into the lobby and almost fall on my face.

CHAPTER THIRTY-TWO

DANE

It all happens in slow motion. One second, I'm trying to ignore the receptionist's comments about how "sweet" my accent is. The next, the door is opening.

Every cell in my body tunes to the doorway where a balding man who looks like he's on the verge of a heart attack stands. He's talking to someone I can't see. I don't have to see her, though, to know it is Neely.

I'm on the edge of my seat, eyes glued to the doorway. My mouth goes dry as I try to remember the little speech I prepped on the plane a few hours ago. I went over it time and time again. Now, when I need it, it evades me.

Her voice is soft as it filters into the lobby. I stumble to my feet, running my hands down the pants I wore last night as I wait for her to come into view.

It takes far too long to happen, but when it does, it happens fast.

She steps through the doorway, looking at Mr. Heart Attack. She says something I can't hear. Finally, she turns toward me.

The smile falters on her lips as her gaze finds mine like it always does. I take a step toward her and she trips. Catching herself on the edge of the receptionist's desk, she blows out a breath.

And then whips her head to me.

"Neely." I gulp, coming to her side. "Just hear me out."

I can't read the look on her face. It's a mixture of fear and embarrassment and more sadness than I care to admit.

Please, God, let this work out. I'll never make her feel this way again.

"Dane—"

"No," I say, shaking my head. "I came all this way with all these things to say. And I can't even remember them all, and I left my notes on the plane." I scratch my head, trying to get myself together quickly before she can tell me no. "I can't do this again. I can't. Everything is wrong now that you're gone."

"Dane—"

"And I realize I might be embarrassing you right now in front of your boss and coworkers, and I hope they will know this is a reflection of me and not of you. I'm the crazy one. Crazy about you."

"Oh my gosh." The receptionist clutches her chest. "I can't even with this."

Neely's eyes water, the lights above reflecting off her eyes. I feel wetness gathering at the corners of mine too. As hard as it is to stay calm, I have to. This is my one chance to fix every mistake I've ever made. My one shot at getting every piece of my life back together.

"I never should've let you leave. I should've manned up and told you flat out how I feel. Maybe it wouldn't have changed things because I know who you are. I know how much this job means to you."

"Dane," she says. "Listen to me."

"Just let me finish. Please," I beg. "I want you to be happy and to get everything you want out of life. But there has to be a way to do that with me and Mia. I know you love us, Neely. I know you love us as much as we love you."

I swear Mr. Heart Attack mumbles something along the lines of "I told you," but I let it go.

Taking a step toward Neely, ignoring the audience we're beginning to attract, I take her hand. "I'm sorry for being a dick when you told me you were leaving."

"Will you listen to me?" she asks. She sniffles back a laugh, squeezing my hand.

"No. This is my moment." I bite my lip to keep from saying anything else for a moment because if I do, I know I'll cry like a pussy. "Life isn't about playing it safe or playing the odds. If I listened to either of them, I'd be home right now. But an old man came by the house late last night and asked what I was going to do about you leaving. I had flights pulled up but hadn't pulled the trigger. Mia had gone to bed, and Haley was on the couch." I look up at the spectators. "She's the nanny, just clarifying."

The lobby rolls with laughter from the five or six people watching. Neely sets her briefcase down and takes my other hand in hers.

I don't want to think this might be working, but it damn sure feels like it. My heart pounds in my chest as I go in for the kill.

"Dad said something smart for once," I say. "He said life is not about what happens to you, but how you react to it. My reaction to you leaving is to come and get you because I don't see another way to live without you by my side. And I know a little girl who thinks the world of you, and I'd be honored if you'd be a part of her life too."

"Just marry him," the receptionist cries. "If you don't, I will."

Neely flashes her a look to stay put before turning back to me. "Can I talk now?"

"Depends on what you're going to say."

She searches my eyes for a moment. I remain as unguarded as I can, completely opening myself up to her inspection.

"I love you, Dane."

"Yes!" The receptionist gets to her feet and claps.

"I like your enthusiasm," I tell her.

Neely laughs, blinking back tears. "I love you. I love Mia. And I love that you're here."

"I had to come. It was a long time coming." I lean forward and press a kiss against her lips. She wraps her arms around my neck and kisses me back like she means it.

For the first time in my entire life, my world feels like it's complete. There's a warmth rising from the center of my chest, and I can't fight it if I try.

Despite being in New York, having Mia so far away, being in the reception area of a company that was my mortal enemy until a few moments ago, everything is right in this moment. In this one spot of time, my world is perfect.

Lifting her up, I spin her in a circle and enjoy the feeling of her in my arms.

"I hope you know I'm never letting you go now," I whisper in her ear.

"I hope you know I'm never going to let you." She lays her cheek against mine and sighs. "I missed you, Dane."

"I missed you, babe." I put her back on her feet as the crowd cheers. Resting my forehead against hers, I laugh. "I didn't embarrass you, did I?"

"Hardly."

Looking up at Mr. Heart Attack, I nod. "I'm sorry if I made a spectacle out of your lobby."

His large belly bounces up and down as he chuckles. "Son, that was the best thing to happen in this building in the twenty-five years I've worked here. I think you've given us all something to think about."

"Yeah, like how I need a guy with a southern accent like that." The receptionist shrugs. "I can't help it. I'd be putty in his hands."

I lace our fingers together and pull Neely against me. The contact is something I need. We went without it for too long.

"Frank," Neely says, "thank you for understanding."

"I'm glad it all worked out." Frank takes a step toward me. "I think the best man probably won this round."

He extends a hand, and I shake it with my free one, which happens to be my left and a little awkward. Still, I'm not letting her go.

Looking down at Neely, I shrug. "Do you need to file something that shows you quit?"

She exchanges a look with Frank and they laugh.

"What's so funny?" I ask.

"She quit before she knew you were here," he says. "You already had her before your speech, but it was nice to get to witness."

My jaw drops. "You quit? Before you came out here?"

She nods. "I didn't come here to quit. I just sat in his office and everything kind of made sense. Or it didn't make sense, I mean." She leans her head on my shoulder. "I kept thinking about you and Mia and Mom, and I realized . . ." She looks at Frank. "I can do what I want to do from other places. It doesn't have to be here. And I don't have to sacrifice my happiness to do it. There's no need to be a martyr. I can have a life and friends . . ."

"And a husband." The receptionist shrugs. "Sorry. It felt like it fit, and I'm totally shipping you two together right now."

"I can have a husband." Neely blushes. "And maybe a daughter that's not my blood, maybe, but is mine in every other sense of the word."

I lower my lips to her ear. "And babies. Tell me you'll have my babies."

The receptionist moans, throwing her head back in her chair. "I gotta get a cold drink," she says, getting to her feet. "Good luck to both of you, although I don't think you're going to need it."

"Bye, Georgia," Neely says, laughing.

She just tosses a wave over her shoulder as she disappears into a back room.

The room thins out, everyone going back to doing whatever it is they're supposed to do. Frank and Neely say a quick goodbye that would've gone easier if I would let go of her hand.

Finally, it's just me and her.

"What do we do now?" I ask. "Do you have stuff to get? Or do we go to the airport? Or do you want to stay in the city for a day or two? Haley will stay with Mia until I can convince you to come home with me."

"I'd love to show you the city, and I do have things I need to get from my apartment. I probably need to cancel my lease too." She bites her lip. "But there's one thing I need to do before I do any of that."

"What's that?"

"I need to apologize to a little girl."

CHAPTER THIRTY-THREE

NEELY

Y ou're going to have to let go of me at some point." I giggle as Dane tries to shut the door behind us without releasing my hand. "I swear I'm not going anywhere."

"Oh, I know that. Trust me. I just spent more time than necessary in a cab in New York. I'm pretty sure that has you owing me for the rest of our lives."

I'm glowing. I know it. If the light were on or if it weren't already dark outside, I'd look at my reflection and laugh, I'm sure. I can feel the joy oozing from my pores. It's weird, but it's so wonderful.

Dane sweeps me into his arms and kisses my neck. "Welcome home."

"Don't say that yet," I warn. "I need to talk to Mia."

"Yeah. Like she's gonna kick you out. She's the one who made me come get you. And her too," he says, nodding toward someone approaching us from the kitchen. "Hey, Haley."

"Hi." She gets closer and I can see her giant smile. "Hi, Neely. Welcome home."

"Thanks. And thank you for insisting Dane come to New York. I was on my way back, but he made quite the scene in my office. I'm pretty sure we're legends there now."

"I wish I could've seen that," Haley gushes.

"It was epic."

"Now that you're back and, I'm guessing, moving in here," she says, "I want you to know I can give you my key."

I look at Dane before glancing back at her. "Why would you do that?"

"Yeah, crazy lady," Dane says. "Why are you giving us your key?"

"I said I would. I don't know how Neely feels about some woman she doesn't really know having a key to her house, and with all the energy we've put into getting you two back together, I'll be damned if I cause any ripples."

"Keep your key." I laugh. "If for no other reason than so Dane can call you and you can come over and talk sense to him. I hear he listens to you."

"Not enough or you wouldn't have been in New York to start with." She heads to the couch and picks up what looks like a giant pink bag. "I'm going back to my house now so you two can have some time alone. Well, with a child upstairs. On second thought, want me to take her with me?"

Dane finally releases my hand. I shake it to get some blood back in my fingers. "That's really sweet of you," I say, flexing my hand, "but I need to talk to her."

She nods. "I think that's an awesome idea." She heads to the door. "I'll just play the next few days by ear. If you guys need me, call. If not, enjoy your time together."

"Thanks, Haley," Dane says. He walks over to her and they share a few quiet words before he closes the door behind her. "You ready to go upstairs?"

"Can I ask you a favor?"

"Sure."

"Can I talk to Mia alone? I know you might not trust me yet, but—"

"Really?" He laughs.

"Well, the last time we talked about it, you said you'd filter through what you wanted her to know, and I get that. She's your child."

He takes my hand again and leads me up the stairs. "The last time we talked about this, I was pretty pissed at you. You were basically breaking my heart, and I was in Daddy Mode."

"I get that."

We stop outside Mia's door. Dane takes my hands and turns me to face him. There's a serenity in his eyes that I've never seen before, but it's a look I never want him to lose.

"I want us to go forward together," he says. "As a family. The three of us—that is, until you let me knock you up."

I swat his shoulder. "Don't say that out here," I whisper. "I need to go in there, and my ovaries are now screaming, 'Open for business,' and that's going to be distracting."

He growls, pressing a kiss to my neck. "Go talk to her. Say what you need to say . . . but hurry the hell up, okay? I need you."

I kiss him lightly, not giving him much of an opening to work with. He narrows his eyes.

I open the door. Dane pokes his head inside, checking on Mia, and smiles. "She's all yours," he whispers to me, retreating across the hall.

Taking a long, deep breath, I go inside.

A night-light shines next to her pink-and-white desk. She's lying on her side, her little lips puckered like an angel's. She's so precious, and my heart aches thinking I hurt her feelings.

I kneel at the side of her bed and brush her hair off her forehead. "Hey, Mia. Can you wake up for a minute?"

"No," she mumbles, tucking her hands under her pillow.

"Mia." I shake her gently on the shoulder. "It's Neely. Can you wake up and talk to me for a minute?"

I barely get the words out before her eyes shoot open. "Neely!" she exclaims, sitting up. "Are you really here?"

"I am."

She throws her arms around my neck. I hold her close, feeling her little back shake as she cries. "I'm so glad you're here," she says.

"Oh, girl. I'm so glad to be here too."

She pulls away, knocking the hair that's stuck to her tears out of her face. Her eyes shine with a mixture of happiness and more tears, as if she can't figure out which way to go with it.

"Dad found you," she says.

"He did. He ran into me just as I was leaving."

"Where were you going?"

I smile at her. "I was coming back here. Hoping you would accept my apology for leaving."

She doesn't answer me immediately. She just places her hands on her lap and looks at me.

"Mia, I'm sorry," I tell her. "I don't know what else to say to you."

"Why did you have to go?"

I try to think of a way to put it so she'll understand. "Do you know how Aerial told you not to put your hands too far apart on your back handspring, but you did it anyway because you think it's easier?"

"Yeah."

"It's kind of the same thing." I rock back on my heels so I can see her better. And so she can see me. "When you become an adult, you don't just have all the answers. Sometimes things are still confusing, and you don't know what to do or you think you know things better than others. And you do what kids do—you do it your way until you fall on your face. Does that make sense?"

"Kind of." She yawns.

"I needed to go to New York to end that part of my life. I needed to realize I'd done everything I needed to do there and that everything I wanted in life was right here. In this house."

A slow, sleepy grin stretches across her cheeks. She yawns again. "So you aren't leaving again?"

I help her back under her blankets and kiss her forehead. "I'm not leaving again until you guys make me."

"Good," she says. "Because it really messed Dad up."

I can't stop the laugh that slips by my lips. "Oh, did it?"

"Yeah. He was being a baby. You should've seen it." Her lashes flutter a few times before they land closed. "I knew you'd come back."

"You did?"

"You told me you'd take me to Manicure Day. I knew you wouldn't lie to me." She yawns. "But I might need ice cream tomorrow to really make sure I'm okay. It cures everything, you know."

I tuck the blankets around her, trying to manage my emotions. "Thank you for having faith in me, Mia."

"You're welcome," she whispers as she falls back to sleep.

I stand in her room a long time, listening to her breathe. I've done nothing in my life to deserve having these two love me, but I'll fight like hell to earn it going forward.

Leaving her room, shutting the door softly behind me, I head across the hall to Dane's room. He's shirtless, sitting on the bed in nothing but a pair of gym shorts.

"That took long enough," he grumbles.

"I had to talk to her. I can't help it."

"You could've not left."

"It's a little late for that now, isn't it?"

He rolls his eyes.

"I brought nothing with me besides my briefcase." I smack my palm on my forehead. "I don't even have a toothbrush in this state."

"There are extra toothbrushes under the sink in the bathroom. You can sleep in one of my shirts after I get you naked for a while."

Sauntering toward him, I toss a playful grin his way. "I like the way you plan, Mr. Madden."

"There will be no reason for you to leave. I guarantee that."

"I need to schedule a moving company to get my stuff from New York. I don't know how to do that, being here."

"Maybe we'll take a little family vacation to the city. That should terrify Mia enough to never leave home again."

I sit on the edge of the bed. "Come on. It wasn't that bad, Dane."

"It smells like piss. There are no trees. Everyone is in such a hurry."

"I'll take you around and you'll at least like it. I promise."

He reaches up and jerks me down beside him. Nuzzling his face in the crook of my neck, he breathes in deep. "I like you."

"I like you too."

"I'd like you better if I was inside you."

"I'd like that too."

Much to my surprise, he doesn't roll me over right away. He doesn't order me to get naked or palm my breasts. He just lies behind me and breathes evenly.

"I need to call my mom and let her know I'm back," I say.

"Tomorrow," he mumbles. "Let me have you to myself tonight."

"You have me to yourself forever, dude."

He yawns, pulling me closer. "I like the sound of that."

I lie in his arms for a long time, listening to his breathing fall into a steady rhythm. It's the most peaceful thing I've ever felt.

Once I'm sure he's asleep, I sneak out of his arms and get ready for bed. It feels different now that I live here. I don't want to stick my stuff in places it doesn't belong, but I don't know where to put my clothes either.

Dressed in one of Dane's T-shirts, I fold my clothes and put them on a chair. I turn back around to see Dane watching me. His hair is mussed, his eyes sleepy. He's a mixture of adorable and sexy, and I know I'll never get tired of seeing this side of him.

"I wasn't leaving," I say, climbing back in bed. "I just needed to get my shoes and stuff off."

"Could've left this off too." He flicks the cotton material away from my skin. "Although there's something inherently sexy about a woman wearing your clothes."

"Is that right?"

"Yup."

He takes my hands and pulls me down. Rolling me onto my back, he situates himself over me. Those green eyes I fell in love with years ago shine back at me.

"I hope you aren't tired," he says, bringing the shirt I just put on up and over my head. "Because it's going to be a long night, Miss Kimber."

I move around so his cock is between my legs. Lifting my hips, he slides through my part.

"Look at you," I say, holding his head in my hands. "You're so erect."

"I'll show you erect."

I laugh for a split second before he makes me forget about anything other than him, me, and this night.

Being home.

EPILOGUE

NEELY

T he glitter is so hard to get off, though." I stick the key in the door and swing it open. "After you."

Mia walks in with her bags from today's shopping excursion after Manicure Day. "I liked the pink glitter, but Madison got that and I didn't want to look like I was copying her."

"I'm sure she wouldn't have cared," I note. "But I still think the navy blue is super pretty on you." We pile the bags near the foot of the stairs. "They make your eyes pop."

"Thanks." She wraps her arms around my waist for the sixth time today. "Thanks for taking me today, Neely."

"Are you kidding? I needed a manicure, anyway. And besides, if I hadn't taken you, I'd have been stuck here all day with your dad."

"Did I hear my name?" Dane comes around the corner. He has a paintbrush in his hand. "Did you guys have fun today doing all the girlie things?"

"Look at this." Mia wiggles her fingers in front of her dad. "Pretty, huh? Neely helped me pick the color."

"I love it." He looks at me and shrugs. "We love it. Right?"

"Yes, we love it." I laugh. "I got it too."

"And our toes are red. Mine is more pinkish," Mia explains, "but Neely got cherry red."

Dane turns so Mia can't see him and grins devilishly. I look away before I can't.

"Why don't you take your things up to your room?" I ask Mia. "And put them away. I don't want to find them thrown over a chair."

"Really?" she moans.

"I can take them back."

She looks like she's going to stomp off and then stops and laughs. "Fine. I'll put them away. Thanks again, Neely."

"You're very welcome."

She gathers the bags that are hers and heads upstairs. Once she's gone, I look at Dane. "Did you ever even look at her? Or have you stared at me this entire time?"

"She didn't notice."

"You're impossible." I sigh. "What did you do today? And why do you have a paintbrush?"

His lips part in a smile. He crooks a finger for me to follow him.

We walk through the living room and into the kitchen. The table is covered with a drop cloth. A can of white paint sits open in the middle, and a long board stretches the length of the table. The words MALONE FARM are printed in old-fashioned letters across it.

"What's this?" I ask. I run my finger down the freshly sandpapered wood. "You doing some work out there?"

"You could say that."

"Maybe I could go out there with you one day. I added a class on Tuesday afternoons starting next week at Aerial's, so that will just leave Monday afternoons clear. But I'd love to spend an afternoon out there, if it works out."

"I think it'll work out." I wait for him to say something else, but he doesn't. He just looks at the sign.

"Man of few words today," I mutter. I head to the refrigerator and pull out the lemonade. "Mom and Gary want us to come over for dinner this week. I told them we'd find an evening. This week is going to be crazy with the show so close. I'm kind of starting to lose my mind."

Dane comes up behind me and pulls me into his chest. "Will you relax, babe?"

"I'm trying."

"I have something to tell you, and I need you to be calm when I say it."

"Oh no." I spin in his arms and search his features for some indication as to what's happening. "What did you do?"

"It's nothing big." He grins. "Okay. It's big. It's really big."

I cock my head to the side. "You always say it's really big."

"And do I lie?"

"Well, no." I laugh. "Just tell me what's going on."

He takes my hand and pulls me back to the table. "How would you feel if I told you we're moving? Or that I want to move?"

I blanch. "Moving? Where? Why?" I shake my head. "I love it here, Dane. You don't mean out of Dogwood Lane, do you?"

"Hey," Haley says, coming in through the back door. She takes one look at Dane and me and stops in her tracks. "Oh. You haven't told her yet, I see."

"You know?" I ask her.

"I'll just be outside." She jabs a thumb over her shoulder. "Come get me when this is over."

"Dane. What in the heck did you do?"

"Settle down, settle down." He chuckles, finding more amusement in my reaction than I do. "I thought, you know, maybe we should start fresh."

"But I love this house," I whine. "And what about Mia? How will she feel about leaving this place? It's the only home she's ever known."

"I can't wait!" Mia shouts from upstairs.

"She knows too?" I walk in a circle, covering my face with my hands. "Why do I feel like there's a big joke being played on me?"

"It's not, Neely. Promise!" Mia shouts.

I look at Dane and we start laughing at the same time.

"Stop eavesdropping, Mia," Dane yells.

"I'm excited!"

"So am I, but give me a chance to do the whole thing, okay?"

"Well, hurry up."

"This is all adorable and all," I tell him, "but I'm starting to lose patience."

He takes my hands in his, swinging them back and forth between us. I sense his nervousness, and that makes me nervous because this isn't like Dane.

"What would you do if I told you I bought Malone's Farm?" He motions toward the board on the table. "Because I did."

My jaw falls to the floor as I look at the board. Then up to him. "I think I misheard you. I thought you said you bought Malone's Farm."

"Yeah. I did." He gulps. "I got a good deal on it. The house isn't in that bad of shape, actually, and I thought it could be our house, you know?"

Tears well up in the corners of my eyes as I propel myself into him, almost knocking him off his feet. "Are you serious?" I ask, looking up at his face for any sign of a joke.

He doesn't flinch. "I'm serious. I bought it. *We* bought it."

"No way." I let out a little screech as I clap my hands. "I can't believe you bought it. Dane! This is amazing."

He still looks nervous. "I'm glad you think so."

"Can we go see it? Today?" I ask, trying not to squeal again. "Oh my gosh. I don't know what to say. I love this."

"Say yes."

"Yes. Of course. I love the idea of moving out there. I'm in shock, I think," I say with a laugh, walking in a circle. "But it's a gorgeous piece of property, and *oh my God*."

When I turn back around, Dane is down on one knee. A streak of white paint down the side of his face, his hair a mess from being under the new Dodgers hat I bought him last week, he couldn't be more perfect.

In his hand is a little black box with a ring in it.

"I wanted to do this somewhere more private, but Mia had definite issues about that. And if I'm guessing, Haley is probably spying through the window right now too." He shrugs. "But it's all because we love you, Neely. But nobody more than me."

Tears don't even warn me this time. They just fire away down my cheeks and drop onto my shirt. I can't move. I can't see the ring or kiss his face or even say yes again because my legs promise me they'll let me fall if I try.

"Did she say yes?" Mia shouts.

"The house is my engagement gift to you. I got you a ring, too, because that's what people do. Maybe because I'm a carpenter, I think a house means more. It's a place we can build our future together. Home is where your loved ones are, and I want a place where we can live together and love each other forever."

"Did she say yes yet?" Mia shouts.

"Will you give me a second?" he fires back.

"If you wouldn't have made me hide upstairs, I wouldn't be yelling."

My laughter comes out in the middle of sniffles and sobs. He places the ring on my finger, and I can't even see it. But what I can see, what I know, I don't need eyes for. I can feel it in my heart.

"Yes," I say, tugging him to his feet. "I would be honored to marry you, Dane Madden."

He kisses me through my snot and all, laughing as he wipes both of our faces after.

"She said yes, Mia," he says, but his words are hung up on a lump in his throat.

Mia squeals as she tumbles down the stairs and launches herself at us. We stand in the kitchen, next to the Malone's sign, and celebrate the first day of the rest of our lives.

ACKNOWLEDGMENTS

I'd like to thank a few special people who helped make this book happen.

First and foremost, I'd like to thank God for His blessings and the ability to do what I love.

I'd also like to express my appreciation to my family for their patience, love, and support. Saul, Alexander, Aristotle, Achilles, and Ajax—you are the reason I get up every morning. I'm so lucky to call you mine.

I've been blessed to have the world's best parents, Mandy and Dennis, and in-laws, Rob and Peggy, and Tom and Violet. I love you all so very much.

I wouldn't be able to create the worlds I love without the help of Kari March, Tiffany Remy, Carleen Riffle, and Kim Cermak.

Thanks to Becca Mysoor for her guidance and to Dana Sulonen for answering all my questions with such enthusiasm and patience.

Sending all the love to Mandi Beck for believing in me and all my wild ideas, and to S.L. Scott for believing in second chances, both in books and in real life.

Jen Costa and Susan Rayner have been with me since book one. Thank you for always being in my corner.

Ebbie Moresco, Kaitie Reister, and Stephanie Gibson manage my various reader groups and deserve all the accolades for keeping everything running smoothly.

Hugs to Keyarah and Madison for inspiring such joy and spirit.

Sincere gratitude to the bloggers who continue to show excitement for my stories.

And to my readers: Thank you for choosing to pick up my books. I appreciate and acknowledge you. XO.

Don't miss a release! Sign up for my Amazon Live Alert or text the word *adriana* to 21000.

ABOUT THE AUTHOR

USA Today bestselling author Adriana Locke lives and breathes books. After years of slightly obsessive relationships with the flawed bad boys dreamed up by other authors, she decided to create her own. She is the author of *Tumble*, the first novel in her Dogwood Lane series; the Exception series; the Gibson Brothers series; and the Landry Family series.

She resides in the Midwest with her husband, her sons, two dogs, two cats, and a bird. She spends a large amount of time playing with her kids, drinking coffee, and cooking. You can find her outside if the weather's nice, and there's always a piece of candy in her pocket. Besides cinnamon gummy bears, boxing, and random quotes, her next favorite thing is chatting with readers. She'd love to hear from you! Look for her at www.adrianalocke.com.